I0658904

Alien Blood Wars

DANGEROUS DANCE

SAMANTHA CAYTO

Dangerous Dance
ISBN # 978-1-78686-359-1
©Copyright Samantha Cayto 2018
Cover Art by Cherith Vaughan ©Copyright May 2018
Interior text design by Claire Siemaszkiewicz
Pride Publishing

Published in 2018 by Pride Publishing, United Kingdom.

DANGEROUS DANCE

Prologue

Scotland, 1750

"I'm sorry, Val."

The sorrowful expression on Harry's face was too painful to look at, so Val focused his attention on the unmoving bundle lying in the man's arms. The castle was eerily quiet except that Robbie's screams still seemed to echo throughout — at least they did in Val's head. He had the passing notion that he would never stop hearing them. That was his cross to bear, as the humans would say. Harry was blameless.

"You did your best," he said to reassure the doctor. "I know that and I thank you for it. I apologize for my lapse earlier."

It needed to be said because their group was small after so many defections. They couldn't continue to survive on this miserable planet if they splintered into more warring factions. Besides, there was only one man to blame for this hideous outcome, and it wasn't Harry.

I did this. I killed Robbie.

The older man inclined his head, a gesture they'd picked up from the humans that conveyed a great deal. "There is no need. I understood your distress."

Val almost smiled at the understated response. It was so like Harry to play the peacemaker and rise above the aggressive impulses of their species. But then, that's what made him a healer rather than a warrior. That's how the man had been able to calmly do his work, even as Robbie lay dying in agony.

Val made himself focus on the proximate cause of his beloved's demise, the primary one being Val's own lust and hubris. The babe had neither Val's paleness nor Robbie's ruddy complexion. It appeared almost blue and perfectly formed — a beauty, like the boy who'd carried him in a body not quite built for such a thing and which had no natural way to expel him.

"Did he ever draw a breath?" he found himself asking, even as he made an aborted attempt to touch the lifeless face.

"No," came Harry's soft reply.

Val stepped back, away from the sight of his fatal decision and a pain so great that he wondered if he could survive it. "Just as well. Would you please take him back to Robbie's side? I must prepare a pyre out in the courtyard for them both."

A heavy, yet reassuring, hand landed on his shoulder. "Let me help you in that."

Val turned to Alex. He'd almost forgotten the man was there — and had been by his side from the moment Robbie's labor had begun. It had taken Alex and two others to pull Val from the birthing room.

"Thank you, sir, but no. This is my last duty for the boy who gave me everything and lost his life for it." His words choked him. He had to stop and gather his wits and courage. The sense of helplessness was utterly alien to him, as much as the whole miserable planet had been from the beginning.

He struggled for control as he addressed his captain, a man he would gladly follow to any destination for any intent. "I know he'd probably prefer to be buried in the ground." The very concept sent a shudder through him. "I can't do that." The idea of Robbie and the babe moldering under dirt for years to come was vile. "Why can't these humans turn to dust with death?"

He cringed at his own mewling, disgusted by how weak and pathetic he sounded. Yet, it didn't change the fact that he needed to burn his beloved to ashes if he was going to keep what the humans would call sanity.

Alex squeezed his shoulder once before letting go. "I understand. Do what you must. No one will interfere, but know that we are here to help, should you want it."

Val shifted his gaze to a nearby window as he nodded. "Thank you, sir."

The sun was low in the sky. It would be full night by the time he finished, and that seemed fitting. The humans were afraid of the dark and preferred to be inside once the sun set. That meant fewer eyes in the surrounding countryside to notice what he did. The primitive creatures also thought evil came out and lurked until dawn. He'd always sneered at their superstitions, but at that moment, he had a keener insight into their beliefs. Something putrid blanketed the castle that might only be purged by the brightness of the sun.

I've been living among humans too long. There was nothing to fear except the actions of people, human and their own kind. And those mutinous men weren't worthy of fear at all, only scorn and fury and vengeance.

"I will see to it now," he added unnecessarily. When he turned to go, Alex stopped him with a touch to his arm.

"Do *not* blame yourself, Val. Robbie made this decision understanding the risks."

Anger flared inside him. He jerked away from his superior in an insubordinate way that would have earned him a harsh rebuke in another time and place. "He was only a boy! I saved him from the horrors of Culloden and gave him a safe place in my bed. He would have done anything to please me."

Val clamped his mouth shut and fought a wave of agony that threatened to double him over. He saw again, as if for the first time, those exquisite green eyes peering up at him with adoration mixed with fear. All that lovely red hair framing a face that was impossible to resist. He'd seen it in the mud of the battlefield then on the pillow where they lay together and yet once again when the human had consented to giving Val his blood then taking Val's in return. Yes, the boy had known what he was doing—giving himself to a man who was really a vampire—to a male whose seed would change the boy's perfect body in a way unnatural to humans.

Robbie had shown incredible courage each time, given the limitations of his human imagination and his society's expectations. But he hadn't known what he was choosing, not really. *Did you finally realize what I'd done to you, my love, as you took your last breath?*

"I know something of how you feel," was Alex's quiet reply to Val's outburst.

Of course he does. Val felt bad that, in his own misery, he'd forgotten Alex's loss from only a few decades ago. "Dracul has much to answer for."

"Indeed."

"Not this, though. Not really. He may have played both sides against the middle with the English and the Jacobites, but I was the one who brought Robbie to this end."

"*Val.*"

With a violent shake of his head, Val made his feet move again. This introspection was useless. "I appreciate your concern for me, sir. I don't wish to speak of this further. Never again, if you please."

With that, he left the room and the castle to gather wood and make his pyre. He hoped the sun would burn his eyes and his skin. Physical pain was far more welcome than this emotional one. He would say goodbye to his human and their son. In his mind, he would think of the baby as Andrew, because that was what Robbie had wanted to call him. He wouldn't think of either of them much, however. The pain was not helpful in any way except one.

If ever he found himself becoming emotionally attached to another human, he would remember this night. Never again would he allow this agony to claim him. Never again would he fall in love with a pretty boy.

Chapter One

Boston, 2017

Normally the throbbing beat of dance music didn't faze Val. The rhythm reverberating in his chest reminded him of the ship's engines pulsing. It had been a thousand Earth years since he'd last felt them, yet he hadn't forgotten. He never forgot anything, and that unusual skill, for humans and his species alike, made his life a misery sometimes.

From the second-floor railing, he surveyed the club like a bird of prey, always on the lookout for trouble. That was the job of a bouncer. Humans had little self-control. Even the men of this upscale private club could get out of hand. That was especially true on a Saturday night when they allowed themselves to cut loose from their weekly jobs. And the pretty boys dancing for them only inspired them to more stupidity, not less.

One in particular was causing quite a stir and the sight of it raised Val's blood pressure in a way that the blaring music never did.

"Mackie's in fine form tonight."

Val almost bared his fangs at the casual remark. Given that it had been delivered by his superior, he kept his impulse in check. Besides, he had a lot emotionally invested in being unconcerned with the redheaded boy's life.

He clamped his fingers harder around the railing. "His arm healed well."

Alex leaned against the barrier next to him. "Yes, although that's not what I meant. The members are delighted to see him back in action. He'll make a killing, even if he only dances on the stage."

The man's gaze bore into him, although Val refused to take his eyes off the patrons. "He's a smart boy. He'll bring some up here and make even more." The words were uttered with indifference, although maintaining the 'I don't give a fuck' tone nearly caused his throat to constrict.

Alex left him alone for about two seconds. "We could still see him settled somewhere else. I'm sure any one of our remaining cadre would be willing and able to keep him safe. That's assuming Dracul has him in his crosshairs at all."

"No."

Val had had this conversation before with Alex. Since the renewal of their endless internecine war a few months earlier, they'd been operating under the assumption that Quinn and Mackie were both at risk. Alex kept his lover safe, of course, and Mackie had been convalescing at the club. The brat had been willing to be kept pampered and happy to return to his old job on the pole. He'd probably been shaken enough by his near-death experience at Adrian's hands to go along with any plan to protect him from further harm.

It was Val who was the problem. He couldn't stand the idea of his former lover being sent away. No one could be trusted with the boy's safety other than him. His feelings on the matter were irrational, he knew. Those of his crew who remained loyal to Alex were all well-trained warriors who had survived human aggression, as well as Dracul's frequent assaults. Yet, any time Val pictured Mackie being kept by another, his head threatened to explode.

"He's my responsibility." His gaze homed in on a club member whose hand lingered a little too long on Mackie's perfect ass. "I will keep him safe, no one else."

"Val…" Alex's tone was one of infinite patience. He only used it when one of his men was driving him crazy. "You can't keep the boy under your watchful eye forever, not as things stand between you."

Val glanced sideways. "Things stand exactly where I want them. Mackie, too. He's made it quite clear he wants nothing more to do with me."

"His feelings are hurt. You know how these humans are. You sent him away with blistering words that his wounded pride won't allow him to forgive."

"They were necessary."

It had been one of the hardest things he'd ever done — tossing Mackie out on his ear to keep him from Dracul's clutches and it hadn't even worked. Harder still had been seeing Mackie battered and bruised in Adrian's hands. He would have torn the fucker to pieces, except that honor had been Alex's. Val still blamed himself for not breaking it off with the boy earlier.

The club member's hand hadn't left Mackie's ass. Every time the boy moved, the man stayed with him. Val's eyes narrowed and his fingers tightened sufficiently to hurt his knuckles. If he wasn't careful, he might splinter Alex's beautiful balustrade.

Alex's voice claimed his attention once more. "At the time, yes, your scheme seemed the correct course. Now, wouldn't it be more prudent—"

Val cut him off as he pushed back. "Excuse me, sir. I'm needed on the floor."

He wanted to vault over the railing. It was the quickest route down and an easy drop for him. It would scare the shit out of the humans, however, so he was forced to use the stairs instead—and at a pace that made his teeth clench. Damn, these upright apes and their slow, puny bodies. Mimicking their weakness infuriated him. Always had.

Still, he fairly flew down the stairs to the first floor and strode over to the small stage where Mackie was thrilling his admirers with his graceful dancing— provocative, as well, his lithe body twisting around the pole as if born to it. His pale beauty was entrancing, even at a distance, though Val had sworn to resist it. During his weeks of recovery, the boy had let the shaved part of his head grow out. He had gelled it into spikes that should have looked ridiculous, but somehow Mackie pulled it off.

Val couldn't help but stare at the red hair. It had been his weakness, and the sight of it set off a pang deep inside him, as it always did, except Robbie had had a fresh-faced look, with round cheeks and wide eyes that conveyed wonder at everything. Mackie's features were sharper, more elfin, and his eyes held a depth of pain that always tugged at Val's protective instincts.

It wouldn't take much, a small slip in Val's resolve, for him to be totally lost. He could not let that happen. He'd been selfish once before to fatal results. He wouldn't be that weak or self-indulgent again. No more human boys would die in agony because of him.

As Val approached, Mackie leaned down and said something to the man whose hand was still plastered against the go-go boy's rump like it had been surgically attached. The man shook his head and leaned in closer, his lips almost grazing Mackie's lightly painted, plump ones.

The room became a hazy red before Val could keep himself in check. Mackie turned toward him, and his eyes fairly popped right before Val lashed out and grabbed the offending club member by the back of his collar. Even with the loud music, the man's squeak of alarm reached Val's ears.

He grinned, careful to keep his fangs from showing as he hauled the man up to his face. "Having fun, Mr. Warren?" The older man sputtered and squirmed. "You know the rules, sir. Boys dancing for your entertainment is not a license to be overly friendly. I believe you were crossing a line just now." He kept his tone moderate, mindful of how much Alex loved his club and living in Boston. Nothing would be gained by causing too much of a fuss.

Mackie all but flew off his stage to join them. "Let go, Val. Mr. Warren was a little overly enthusiastic. He wants a lap dance so badly that he was having a hard time waiting for my time on the stage to end."

The boy's proximity was like a magnet for Val. He hated how impossible it was to escape his lure. Reluctantly, Val took his gaze off the patron and swung it over to the little spitfire. Mackie flashed him a grin that was also a warning to knock it off. Smaller than most human men, the boy had never been one to back down, not even when up against someone half-again his height and almost twice his weight.

Mackie placed one delicate hand on Val's arm. "Come on. Everyone's glad to see me back. You're putting a major crimp in my style. You know I can handle myself."

For a few frightening seconds, Val lost himself in Mackie's green eyes. It had been so long since they'd interacted directly, Val having been careful to keep his distance. He'd almost forgotten how compelling those human eyes were. The light touch of the boy's fingers burned through the sleeves of Val's Armani suit and right down to his flesh. His stupid dick stirred with the memory of what those clever fingers could do.

A tug from Warren, along with a few more sputtering sounds of indignation, forced Val to break free of Mackie's influence. Loosening his grip, Val eased the club member onto his feet. Val fussed with straightening the man's jacket.

"My apologies, Mr. Warren. It seems I misconstrued the situation." Before the man could utter a response, Val whipped out his wallet and pulled a hundred from it. "Please have a few lap dances on me."

The wealthy man hardly needed the gift but that wasn't the point. Val turned away and peered down into Mackie's blazing gaze. He kept staring as he bent to tuck the bill into the already stuffed G-string the boy wore. It was some frilly bit of fabric that was more effeminate and less Goth than Mackie's previous look had been. It, along with the heavier makeup the boy had plastered onto his face, should have been a turn-off. Val had always preferred males to females. Somehow, on this particular human, the new look only served to make the boy more enticing.

He slid his fingers along the silky skin moist from the boy's recent exertions. It was how he remembered that flesh. He'd once spent hours trailing his fingers along every inch he could reach, Mackie always purring like a cat at the touch. He'd craved the contact like a starving man did bread.

Yes Val, the one who never forgot, got a jolt of nostalgia. It was a dangerous game he suddenly played. The look in Mackie's kohl-rimmed eyes confirmed that the human remembered, too. It would take nothing for Val to lean down farther and take those plump, painted lips in a searing kiss that would leave them both breathless.

That way lay madness, however. He had to be strong for both their sakes. So, tucking in the bill, he straightened once more and hastened away with as much dignity as he could muster.

Mackie watched Val leave, the man's broad back set firmly and his gait confident. *No, not a man, an alien.* Val was from another world and another time, as well, when one considered that he had been on Earth for a thousand years. And Mackie had thought about it—a lot. His slow recovery from that awful night when his world had turned upside down had left him with plenty of time to ponder the situation. Nearly everyone in the club that he'd started to think of as his family was otherworldly in the literal sense of the word.

I've been fucked by an alien. A vampire. I gave my blood and heart to him.

Those notions had been reeling around in Mackie's head for weeks. It left him slightly queasy and totally confused. He should have been petrified, especially after what he'd suffered at the hands of one of their kind. Alex had killed the asshole in a battle worthy of the best Marvel Universe movie. Mackie had been awed and terrified in equal measure. A sensible person would have blabbed to the police—or at least run fast and far. Mackie had done neither of those things. He'd chosen instead to keep his mouth shut and allowed himself to be installed back into the one place in his life where he'd finally felt safe.

For, despite how Val and his cohorts could make the bravest person's blood run cold, Mackie didn't worry for a second that he was in danger with them. Maybe it was because Val had shown such amazing restraint when they'd played upstairs in one of the private club rooms. Mackie had been at the man's mercy hundreds of times and yet Val had always only brought him the kind of pain that elicited pleasure. Although Mackie had never used his safeword — a point of pride — he'd also never doubted that Val would heed it.

Val had been the first person to treat Mackie with respect, and even affection, albeit in a gruff and remote way. Perhaps that was why Mackie had fallen in love with him. An armchair psychologist would probably say so, not him. Mackie had always felt he and Val had been destined for one another. Together they could tackle anything…until Val had thrown what they'd had away. The man didn't deserve Mackie's love or even a second more of consideration.

Mackie forced himself to turn from the sight of Val's retreating back and focus on someone who appreciated him. He flashed a smile at Warren that was guaranteed to harden a man's dick and loosen his wallet.

"Sorry about that, sweetie. Val always has a stick up his ass. Let's go have some fun."

The older man's expression changed from indignation to delight, as Mackie expected. And yes, the guy's thousand-dollar trousers had tented nicely. He understood Mackie's worth and appreciated getting to spend time with him. Mackie took his somewhat-sweaty hand and led him through the throng of men milling about the dance floor area. Everyone he passed gave him a broad smile or a suggestive wink. They were happy to see him back in action, and the attention lifted Mackie's spirits.

The money didn't hurt, either. His new gender-bending HommeMystere thong was packed with bills. They made satisfyingly crinkly sounds as he strutted, careful to put a provocative swing to his hips. It was like a constant musical accompaniment to his sexy strut. He also liked the tangible feel of the cash against his skin. Knowing he had money eased the one thing that he was truly terrified of—poverty. Not having had much money during childhood, he'd known real hunger and homelessness once he'd been kicked out of his house. Blood-sucking aliens didn't hold a candle to the kind of terror that comes from not knowing where his next meal was coming from or whether he would freeze to death in an alley.

Since he'd started working at the club, he'd found financial security for the first time in his life and not only because Val had kept him as his boy. Mackie was capable of earning his own money, dancing coming naturally to him. Now he had a way to make a great living and a surprisingly plump bank account.

Of course, the one bill that his body somehow distinguished from the others was the hundred that Val had tucked in. *Damn the man.* Even with their relationship in tatters, he still managed to make Mackie feel owned by him. Not in a way that was demeaning… It was more like being cherished. Worse, a significant part of Mackie was thrilled at the idea. Try as he might, he couldn't quite quash his love for Val and the need to be dominated by him. All this was despite the vicious way in which Val had cut their bond.

Stop it! Don't think about him.

Mackie sprinted up the stairs to the second floor, dragging Mr. Warren behind him. "Let's go find a quiet corner and get reacquainted."

There were lots of big, comfy seats designed to allow a go-go boy to straddle even the widest of hips. A couple of boys were entertaining clients already. On a Saturday night, it was all hands on deck and Alex had recruited a few more dancers in the months during Mackie's recovery. Normally, Mackie didn't care about being seen. He would grab the first free space. For some reason, though, he was feeling uncharacteristically shy. So, he went all the way to the far end before depositing his guest on the red velvet seat.

Warren grinned up at him with obvious glee as Mackie climbed up on his lap. "The bouncer gave you a hundred. That's five songs, right?"

"You know it is, Daddy." Mackie fluttered his lashes, a move that normally came easily to him, yet felt oddly forced now.

Warren licked his lips. "I want to spend the time touching all of you." He raised his meaty hands and ran them down Mackie's back. "Maybe we can get rid of all these pesky bills? They're getting in the way."

"Sure, sweetie." Mackie usually would have already pulled the bills out to form a pile on the seat. For some reason, he'd felt like keeping them in place. They did present a little bit of a barrier.

He inwardly scoffed at the idea. His job involved allowing the patrons to cop a feel, and the more they did, the more they paid. He hadn't been out of commission that long to have forgotten what the deal was. Making short work of clearing the way for his patron's grabby fingers, Mackie began to sway his hips in time to the music.

It was like riding a bicycle — not that he'd been on one of those for years. His body knew what to do, the same way it had remembered his routines on the pole. He undulated against the man's tented pants, rubbing the hard-on inside them with light brushes up and down and side to side. Warren pressed his fingers into Mackie's ass, hard enough to make him wince. He recovered in time to turn it into what he hoped was a seductive smile.

"Oh, Daddy, I missed you," he moaned against the man's ear. He knew what men liked from him. "No one treats me the way you do." He was there to satisfy club members' risqué fantasies without running afoul of the law. He could play the slutty boy for them.

"Baby…" Warren's whiskey breath wafted into Mackie's face before the man ran his tongue along Mackie's jaw.

The intimate touch caused Mackie to jerk back. He surprised himself as much as Warren. The man frowned and clenched his fingers even more. "Something wrong?"

To cover up the insulting response, Mackie said, "Sorry, Daddy. I only want to loosen you up a bit. It's hot in here, don't you think?"

Warren licked his lips and groaned. "Yeah, so hot."

Mackie made a fuss about undoing the man's shirt buttons to expose his chubby, smooth chest. Then Mackie moaned and fawned over it by running his hands down the sweat-slicked skin. All the while, he gyrated against the man's lap with a fake smile plastered on his face.

What's wrong with me? This is the job I love.

But, try as he might, he couldn't work up any genuine enthusiasm for the lap dance. He found himself counting down the songs so he could finish up. Warren, on the other hand, was just getting started. The man bucked up his own hips to meet Mackie's lap. Their dicks rubbed together, making the man moan with heavy-lidded eyes. Mackie's cock remained soft, the movement doing nothing for him.

Because it was the wrong dick touching his.

The fifth song was playing when Warren really upped the ante. He slid a finger underneath Mackie's thong and pressed it against Mackie's hole. Mackie froze mid-swivel and glared down at the man.

Warren stared back at him with blown pupils. "Come on, baby. Let's go to one of the private rooms." He licked his lips again. "I'll make it worth your while."

Mackie gave the invitation about two seconds' worth of thought before practically vaulting off the man's lap. "Sorry, sweetie. That's not on the menu tonight." He grabbed his money and made a show of stuffing it back in his G-string. "I'll see you later."

"Hey!" Warren grabbed Mackie's arm before he could leave. "What gives? Word is you're not with the bouncer anymore." He heaved to his feet. "Don't be a tease now. I said I'd pay you well."

Mackie let his eyes flash his annoyance. "I'm not teasing. I'm refusing." He looked pointedly down where the man's fingers still gripped his arm.

With a sigh, Warren let him go. "Okay, I hear you, but if you change your mind..." The man pulled out his wallet and removed a hundred. "Here. I don't like another guy paying for my dances. And, it's a little reminder that I can make your life very easy if you'll let me."

Pride waged war with practicality for about three seconds until Mackie remembered that he was an undereducated gay kid with no family to speak of.

Snatching the bill, Mackie said, "Thanks. I'll keep that in mind."

He stuffed it down the front of his thong before sauntering away, to show how unaffected he was by the exchange. He made sure to keep his gait slow and provocative, hiding the sudden turmoil and sadness whirling around inside him. The night had started out so well. Why, then, did he feel cheap and miserable?

Unable to face the rest of the club members—or a particular bouncer—Mackie made a beeline for the boy's locker room in the back of the club. He'd hoped to find it empty, but no such luck. Quinn and Shawn were there, Quinn still dressed in work 'clothes' from their shift. Even though Quinn was banging Alex on the regular, he still insisted on working. He simply didn't do lap dances anymore, in order to keep Alex from losing his alien shit on club members. Shawn had obviously just taken a shower and stood with a towel wrapped around his hips. They were staring at the flat screen on the far wall.

"What's up, guys?" While Mackie didn't feel like socializing, he also didn't want to let on that he was anything other than happy to be back to work.

Shawn glanced over his shoulder. "Girl, you've got to see this."

Mackie didn't bother to object to the feminine pronoun. Shawn always spoke like that. Besides, the way Mackie was styling his hair and makeup—not to mention the new outfits—there wasn't much to complain about. Mackie hadn't thought hard about his new gender-bending look, although he supposed it was intended to piss off Val or something.

He stepped closer to them. "What's going on?"

"Some guy is so freaking high that he's hanging off a balcony at Copley Place."

As he came abreast of them, Mackie could see and hear the breaking newscast. A young white guy with blond dreadlocks was holding on to the railing with one crooked arm. He was grinning like a maniac and waving like he was on the Jumbotron at Fenway. Although his middle was blurred out to protect the viewing public's sensibilities, it was obvious that he was buck-naked.

Mackie leaned in to get a better view. "What the fuck?"

"I know, right?" Quinn nudged Shawn. "Turn up the volume. I can't hear what he's saying."

Shawn pressed the remote, and they all got an earful. "I'm a superhero!" the guy called out. "Have no fear, people of Earth. I can fly. Your puny buildings can't hold me."

There were a few screams as they guy leaned over. Behind him, police were trying to edge closer. He swung his head wildly in their direction. "You have no power over me. I have the strength of ten of you." The camera zoomed in the moment the man turned his head back to peer down from where he hung. Mackie's heart skipped a beat as he got a good look.

"I am more powerful that you can imagine!"

Those were the man's last words before, spreading his arms out wide, he swan-dived down. The screams were deafening, but Mackie hardly noticed. Instead, he grabbed at Quinn's arm.

"Did you see his eyes?"

Quinn turned a horror-stricken face to him. "It couldn't be."

"What?" Shawn asked. "His eyes were bloodshot. Big deal. Must have been on bath salts or something."

But no one was listening to him. "We need to tell Alex and Val," Mackie said. Mackie didn't wait for Quinn to move after he nodded. Instead, Mackie headed for the door with more speed than he'd used to enter it. His melancholy from moments ago had fled in the face of a possible new stage of the alien war.

Chapter Two

"Why don't you knock off for the night?"

The suggestion surprised Val. He shifted his gaze from the security monitors to his boss. Alex sat behind his massive desk with his feet propped on the edge and his hands linked behind his head. The man had become surprisingly laid back since he'd started getting an uninterrupted supply of sex and fresh blood. He was happy, as well, and that fact alone made Val inclined to appreciate how Quinn had entered their lives. The human boy was good for their leader, accepting of their ways and naturally exerted a calming influence over Alex, even with Dracul active again.

"For what reason? The club is still in full swing." He returned his attention to the screens, although nothing of note was happening.

"You're tense and edgy, making the members tense and edgy every time you come near them."

"Is that why you asked me to come in here, to keep me away from the floor?" Not waiting for an answer,

Val faced Alex full-on and added, "You don't trust me to keep my shit together?"

Alex gave him a pained look. "Val, you have many fine qualities, not the least of which is your dogged loyalty and ability to keep others in line. That's what makes you the perfect second-in-command to our cadre and chief bouncer to the club. Holding your temper, however, is not one of your strengths."

Val grimaced, biting back a quick retort. "I didn't toss Warren out on his ass, though, did I?"

"No," Alex allowed. "But the thought did cross your mind."

Before Val could work out a response to that observation without sounding any more defensive than he already did, the door to the office flew open. Quinn rushed in. "Alex!"

The boss sprang up and was by his lover's side with a speed that would have left a human seeing a blur of movement. "Darling boy, what is the matter?"

Val didn't hear the answer over the sudden pounding of his heart. His gaze was trained on the doorway. The sight of Mackie appearing a second after Quinn sent a dizzying relief through Val. Whatever had caused the boys to breach Alex's business sanctum hadn't involved personal danger. Val didn't want to care so much, yet his unchecked reaction told him he was fooling himself if he thought he was over Mackie.

The boy caught and held his gaze with cool distain as he closed the door behind him. The expression on that pretty face made Val want to drag him upstairs, bend him over the spanking bench and beat it off him. When they'd been together, Mackie had many times given him that look specifically to bait him into that response.

But, they weren't together anymore, and Val wasn't in a position to react in his usual way.

Mackie fluttered his lashes a couple of times before turning his attention to where Alex and Quinn stood in front of the flat-screen television against the far wall. Val was momentarily distracted by the sight of the boy's perfect ass outlined by that ridiculously frilly thong still stuffed by other men's money. Val's own hundred-dollar bill was mixed with the rest of them as if he meant nothing more than the grubby-handed letches that frequented the club.

"Val!"

He realized with an inward start that he'd again been distracted by something he should be indifferent to. Some*one*. "Sorry, boss. What's up?"

Alex pointed to the TV and turned up the volume. "Watch and listen."

Some breathless local reporter was outside what he recognized as the Huntington Avenue entrance to the Copley Place shopping mall—one of those ridiculous places where humans loved to spend time and money. She was nattering on about a guy committing suicide by leaping off one of the interior balconies. No, it was more that he was high on something that had led him to believe that he had superpowers. Whatever... Foolish humans bored him.

He wandered closer to the screen. "What's the big deal?"

It was Mackie who answered, giving him a disdainful roll of his eyes. "You need to pay better attention. The guy eluded security with surprising speed and even managed to out-muscle two of them at once."

Val tried to glower at the boy, yet worried it came off as more of a sexual invitation. "I still don't get why this matters to us."

Mackie folded his arms. "Because Quinn and I saw him before he jumped. Someone was filming the whole thing while they were trying to talk him down. And," he added with an insolent flick of his one-sided bangs, "his eyes were red."

Val frowned. "Bloodshot?"

"No. Red, as in pissed-off-alien red."

That got Val's attention. He focused on Alex, who clicked off the television. "He was one of us?" He shook his head at his stupid question. "No, obviously not, or we'd be listening to a report about how a man suddenly disintegrated right in front of everyone."

Alex also shook his head and returned to his desk with Quinn in tow. He deftly tumbled the boy onto his lap as he continued. "Quinn said the man was definitely human with a golden skin tone and light hair." He cuddled his lover with enviable nonchalance and lack of self-consciousness. For his part, Quinn lounged against Alex with obvious ease and trust and also without any evident discomfort over a public display of affection.

Ignoring the pang he felt at the sight, Val focused on the weird topic at hand. "This doesn't make any sense. If he wasn't one of us, then his eyes couldn't have turned red. You must have been mistaken in what you saw," he added cautiously. Alex was so protective of Quinn. Val didn't want to test the waters of how far he could challenge the boy in anything.

It didn't even matter because it was Mackie who took offense and answered for both of them. "We know what we saw, don't we?" the boy asked his friend.

When Quinn nodded in assent, Mackie turned his ire on Val. "We're not stupid."

Val huffed. Nothing and no one on this miserable planet had managed to get under his skin in so little time the way this pint-sized boy had. "I never intended to intimate you were. It's just not possible for this dead man to be one of us."

"We didn't say he was. Clearly, he was human, and yet," Mackie added, stepping up to Val, "his eyes were red, the same way that Adrian's were right before he snapped my arm like a twig. I'm not likely to forget that, am I?"

Val winced inwardly at the reminder of the way Dracul's lapdog had tortured Mackie in order to lure Quinn into a trap. The painful memory of realizing how hurt Mackie had been still plagued Val. He also admired how, despite feigning a self-indulgent attitude, Mackie had had the courage to warn Quinn. If Mackie hadn't, both boys would have ended up dead, and that would have led Alex into a crippling emotional tailspin. Everyone had underestimated Mackie, Val included. He was as proud of the boy as he was furious at himself for letting harm come to him.

Except Val didn't have the right to feel anything about this human because he'd thrown him away. He turned his attention to Alex, a safer place to focus. "What do you make of this, sir?"

The man ran his fingers idly up Quinn's arm as he considered the question. "I don't know. It could have been a trick of the light."

Both boys said no at the same time. Their certainty was disturbing.

"It's possible, "Alex continued, "that the dead man was a turned human. I'll have to ask Harry if eye color can be affected by the change. I've never heard of it or seen it for myself, but then, unlike Dracul and his boys, we haven't turned many humans." The man flicked a guilty look in Val's direction.

Val knew what thought had flitted across Alex's mind. His own had gone there, as well. *How could they not?* Normally, he pivoted away from any memories of Robbie, the pain cutting too deep for him to weather, despite the passing centuries. For Val, nothing had faded. Each experience in his life could be revisited with the same clarity as if it had just occurred. At the moment, though, too much was on the line for him to indulge his cowardice. He forced himself to picture the one changed human he'd actually known intimately. All he saw were green eyes staring back at him with love and trust. *So much misplaced trust.*

Putting those biting and unhelpful memories aside, he focused instead on the other turned human that he knew well. Harry's husband had deep brown eyes that, as far as Val knew, never changed color. Then again, the couple didn't seem to ever be at odds with one another. If they fought, they did so quietly and in private.

"Lucien is so mild-mannered," he observed. "I'm not sure he's constitutionally capable of feeling the kind of rage that manifests in us as red pupils."

Alex snorted. "I agree. And with Harry totally smitten and doting, why would Lucien ever need to work up a head of steam? Still, we can't discount what these boys saw." He stood with his usual grace, bringing both himself and Quinn to their feet. "Come, dearest boy. Let's go wake Harry and ask. He's not going to like being roused so late, but doing it in person is going to help us convey the urgency. Perhaps Lucien will be angry, as well, and show us his red eyes, if they exist."

Val quelled a spark of irritation that Alex immediately asked Quinn to go with him and not him. Security was his domain. No way he wanted to sit around twiddling his thumbs. Never good with downtime, it was particularly hard for him to remain passive when a potential crisis was at hand. If he went out onto the club floor to play bouncer now, he'd probably do something Alex would hate and he would regret. Humans always managed to irk him.

An idea struck. "I should call Duncan. It's not homicide, but he must be able to get access to inside information, including an autopsy on the jumper. If there is some connection to our people and this human, we'll want someone we trust on top of it from the inside, anyway. Not that I'm entirely sure we can trust the sergeant."

Alex hadn't quite reached the door. "Excellent idea. I agree that our uneasy alliance with the man hasn't been put to the test, but we have to assume he will come through for us. Call him. We'll meet back here as soon as I've spoken to Harry."

Taking out his phone, Val eyed Mackie. "No need for you to stay."

The boy's eyes flashed. "Says you. I'm not leaving unless Alex asks me to. This isn't only *your* fight, you know."

"Fine," Val bit out. "At least go put some clothes on."

It was the wrong thing to say. He knew the moment the words had left his mouth that he'd shown a modicum of weakness. With a provocative swivel of his hips, Mackie ran his hand down the front of his thong.

"What's the matter, Val? Missing what you can't have anymore?"

The little shit batted his eyelashes.

Val reacted without thought or sense. He closed the distance between them, and swatted that impertinent rump with a loud single smack of his palm. Mackie gasped with a satisfying tone of outrage and fury in his eyes.

"Don't push me, Mackie. I'm still your boss, even if we're not playing anymore."

They stood in a brief staring contest until something in the boy's expression softened, became almost seductive. "Fine." The one-word response was breathy.

Val didn't want to, but he couldn't help glancing down to see that the boy's dick had thickened. Whether it had been the smack or the stern command — or likely both — Mackie still found Val arousing. Val would have been more pleased with that information if weren't for the fact that his own pants had gotten considerably tighter from the interaction. Mackie wasn't the weak link in what was left of their relationship. Val didn't have as tight a grip on his own needs and emotions as he would have liked.

"I'll be back." Mackie turned on one heel and walked out.

Trying not to watch, Val fumbled with his phone until he pulled up Duncan's contact info. The Boston police sergeant was privy to too much information, as far as Val was concerned. But this was a problem that they'd dealt with ever since crashing on Earth. As much as they would have liked to remain well-hidden, Dracul had forced them into the open. Alex had no choice but to accept help from humans from time to time. Not all of them had proven trustworthy. Up until now, however, any efforts to expose the aliens living among them had been dismissed by other humans as lunacy or lies. With humans having reached space and actively trying to make contact with other species, there was a greater threat of someone like Duncan being believed.

And, despite all those efforts to reach out to aliens, how would humans really react to finding them on Earth already? It was not in Val's nature to trust easily. He didn't expect to be greeted with flowers and handshakes. Incarceration and vivisection seemed more likely. He had no choice at the moment, however, except to assume Duncan was reliable.

The man picked up after a few rings. "Christ Jesus, this better be good."

Val smiled at the angry greeting. Val wasn't sure how he personally felt about the human ally. Over the centuries, there had been those few that he had actually liked, as well as trusted. Kitty was one. They were rare, however, and sometimes proved duplicitous, despite Val's feelings toward them. It could be hard to read these creatures. It wasn't worth investing a lot of emotion in the relationship. That was another reason for keeping Mackie at bay. Even the ones who were steadfast were far too easily killed, and they always died in such a short period of time.

The one thing he was sure about with Duncan was that the man was smart and courageous. The fact that he was being surly also implied he wasn't playing some game at being on their side. Val was never more suspicious of humans than when they were acting overly nice and accommodating. He preferred straightforwardness in any event.

"Apologies for the lateness of the hour, Sergeant. There's been a development in which your position on the force may come into play."

A loud breath sounded over the phone. "Has another round of serial killings started?"

"Not exactly." He relayed what he knew about the man in the mall, little as it was.

Duncan didn't say anything for a few seconds. "Normally I'd say it was another pathetic case of someone dying from bath salts or something. The eyes, though… I haven't forgotten any of the details of how that night by the harbor went down."

Val could well imagine how seared that event was in the human's mind. "Yes, that is the disturbing part. Pupils in my species change color based on strong emotions. Red is for fury."

"No shit. Give me a second." There was some rustling, then a voice droned in the background. "Yeah, so according to the news, it sounds like my brethren on the force are treating it as a drug-related death. Not exactly my beat."

Val tamped down his temper. "Yes, I know. We have television here at the club."

"Don't get your panties in a twist, bouncer boy. What I mean is that I can't do anything about it tonight. It would look suspicious if a homicide cop suddenly turned up at a crime scene without being called in, especially as it's not a murder case. I'll get in early and ask around. I'm sure I can come up with some possible tie-in theory to a probable gang killing Karl and I have been investigating."

"All right. I'll let Alex know. Thank you," he made himself say, because the cop didn't have to help. And, although the man had been essentially forced into staying quiet about aliens living among humans, he had been fairly gracious about his situation, at least as far as they knew.

Hanging up, he flopped down onto the couch Alex kept for his guests. There was nothing to do but wait — wait for Alex to return with Harry's take on the red eyes and wait for Mackie to return. He didn't like the way his cock stirred at that last thought and how his heart thudded a little bit harder, as well.

He especially didn't like the way his sense of danger rose to an almost panicky level. Dracul had launched the next attack in the renewed war. Val didn't know how, exactly, yet nothing else made sense. Normally, he would have been merely irritated at the endless need to fight. His time with Robbie had been during a lull. Val had had ample time to secure his secret lover in a safe location, even though he'd ended up not staying. Now was different. The club was exposed, out in the open, their lives on display if Dracul cared to look. And he had given the taunt of Adrien's killing spree.

Then and now, Val felt a true sense of dread because he had more to lose.

* * * *

As tense as everyone was over the new development, there was something comforting about hanging with what Mackie thought of as *the family*. They'd reconvened in Alex's office within a half-hour of his and Quinn's barging in with their tale of a red-eyed man. Val had remained, sitting like a pissed-off sphynx, his gaze tracking Mackie's every movement. There had been no time for him to consider how he felt about the scrutiny because Alex had returned with Quinn and a sleepy-eyed Harry. Then Alex had declared that Quinn needed feeding, so they'd trooped down to Emil for a late-night meal.

Mackie tried not to feel jealous over Alex's treatment of Quinn. The obvious love and caring the man showed was enviable, the kind of thing Mackie had secretly hoped he would find with someone. Not Val. There was nothing cuddly or goopy about how he'd treated Mackie when they'd been an item, and that had been fine with Mackie. It had been enough that he'd treated Mackie with respect and that Mackie had always felt safe with him. It had certainly been a far cry from the scary life he'd led at home and on the streets.

Still, there was something appealing about the hearts and flowers kind of relationship. Maybe someday he'd find that, although he still liked the dominance and discipline aspects of his time with Val. Could he fall in love with someone who would be both? Perhaps, although nothing would happen until this nightmare with the dreaded Dracul asshole was over.

The chef put a plate of food in front of Mackie. "Here, eat. You're too skinny." Emil grimaced after he spoke.

Mackie put on a show of being affronted. "Says you. The club members think I'm perfect." He hid a grin as he picked up his fork.

"That's because they're pervs," the man grumbled and went to get more food.

Mackie took a moment to appreciate how Emil had turned the stack of pancakes into a face with a whipped-cream smile and chocolate-morsel features. Although Mackie was coming up on his twentieth birthday, he hadn't known enough of a childhood to be past such cute touches. Plus, he had a massive sweet tooth. He indulged it further by smothering the stack with maple syrup. It was the real kind, not colored corn syrup. The Stelalux boys were high-end on absolutely everything. When the time came for Mackie to leave — and it would — he was going to miss the creature-comforts of the super-rich.

"Mmm." The moan escaped without him thinking about it. As he chewed his mouthful, he felt eyes on him. Glancing up, he saw Val's hawk-like gaze boring a hole into him from across the table. Never one to stifle an impulse, Mackie licked his lips with a slow turn of his tongue.

Val bared his teeth, showing his fangs and everything. It was a mark of triumph for Mackie, proof that the badass bouncer wasn't made of stone. There was a power in being able to bring a man to his figurative knees. It wasn't much, but it was all Mackie had. Somehow, he just couldn't help himself. He wanted to bait the man because he was still smarting over the brutal way in which Val had tossed Mackie from his life.

He would never forgive Val for the awful things he'd said. Never.

"I beg your pardon, ladies and gentlemen." Alex's voice boomed down the table, even though he hadn't shouted. "I hate to disturb your eating or whatever it is you're doing," he added with a narrowed gaze that encompassed both Mackie and Val. "We need to get up to speed on this matter at hand.

"Harry, will you please repeat for everyone else's benefit what you told me?."

Besides Quinn, the everyone else Alex addressed included Emil. The cook had dismissed the rest of the kitchen staff and had joined them at the table with his own plate of food. Kitty, too, was there because she'd been supportive of Alex and the others for a few years now. There was nothing about them that she wasn't privy to. And lastly, Logan huddled at the far end, removed in an emotional way from the rest of the crowd except Emil, whom she seemed to like.

The veteran was mostly living onsite, although she took off when she wanted — kind of like a feral cat who was willing to pretend to be domesticated when she wanted. Given how she'd saved Quinn and Mackie with amazing courage when she hadn't needed to, everyone was willing to cut her in on the meeting. Whether she cared enough to be a part of whatever they were going to do was another matter. Her default and constant expression was one of distrust.

Harry rubbed his eyes. "Well, as I said, I know of no reason why a human's pupils would mimic our mood changes. It's never happened that I know of. Certainly Lucien's remain the same brown that they've always been."

The man took a long gulp of coffee. "And, before you ask, yes, he's been angry enough for it to happen." He chuckled. "Definitely so. I do seem to have a penchant for getting under his skin, despite my efforts to the contrary. No human would have enough patience for me."

Mackie got the joke. Harry's human husband was the epitome of Zen-like calm. Although Mackie didn't know the man well, he'd always liked him and admired how well he weathered being among the strong impulses of his family by marriage.

"Demi's haven't changed either, for that matter," Harry continued. "Of course, he's not fully mature, so I can't say for certainty whether it will or won't happen with a hybrid."

Mackie concentrated on eating and listening. He really had nothing useful to add and was happy to be included in the meeting instead of being sent off. He tried to hide his automatic frown, as well, at any mention of the brat that was Demi. If men thought Mackie was too full of himself, they hadn't met Demi. He was a constant trial to everyone, although knowing as he did now that the boy was living in-between worlds, Mackie was inclined to cut him some slack. It couldn't be easy navigating life on Earth as a half-alien. And, while Mackie's understanding of this alien race was slim, he did know now that Demi was a lot older than he looked. There was a weird interaction of his mixed blood that both sped up his maturity and slowed it down, depending on which race you viewed it as. It was like he was living out adolescence for decades. A few years of that drove most humans a little crazy. How much worse must it be to live with it for longer?

"Have we ever known of a half-breed to favor human hair and skin coloring?" Val asked. He was plowing through a pile of food that made Mackie's plate appear to be a dainty snack.

Harry looked down his nose at Val. "I prefer to use the term 'hybrid'. 'Half-breed' is demeaning."

Val cocked an eyebrow. "You think so? Have you ever asked your kid if he likes being referred to as if he's some kind of fuel-efficient car?"

Harry looked as if he was about to launch into a counter-attack when Alex intervened. "Gentlemen, please. We're veering off track. While it's possible that Quinn and Mackie were mistaken in what they saw, we must operate on the assumption that they weren't."

"His eyes were Nancy Reagan red!" Mackie interjected before good sense could stop him. If he'd dared to do something like that in his birth home, he would have earned himself a slap at best, a beating at worst. No, not worst. There had been worse done to him than a hiding, but he tried not to think about that.

In any event, no one here cuffed him or even berated him for his outburst. Instead, Emil smiled at him in encouragement and Alex nodded respectfully. Val simply scowled, but that didn't count. It was one of the man's default expressions, along with grim.

"We believe you, dear boy," Alex soothed. "We simply have to keep an open mind. The implication of all of this is disturbing."

"Duncan may have more for us tomorrow," Val added.

Alex nodded. "I'm gratified to hear that he's keeping his word about helping us. We've never had a cop on our side before, have we?"

"There was that Metropolitan Police Officer who helped us when one of Dracul's whelps cut up those women," Emil replied.

"Oh, yes. I suppose that does count, although the poor man died very quickly for his trouble. We didn't do well by him at all."

"What women?" Mackie couldn't help asking. "And, do you mean this Dracul dude has children?"

"Two sons. Twins." It was Val who answered. "He turned a Welsh boy long ago."

Mackie made a face. "You mean a human gave birth to them, like Lucien did Demi?"

During Mackie's long convalescence, Quinn had told him everything he knew about these vampires who were really aliens. The idea of a human male being able to become pregnant and give birth blew Mackie's mind, his relationship with Lucien and Demi notwithstanding.

It was still easier to believe that Demi was adopted or that Lucien was really transgender, even though he knew neither of those things were true.

Stranger still was that Quinn was seriously considering allowing Alex to 'turn' him by feeding Quinn the alien's blood. It wouldn't happen right away. It might take years for Quinn's body to undergo the transformation that would allow him to conceive and carry a baby to term. *How would that even feel, to be both male and female at the same time? Then, having someone grow and wiggle around inside you?* Mackie put a palm to his stomach at the very thought of it.

Val's gaze took in the movement before his lips thinned. "Yes. He managed to survive it, the way Lucien did."

There was a sudden stillness among the aliens that weirded Mackie out. Val's expression went extra grim and even laid-back Emil focused on his food as if it contained the secrets of the world. Mackie wanted to ask what was wrong, but instinct had him holding back for once. Instead, he returned to his first question. "So what was up with the women who got hurt?"

Val speared a forkful of eggs before answering. "You've heard of Jack the Ripper?"

It took a second for the meaning of his answer to sink in. "Shut up! You're telling me that the Ripper was an alien?"

"Half-breed."

"Hybrid," Harry interjected. "We put a stop to him, sent him whimpering home to Daddy's castle in Wales with his figurative tail between his legs."

Sitting back, Mackie tried to absorb the news. "So, just how much of human history are you guys tangled up with?"

He glanced at Quinn, who was equally open-mouthed at the news. Apparently pillow talk between him and Alex hadn't gotten very far yet. Kitty looked unimpressed, probably because she knew it already. Logan was studiously eating and looked to be not quite plugged into the conversation at all.

It was Val who answered. "Not so much. We wouldn't be at all if not for Dracul always trying to stir the pot. Fucker," he added, his words swallowed by his mug of coffee.

Mackie scraped his teeth along his lip. "But, if you know where he hides out, why don't you take the fight to him? You know, attack the castle or whatever."

"We have considered it," Val replied, staring at his coffee. "We've also tried on numerous occasions to neutralize him and his men by stealth. It hasn't always ended as it did with Adrien." He shook his head. "We are evenly matched in number and the outcome of a full-on assault would be uncertain."

He switched his gaze to Mackie. "If we were to lose, there would be nothing to stop him from taking over this world and enslaving your people. He would slaughter millions purely for his own perverse amusement."

Mackie blinked at that stark appraisal. "Oh." It was hard to believe that the men sitting around him could ever be vulnerable. Hearing Val admitting he could lose a fight made Mackie appreciate more what deep shit they were all in.

"Well," Alex said, "there's no point in dwelling on the past or our lack of invincibility. We will continue to parry Dracul's thrusts as best we can. In the meantime, there's nothing for us to do until we hear back from Duncan. We are assuming this is tied to Dracul, but that was only a theory at this point. We must not get ahead of ourselves. It would please him greatly to know he's always on our minds."

Harry hummed in agreement. "You are right, of course, sir. In this case, however, I have to believe there's some connection with our blood. It's the only thing that makes sense. There will be an autopsy, I assume, given the circumstances. I wish I could be in on that. So much can be learned from that, more perhaps than we want the humans to know. It all depends on whether we are dealing with a hybrid or not."

There was a pointed silence for a few seconds in which Mackie could tell the aliens were pondering issues that the humans in the room weren't privy to.

"I'm with Harry on this, sir," Emil said around his mouthful of food before Mackie could work up the courage to ask questions. "It's got Dracul's fingerprints on it. He's involved somehow."

"You *think*?" Val shook his head. "The guy's a tricky fucker. Spectacular murders didn't work, so now he's onto something else, something to screw us with…again."

Alex sighed. "Yes, yes, gentlemen. Odds are it's Dracul behind whatever this is. I simply caution against precipitous conclusions. Working everyone up into a frenzy of worry won't help." He punctuated his caution by gesturing around the room with his fork.

Mackie got it. Alex didn't want to upset Quinn or any of the other humans in the room. While he appreciated the effort to shield him from worry, that ship had sailed a few months ago for everyone except Kitty. Once he'd actually found a monster under his bed, he couldn't help but keep looking for it night after night. A shudder ran through him.

Val's hawk-like gaze pierced him. He must have seen Mackie's moment of fear. The look somehow gave Mackie a brief sense of security.

"We could simply let it go," Val said to Alex. "He's not attacking us directly, the way he did before."

Alex tsked. "We've had this conversation before, Val. We can't leave him unchecked. He's not like a human child who will give up his tantrum simply because he's being ignored. He will keep poking and prodding until he gets a reaction. And," he added, cupping Quinn's face and staring adoringly at him, "we have soft spots again that he won't hesitate to exploit."

The alien's words hit Mackie hard, making it difficult to swallow his food. Alex would fight to protect Quinn because he loved the boy. As much as the family in general was keeping him safe, though, no one was emotionally invested in it. He was no different than Logan or even the London prostitutes that the Ripper had preyed on. The Stelalux men had a strong code of honor and that's what drove them to intervene where humans were concerned. There was nothing personal in it, simply a chore done out of duty and a strong moral sense of what was right.

And thank God for it. Still…it would be nice to matter to someone. Just as he had the thought, Val's gaze swung on him again. The guy had beautiful eyes, Elizabeth Taylor violet ones. Mackie had always loved looking into them, not that he had ever been able tell what Val was thinking. He still couldn't. All he knew was that it was hard to look away. He dropped into the deep pools of color and got instantly lost—his food forgotten, the others around the table so many buzzing insects to his ears. A sense of calm descended over him, a blissful trip into a kind of subspace without Val having to lift a finger to put him there. That was the strength of the man. Regardless of how mad Mackie got at him, that power was a magnet Mackie couldn't break free from.

Not now, and he feared not ever.

Chapter Three

"This is kind of a long shot, don't you think?"

Sergeant Trey Duncan gave his partner a bleary-eyed side glance. After the alien bouncer's middle-of-the-night call, sleep had proven elusive. It had only been a few months since the horrible night he'd learned that aliens did walk the earth and were waging a vicious war with humans suffering as collateral damage. Enough time had passed, however, that he'd almost convinced himself that he'd imagined the whole thing. *Almost.*

Of course he hadn't. No amount of desperate efforts to rid his mind of the memories had worked. He could still see the epic battle waged near the water in which gravity and other natural laws had been defied and with the loser literally turned to dust. The best he'd managed was to bury the information deep inside his brain while living his normal life of putting away human monsters. Those, he could live with. He was good at his job. Although there was no end to the horror of what humans did to other humans, at least he was confident in his ability to stem the tide. He had no such certainty when it came to dealing with aliens. And now the fuckers might be back at it, starting a new litter of dead human bodies.

He slurped a mouthful of scalding coffee before answering. "What have we got to lose, Karl? We've been chasing our tails on this latest case. Given that we know Murphy was into drugs and this poor bastard who took a header at Copley seemed hopped up on something…" He shrugged. "Could be a lead. Got any better ideas of how to spend our morning?" he asked as he opened the doors to the morgue.

Karl sighed. "Guess not. I saw the footage from last night—the uncut Internet one."

"What was your impression?" Trey kept his tone casual, waiting to hear from his partner what he'd seen.

"The guy was tweaking badly, that's for damn sure. Strong with it, too, and feeling no pain, probably not even when he hit the ground."

"Did he strike you as being maybe homeless?"

"Yeah, maybe. Hard to say with those dreadlocks. I mean, it could be he did it on purpose, or it could be the effect of not washing or combing it."

Trey silently agreed. That kind of deliberate cultural appropriation by white guys never made sense to him. He'd always liked keeping his own somewhat kinky hair cropped close. He ran a hand over his head and remembered he needed to get a tune-up. "The coroner will be able to tell us what kind of shape he was in."

Pushing the elevator button, Trey fiddled with his coffee before deciding to get to the point, which had nothing to do with hair or homelessness. "Weird about his eyes, though, huh?"

Karl snapped his fingers just as the doors opened. "Right. Now that you mention it, his eyes did look kind of red. Maybe that was a trick of the light."

They got inside and Trey pushed for their floor. "I thought of that, but it also could have been an effect of the drug."

"Pot will do it, but stoners don't usually go nuts like that. Coke, maybe."

Hearing his partner's logical explanations made Trey feel a little better. Perhaps all of this was nothing more than a cokehead thinking he could fly. The coroner would probably have little to tell them, given how long toxicology took, except that if the guy had been a long-term drug user, there could be other possible physical signs of it. Just because the club-owning aliens thought this was about them didn't mean it was.

The elevator doors opened, and they found themselves running smack up against two vice detectives. Trey and Karl pulled up short as there was no way into the autopsy room except through the two women who eyed them with suspicion.

Trey went for a little charm, even though he knew when it came to women, in particular, he had none. "Bronner and Diaz, how's it going?"

Bronner gave him a narrow-eyed assessing look. "What are you doing here, Duncan? The guy on the slab wasn't murdered."

"We don't know that yet. In fact, Karl and I are investigating Brian Murphy's death. Given that he was known to run drugs, we thought there might be a connection."

Diaz snorted. "That's it? You working on a hunch or something, 'cause I can't see how those dots connect at all."

Trey gave the woman a tight smile. "Indulge me. We're bone dry on this one and you never know." He gave her a sheepish smile, like he was desperate for any lead, no matter how slim.

"Fine," Bronner replied. "Let's all go see what Almadeo's got. He told us to chill for a few minutes while he did something inclined to splatter."

They all trooped down the hall and into the cold, sterile world where doctors practiced a bedside manner that never failed to please their non-judgmental 'patients'. Never a pleasant place, it was particularly grotesque when the victim was as banged up as this one. Trey tried not to look too closely.

"What have you got for us?" Bronner asked.

Almadeo looked up and over the DB at them. If he was surprised by the detectives doubling in number since he'd last seen them, he didn't show it. "I'm about done here." He snapped off his gloves as he spoke and walked away from the table. "I've taken samples for a tox screen, but you know those results can take weeks."

Trey couldn't help stepping up and possibly on the vice cops' toes. "Based on observation, can you make an educated guess?"

Almadeo raised his eyebrows. "Pressing for conclusions before I'm ready, as usual, Duncan?" The coroner sniffed. "I can say that he was on something. I'm not sure what."

Diaz frowned at Trey before saying, "What makes you think so?"

"For one thing, he took a swan dive off a balcony after calling himself a superhero. We in the medical profession would typically view that as an indication that someone was under the influence of a drug. For another, his blood was like sludge, very much like you'd see after a long-term heroin addiction." The man furrowed his brows. "Although his euphoric mood, manic activity and unusual strength points to meth or bath salts."

He shrugged. "Like I said, the tox report will tell us for sure. Besides that, his organs showed significant damage. Normally with such a physically traumatic death I wouldn't find that surprising, except his brain was in the same condition, even the parts where the skull was reasonably intact. It looks to me as if everything suffered on a cellular level, although I know of no drug that does that...*yet*," he emphasized.

"What about his eyes?" Trey pressed, aware that he was risking something by focusing on the one thing that seemed to be freaking out the Stelalux boys.

"What about them?"

Trey shrugged and tried to appear casual about his interest. "I saw the video of his swan dive, and right before he went over, it seemed like his eyes were pretty red."

"I didn't notice when I viewed it, but he certainly has subconjunctival hemorrhaging in both eyes on account of landing face first on the floor. No mystery there, Duncan."

Trey wanted to push the point, except Karl changed the subject. "What can you tell us about him in general? Like, was he in good condition?"

"Not particularly. My assessment is that he's been living rough for a while. There was ingrained dirt on much of his body. I take that to mean he wasn't able to bathe routinely. Calluses on the soles of his feet indicate a lot of walking in poor footwear. He had gum disease and rotted teeth. That is typically a function of prolonged meth use. Sallow, acne skin points in that direction, as well. Liver's seen quite workout for a few years. So, alcohol may be another factor."

"Okay," Bronner interjected, "addict and probably living on the streets."

Almadeo sighed. "Yes, and a shame, because he appears to be in his late twenties, although some of his organs peg him as a lot older. He had to have been using various substances because there are signs of so many things. And, there was an odd odor to him when I first cut him open."

That observation had Trey perking up. "What kind of smell?"

Almadeo gave him a pained look. "Like I said…odd. A sickly sweet one, kind of like honeysuckle but mixed with a sharp pine scent. Not something I recognized, and it dissipated pretty quickly."

"What drug would create such a smell?" Trey pressed.

"None that I'm aware of."

Bronner clapped her hands once. "Well, the guy died because drugs made him stupid. No mystery about that. And, as no one has found his clothes, he's a John Doe. Hopefully someone will see the video and recognize him, although I don't hold out much help of finding his dealer. God knows there's plenty out there. His body isn't telling us anything pretty, regardless."

Turning to Trey, she gave him a pointed look. "I have no idea what this Murphy vic's life story is, but surely this poor boy has nothing to do with your case."

Trey rubbed at his chin. "I guess not. Seems like at best he was a user, not even a dealer." He gave her a tight smile. "Thanks for letting us tag along."

"Any time, and by that, I mean let's not make a habit of this. We've got enough on our plate."

"Right. Thanks anyway. Doctor," he added with a nod.

"Waste of time," Karl said once they'd left the room.

"Yeah, I guess." Trey made himself busy finishing his coffee to hide how he was thinking through the rest of his day. The Stelalux boys would be waiting for him to get back to them about what he'd learned. It hadn't seemed like much to him, but there might be something meaningful to them.

"Trey!"

"Huh?" He glanced at his partner, realizing that Karl had been trying to get his attention for a few seconds. "Sorry, what?"

"I was asking what you think our next step is. I vote for going back to Brigid's Place and rattling Murphy's cousin some more. He knows something. I'm sure of it."

"Yeah, sure. That dive is always open early. It depresses the hell out of me to see so many people drinking Scotch in the middle of the morning, but I agree that the cousin is holding back."

As they entered the elevator, talking and planning out their strategy, all Trey could really think of was another bar in the middle of a private club—an upscale one with pretty boys and humungous aliens.

* * * *

The cool elegance of Lux was a world away from the old bar in South Boston. Here was muted lighting with classical music playing low. His cop's feet tread on a deep pile carpet instead of sticky linoleum. And, no sad people sat nursing their second or third drink of the early day, making their own kind of *Boulevard of Broken*

Dreams. There'd be no surly, uncooperative owner, either, giving him and Karl mostly 'no comment' answers that pissed him off yet didn't give him cause to haul anyone down to the station. Here in the quiet space was only one clearly agitated, massive, otherworldly man prowling near the bar.

The bouncer with the girly name, Val, stopped on a dime and whirled to pin Trey with a hard stare. It was difficult not to flinch. Trey had faced down plenty of scary, murderous perps in his day. It wasn't the size factor so much, although that was significant. It was more the knowledge that what confronted him now was something that should only exists in fiction. He hadn't seen any of these 'men' since that mind-bending night a few months ago, and he wasn't prepared for how nervous he felt in doing so.

He pushed that weakness down and plastered the same 'don't fuck with me' look he'd given Murphy's bartender cousin. Not that it had worked, but the point was he could not allow Val to see the effect he had on him. Pride and all that, plus Trey wanted to show these aliens that humans could hold their own.

"You have something for us?" Val barked out.

"Yeah. I only want to say it once, though. Where's the boss?"

"This way." Val strode off, heading for the elevator. If he was irritated by Trey insisting on taking this to the top man, he didn't show it.

Trey hurried to keep up. He didn't know much about the alien's society, yet he'd seen enough to know that Alex was in command. The guy seemed to have the respect and loyalty of those around him. There was no doubting his love for the boy, Quinn, either. Whatever else these creatures were, they had the capacity for the best of human characteristics and emotions. That said a lot to him, even though he still struggled with keeping such a monumental secret from his own bosses and his partner.

He followed Val into the roomy elevator and couldn't help comparing it to the dingy one he'd used earlier with Karl. That memory, in turn, gave him a thought. "I don't think I ever thanked you."

The alien looked at him through the reflection of the polished stainless steel of the door. "For what?"

"Saving Karl, my partner," he added, probably unnecessarily. "If you hadn't dived into the harbor and hauled him out like you did, he would have died. So, thanks for that."

"You are surprised that I did." It wasn't a question, and there was an undercurrent of reproach.

Trey cleared his throat once. "I don't know anything about your, um…species." That wasn't much of an answer, yet the best he had and the least offensive way he could think to put it.

"Alex would have been most displeased if I hadn't at least tried to save your partner. It was my…duty," he finished.

"Okay, well, thanks anyway."

The elevator stopped and, before the doors opened, Trey said, "It's hard." The words rushed out before he realized what he was doing. When his companion gave him the side-eye, he felt compelled to explain. "Not telling anyone. Sneaking around on Karl, making up a story about going to the doctor, for Christ's sake. He and I depend on each other for our very lives, and here I am treating him like I don't trust him."

Val stepped out. "We appreciate your discretion… and your help."

Trey grunted because he couldn't think of anything polite to say to that. He hadn't been given any real choice about keeping the alien's secret. Without another eyewitness to what had happened months ago by the harbor and with no evidence, either, anything Trey could have said about aliens would have made him sound crazy. Once that die had been cast, helping seemed the best course of action, though it still didn't set well with him.

"I'm doing this to protect my people." It was petty of him, perhaps, but he was on edge enough to let it out. He stepped forward.

The bouncer blocked the way by slamming his hand against the frame. He glared down at Trey. "Believe it or not, that is what we've been doing, as well—protecting your people."

Trey jutted his chin, refusing to be cowed. "Why? I mean I get why your boss went all out to rescue his lover and cover the tracks of the killer. Saving Karl was part of all that, I can only assume. What's in it for the rest of you and why didn't you all simply take over this world when you had the chance?"

Those violet eyes went flinty. "As I said, it was a matter of duty. Alex is an honorable man and those of us who follow him, and not the other, do so because we share that same sense of responsibility. I will never see my family again, yet I feel their presence always. I will do nothing that would make them ashamed. You understand those things, do you not? Honor, duty, family?"

"Yeah. I get it."

"So, we are allies, even if we're not compatriots."

Trey stuck his hands in his pants pockets. "Guess so."

The bouncer pulled away from the elevator, giving Trey room to leave and enter a luxurious vestibule that would have been a step up from Trey's entire apartment. At the opposite end was a wide-open door. He followed Val past it and into an apartment that mirrored the décor in the club. He stared down into a large sunken living room. Here was the boss, Alex, with his lover cuddled up against him on a long couch. The boy looked happier than Trey had ever seen him before, and that alone told him that these aliens weren't necessarily something to be feared.

The bouncer's ex, Mackie, was sprawled in a big, comfy chair. The last time he'd seen the boy, he'd had an arm broken by the enemy alien. The trauma of injury, coupled with the knowledge that it had been inflicted by someone otherworldly, must have left the boy shocked and terrified. And yet, he'd still managed to resist the demand to lure his friend, Quinn, into a trap. The balls it must have taken with the alien breathing down his neck impressed the shit out of Trey. Underneath that affectation of the pampered brat was a smart, stand-up guy.

He was pretty, too, with his red hair growing out and a hint of makeup accentuating his eyes. There was a lot of creamy skin on display, given the crop-top he wore. The light caught something shiny around the navel area. Normally a belly ring wasn't anything he found attractive, but the idea of flicking his tongue around this one popped into his mind. Something of what he was thinking must have shown in his face because Mackie fluttered his eyelashes at him and the boy's lips curved up into an enticing little smile.

Trey returned the look for the few seconds it took him to enter the room. A low growl penetrated his ear.

Startled, he turned his attention to Val. For a split second, there was an 'I will kill you' warning in the alien's eyes before it was replaced by placidity. Trey might have chalked it up to his imagination if his cop-nerves weren't screaming that he should take cover. Then, he relaxed in the next instant, understanding that despite the break-up between the two, the bouncer still had it bad for the stripper — go-go boy, rather. The same boy who by all accounts liked to be bent over a bench and beaten.

"Is there a problem, Valeriu?" Alex called out.

"No, sir." With that deceptive response, the bouncer stepped into the living room area and planted himself at the far end of the couch. He stood there with arms folded, ever the sentinel, guarding his master.

Alex's expression conveyed how much he wasn't buying the act, either. "Do come in, Sergeant Duncan, and make yourself comfortable."

"Thanks." Trey took a seat in a chair opposite Mackie and flashed him another smile, just to fuck with the bouncer.

"Emil has provided us with a light luncheon of sandwiches, if you're hungry."

Trey nodded. "I could eat."

When he started to rise again, the chef called out from the small kitchen area of the suite. "Stay. I'll bring it to you."

"Thanks again." Settling back down, he took in the rest of the room and those who occupied it.

The older alien, the one who posed as a doctor, sat on one of the high-back stools at the counter, munching on a sandwich, yet giving Trey his stern attention. Trey had only ever met him once, during the initial interviews after the first of the serial killer's victims had been found in the alley next to the club. At the time, Trey had felt a bit of excitement, along with sick dread, at catching such a juicy case. Now he wished someone else had. He could be living his life none-the-wiser about how aliens walked in his world.

He knew that the man, Harry, was married to an exquisite human who had answered Trey's questions with quiet dignity and understated sharpness. They had a kid, a boy whose brattiness gave Mackie a run for his money. Trey wasn't sure what the deal was with the kid's lineage. He looked alien, to be sure, yet with a touch of Asian features. Given that all the marooned aliens were male, that had to mean that somewhere along the way a human woman had come into the doctor's life. Maybe it was something as simple as using a surrogate who could keep her mouth shut. The boy had far more appeal for him than was healthy. If he never ran into the kid again, it would be a good thing, and Trey was relieved that the kid was nowhere to be seen.

"Here you go." The brutish chef handed Trey a plate piled high with food. "It's only pastrami on rye with German potato salad and slaw, but I cure the meat myself and everything else was made in my kitchen, too."

This is a light luncheon? Centuries on Earth had certainly given these guys a lot of wealth and time to hone their respective skills. "It looks great."

"I'll get you a bottle of water." Emil smiled broadly and fangs peeped out, reminding Trey again that he wasn't there for a date.

As he bit into his sandwich, he saw that the homeless vet, Logan, ate her own meal in the back of the kitchenette area. She looked clean and calm, although she stared at him with suspicion. He supposed her presence was yet another indication that the aliens were stand-up guys. She had helped them, and now she was inside their protective orbit.

Alex's throat-clearing caught his attention. "Sorry to force you to speak and eat at the same time, Sergeant, but we're all waiting with bated breath about what you can tell us concerning that unfortunate young man."

"Mmm." Trey swallowed his mouthful. "Right." He took the water offered by Emil and slugged some down before wiping his lips and setting the plate and the bottle on the table next to his chair. "So, I horned in on the autopsy. Vice has caught the case because it's a drug crime, not a homicide, like I told Val last night."

Alex opened his mouth and Trey held off the obvious response. Yeah, I know. There's an argument to be made that whoever gave him that poison is guilty of murder. Regardless, I pretended that it might tie into a case I do have. A drug dealer named Murphy got his throat slit a few days ago. I used that as excuse to poke around the autopsy of last night's victim. The coroner and the two detectives on the case bought it and were willing to let Karl and me ask a few questions."

With a fleeting look at his lunch, he continued. "Anyway, the vic was definitely human, on account of his...you know, not turning into a pile of dust." That aspect of the alien's nature was possibly the creepiest one of all.

"We know that already," Val barked out.

Alex held up his hand. "Patience, please." He nodded graciously at Trey. "I appreciate your observation, but we were more interested in whether he had any unusual characteristics. Besides his possibly red eyes, that is."

Trey frowned. "Such as?"

Alex seemed uncharacteristically uncomfortable. "Well, I…"

Mackie piped up. "Like did he have only boy bits or were there some girl ones, too, mixed in?"

Trey frowned. "You mean, was he transgender?"

Mackie grinned. "Yeah, like that."

"No, the coroner would have mentioned it. I asked what details he could give me about the vic. Sex-reassignment would definitely have come up."

That answer seemed to settle down most everyone in the room. There were a lot of shared looks.

"And, what about his eyes?" Alex asked.

"The redness, you mean? I asked. The coroner chalked it up to trauma from the fall. Hard to argue with his logic. Then there are some drugs that give people red eyes."

"Not pupils," Mackie scoffed. "That guy looked like his picture had been taken by an old camera or something."

Trey held up his hands. "I hear you, but it's probably a good thing that it's not going into the official report as anything weird. They're doing a tox screen, of course. We'll eventually know what was in his system to make him act that way, if anything. He might have simply been mentally ill."

No one challenged that statement, although their demeanor conveyed how much they disagreed with him. The tension in the group was hovering around DEFCON Two, waiting to climb to One the moment he said something relevant. Although what that would be, he couldn't imagine, except… "The coroner mentioned that when he first cut into the guy, there was a weird smell."

That perked up the aliens, at least. The doctor slid off his seat. "Describe it, if you please."

"I can only tell you what the coroner told me. It dissipated quickly, apparently, and I didn't detect it over the general icky smell of the morgue." He shrugged. "He said it was a honeysuckle and pine kind of combination."

And there it was. The aliens' worry hit full alert. They were silently conversing with eyes and hand gestures. Most of it seemed focused on the doctor, who didn't look happy. Trey wasn't the only one to notice.

"What?" Mackie demanded, sitting up straighter. "Why is everyone freaking out?"

"We're not," Val insisted.

Twisting in his seat, the boy glared back at him. "You sure as fuck are. If I had lied that way to you, back in the day, it would have meant a paddling and lockdown in chastity."

Amused, Trey watched the bouncer struggle to keep his cool.

Those words should not have had any effect on Val, yet his blood pounded down to his cock. It hardened, giving him the urge to adjust his slacks. Knowing that Mackie would be sure to see the movement and take it as a win, he settled for clasping his wrist with one hand in front of his fly.

"I can arrange for that paddling even now, boy. Show some respect for your elders."

Mackie rolled his eyes. "Whatever you say, *old man*." He shifted his attention to Alex. "Sorry, but I can tell you are all bothered by what Sergeant Duncan just said. I'd like to know why."

"Me, too," Quinn added, and that settled that. Alex denied the boy nothing.

"You're right, dearest one. The presence of a scent unusual to humans may be relevant. We're simply deciding on the best course of action. I apologize for our rude internal conversation."

"Wait. Can you read each other's minds?" This from the cop, who'd reclaimed his plate and munched on another bite of his sandwich.

Now, it was Val's turn to roll his eyes. Many humans believed that vampires had telepathic abilities, when really it was a matter of humans being too easy to sway with force of will alone.

"No, Sergeant," Alex answered. "We're a crew, remember? We often communicated with expressions and gestures while onboard ship. Over the centuries, we've honed that skill to keep humans in the dark. Our native tongue is too jarring for humans to accept as natural to this world, so this is the only real privacy we have when among you."

"I've texted Lucien," Harry interjected. "He's on his way." Poor Harry. He was so protective of his husband and really hated bringing him into anything unpleasant.

Within a couple of minutes, the man appeared by way of the back stairs. He was, per usual, dressed casually in jeans and a long-sleeved shirt. His black hair lay in a tight braid down his back. Lucien was the epitome of grace and didn't need to wear expensive clothing to look elegant. Harry had lucked out with his boy, who would have been long-dead if not for consuming a steady diet of Harry's blood.

He also had the distinction of having conceived and survived childbirth. It had been a close call, and thinking of it brought up a stabbing pain in Val. He'd barely been able to stay in the same house as his brethren during the ordeal. It had brought back the memories of... No, he couldn't think of that now.

Lucien approached Harry. "What do you require?" He didn't add the 'sir' but it was implied. The couple had their own kind of dominant and submissive relationship, except that Harry never laid a hand on Lucien's head. He'd rescued the boy long ago from a San Francisco brothel where powerful men had used young boys for sexual pleasure before American law had forbidden it. Lucien had been sold into servitude by his family and forced into docility, although it seemed to be natural to him, as well. As near as Val could tell, Harry had never abused his power. It was all about consent and control, however. Anyone could see their mutual devotion.

Cupping his husband's chin, Harry gazed into the man's eyes. "I must ask of you something that would normally be unthinkable." Leaning down, he spoke softly into his ear, explaining the situation and what was required. The humans couldn't have heard it, and Val did his best to block it out. It was too intimate for eavesdropping.

Lucien bowed his head. "If you say this is necessary, then, of course, I will do as you ask."

Harry placed a tender kiss on his head. "Emil, a napkin, if you please." He took the proffered cloth and led Lucien over to Duncan. "I would ask that you stand, Sergeant."

The cop got to his feet, uncertainty written on his face. "Sure. What do you need? Nice to see you again, Mr. Stelalux," he added with a nod at Lucien.

"And you, as well, Sergeant."

Harry lifted Lucien's arm, careful to place the napkin under the forearm. He brought the wrist to his mouth. "Please take a sniff quickly, as I don't intend to waste my husband's precious blood any more than is necessary."

"I'm not sure I understand," the human said right before Harry struck.

Val had to avert his eyes. The sight of one of his kind taking blood from another was also too intimate. To watch, even in this circumstance, was a kind of voyeurism that he couldn't stoop to. He assumed the others were doing the same, but what did the humans think of it? Quinn would understand. Mackie, as well, given that he'd let Val feast off him often enough. Logan had probably seen so much horror in her life that this little show would make no impression. Indeed, he looked in her direction because it was the safest one. Her expression was entirely neutral.

But Val couldn't remain detached from what Harry did. What he could not see, he could smell. The luscious scent of fresh blood made his nostrils flare. His softening dick went rigid once more. He became aware of the steady beat of a heart. Not just anyone's — Mackie's. On a deep inhale, he swung his vision over to the boy and latched onto the tiny pulse at the base of the boy's throat. No human would have been able to detect it. He could. The sight caused saliva to pool in his mouth and his fangs descended.

"Holy fuck!" That was the cop.

"Breathe in the scent. Quickly now."

The strain in Harry's voice pained Val. How was the man able to score his husband's wrist and not drink deeply from it? The self-control required was impressive. Val doubted he possessed it himself. He flicked his tongue across his fangs and kept his sight peeled on Mackie's jugular.

His interest must have been felt by the boy because he turned his own gaze away from what Harry was doing and focused on Val. His green eyes went wide before they narrowed to sultry. He lifted one small hand to press a finger right over the pulse point. The brat knew exactly what Val was thinking. It would serve him right if Val marched over, lifted him up, sank his fangs into that delicate flesh, and drank, and drank…

"Val!"

The sharp tone snapped him out of his reveries. He focused on Alex. "Sorry, boss." He understood by the way the others were looking at him that he'd missed something.

Alex raised his eyebrows. "Sergeant Duncan was confirming how Lucien's blood smells the way he would interpret the coroner's description."

"Oh." He looked over at Duncan, who was sitting back and, by all appearances, wasn't going to be touching any more of his lunch.

The man ran a hand down his face. "Yeah, I mean, I guess. I wish I'd smelled it for myself back in the morgue. All I can say for sure is that I've smelled blood plenty of times, and what I just got a whiff of is way different." He shot Lucien a wan smile. "No offense."

Lucien nodded graciously. "Of course not. I *am* different, after all."

Having already lapped the wound closed, Harry kissed the inside of his husband's wrist before letting it go. "Thank you, my dear. I'll meet you upstairs in a little while."

"I would prefer to stay, if you will permit it."

Harry clearly didn't like that idea. "This is terrible business. I would not have you be a party to any more of it than is necessary."

"I am not so delicate, husband. Please." That was the end of that discussion. Harry was too smitten to deny Lucien anything.

The love between the two men was another painful thing that Val couldn't watch for long. He asked the obvious question for the humans' benefit. "What does this tell us?"

"I'd like to know that myself," Duncan added.

Alex answered them both. "It implies that the dead man had ingested our blood."

"Is that all?" Duncan asked. "What does that mean for a human?"

"It lengthens their life, for one thing," Alex replied.

Duncan scoffed. "Not in this case."

"Clearly," Alex conceded. "It doesn't normally cause a human to go mad, as you can see from Lucien's well-being."

"So, what are the other things?"

Now everyone else in the room, save Logan, made themselves busy looking elsewhere. This was a bad time to share all the details of their lives on Earth with the cop. He had proven to be reliable in many respects, but there was no certainty that he'd keep their secret forever. The less he knew, the better.

Val stepped into the silence, for once taking the lead when Alex normally would. His boss was sometimes too diplomatic and too trusting. "Nothing relevant, except it doesn't normally change their eyes red, and that's the important point here."

"What would do that?"

"We don't know," Alex replied.

"And, that's what's got us worried," Val added. He really wanted to say scared shitless because he, for one, was. In a thousand years, this was a new development, and when it came to Dracul, new was always bad.

Duncan sighed. "Maybe the tox screen will tell us something, although would it tell them that he had alien blood in him?" His eyes brightened. Clearly the prospect of the secret getting out in an evidenced-based way pleased him.

"It presents no differently than purely human blood does chemically, because once it leaves a living host, our species' component dies and disintegrates." This from Harry, who was forcing liquids on a patient Lucien as if he'd bled him heavily. "Unless it's immediately suspended in a saline-based solution," he added, treating his husband to a love-infused smile.

Duncan visibly deflated. "Oh. Well…maybe what's left of the human blood will tell us something useful. The only other thing I can say about the poor bastard is that the coroner thought he was homeless. His physical condition indicated it."

"How so?" Alex asked.

"Um…" Duncan shrugged again and picked up his plate. Apparently the man's stomach was stronger that it had appeared, or maybe the topic had reminded him that he was lucky enough to have food available.

"He was dirty, right?" They all focused their attention on Logan. The woman rarely said one word, and that was mostly to Emil. Now she'd risen from her seat and come into the living room. "It was ingrained within the folds of his skin and under his nails because bathing means a quick splash in a public toilet before you're rousted by cops or security.

"His feet were bad because he doesn't have shoes that fit and he spends a lot of time walking around the city. If he lingers too long anywhere, the same cops and-or security move him along." She folded her arms and asked Duncan, "Does that about cover it?"

"Yeah," he answered around his mouthful of food. He didn't seem any too happy about the situation, nor should he. The humans had never been good at taking care of their own people.

On Val's home world, the concept of homeless didn't exist. Everyone lived in a lesser hive that made up the greater hive of their species. No one ever lived alone. Humans had been mostly like that when they'd first arrived, living in multigenerational homes. It had changed in the last century and the idea of the elderly and the sick being left to fend for themselves was abhorrent to him. To all of them. The pain underscoring Logan's recitation was clear to their ears. Duncan had heard it as well, and that empathy made him a cut above the average human in Val's estimation.

Logan changed her focus to Alex. "I can ask around and see if anyone knew the dead guy."

Alex inclined his head. "I appreciate the offer. Are you sure you wish to become involved? You know what this is likely to lead to."

Logan bared her teeth. "A fight. I'm good at those. You aliens don't scare me much, either. And you sure as fuck haven't cornered the market on horror. We humans do fine with that on our own."

"Very well. Thank you."

"Hey!" Duncan spoke up. "Don't I get a say in this? The streets are dangerous even without aliens mucking around. You're safe here. Leave this investigation to me. I've got contacts out there."

"You only think you do." Logan sneered. "They won't talk to you the way they will me. If the dead guy has a name, I'll find it out. If he was up to weird shit, I can find that out, too. It's a matter of time, that's all. I don't like being inside anyway. It makes me twitchy."

Emil came up. "Let me go with you."

Logan smiled. The woman actually raised her lips and exposed her teeth in something other than a snarl. She put her hand on Emil's biceps. "Naw, thanks for the offer, but they'd only mark you as a narc. You're too clean-cut."

That was the first time anyone had used those words to describe Emil that Val knew of. The guy went all sheepish on her, as if he were embarrassed by the observation. Not for the first time, Val wondered what their relationship was. Emil had played with human males from time-to-time, yet mostly kept to himself. It was probably no more than an affection for a female in a hive-bonding kind of way. Females had been few and far between in their circle.

"I can take care of myself," she added, stepping back and heading for the elevator.

"Don't forget the phone I gave you," Emil admonished to her back. She waved at his words and kept going.

"Well," Alex said, "I suppose it's as good a plan as any. There's nothing we can do ourselves anyway."

"Except wait," Val reminded him. "If this is a Dracul move, it's only the first volley. There will be more coming."

It was the cop who expressed their collective sentiment. "Fan-fucking-tastic."

Chapter Four

Because the club members were well-heeled men, they tended to behave themselves. Being the bouncer didn't usually give Val much to do except wander around, making sure the boys weren't being harassed. Being a warrior, he needed physical activity to release his energy and relieve the boredom. It had been different for most of his time on this miserable planet. There had been endless wars for him to wade in on. Any time the humans had produced a lull, Dracul had always been there to stir the pot. As grizzly as war was, it did keep one busy and tired.

Now he had to rely on the club's workout room. The moment humans had any free time, they started finding ways to spend their own nervous energy and keep off the fat that plagued them. Val found the idea of using fancy machines ridiculous and avoided them when he could. The punching bag, however, was another story. Hitting something inert satisfied his restlessness without hurting anyone. Nothing for him to feel guilty about, and it kept him from being overly aggressive with the club members.

Especially the ones who hovered around Mackie.

Yeah, if he were honest with himself, it was the redheaded brat who drove him to punch the shit out of the boxing bag. Screw Dracul and his world domination crap. Val had, and could a thousand more years, faced down the traitorous male. But a diminutive boy with a fuck-you attitude gave him fits and had since the first time he'd laid eyes on him. He could still picture the skinny boy shivering in the middle of a brutally cold night, offering to do anything for a chance to get out of the frigid air.

Having lived among humans for so long, Val had developed an ability to see their emotions in their eyes. Mackie had been scared shitless of Val, yet had been more scared of freezing to death. There had also been something more there — desire. Despite the cold and the fear, the boy had wanted Val. So, Val had taken him — not to his bed, not that night or for many more after that. Instead, he'd brought him to Emil for food then to Alex for a job.

If he'd been smart, he would have left it at that. He hadn't been. He'd dismissed the warning bells in his head and had invited the boy not only to bed, but also to the play rooms that Val had developed a taste for. Amazingly, Mackie had taken to the BDSM play with ease. The boy was naturally sensuous and submissive, which made him dangerous — for Val, anyway.

The workout room was empty, thank Christ. He wasn't in the mood for chatting or sharing. He stripped to the waist and headed right for the punching bag hanging in the corner. There were gloves, although no one ever used them. The boys didn't like boxing and

Val certainly didn't need them. Balling his hands into fists, he started in with a few warm-up jabs. Seconds later, he was beating the crap out of the thing.

He pummeled away, giving free rein to his natural speed and force. He knew the bag could take it as he'd set the thing up himself. With no one else currently in the club, other than those in the know about his true nature, he had no fear of discovery. He needed the outlet, to attack the bag as a substitute. Not of a person... He didn't picture Dracul's smug face or any other. No, his target became his perception of himself, all his emotions contained in one big, stuffed piece of leather.

The vicious blows he landed were against his damn feelings of longing for his home world and the hive. He punched out with his fists at the constraints of being trapped on a planet where he was forced to hide in the shadows. The hot, bright sun, the uncomfortable heat... The constant squabbles that humans had, giving Dracul easy ground to sow his deadly meddling. He hated it all and wanted to beat it to bloody remnants.

Val held nothing back, his arms and fists a blur to his own eyes. The bag shimmied with equal speed. The metal chain holding it up creaked ominously. His breath puffed out like the driving rhythm of a ship's engines. His grunts turned to growls, his growls to a roar. He jabbed left, then right—short, vicious blows driven purely by power and no finesse. He attacked the bag without mercy, driving it up and out. There was no stopping the need to vanquish his emotions.

Pain. Loss.

His last punch sent the bag flying from its tether. It hit the opposite wall with a crash that he couldn't even hear over the deafening sounds of his own demon thoughts and his harsh breaths. He stood staring, yet not seeing, trying to calm himself, then wondering what difference did it make anyway?

"Holy shit!"

Val whirled at the exclamation and had trouble processing who he was looking at through the lingering haze of his rage. He saw red, literally, and creamy pale skin surrounding wide, green eyes. *Mackie*. Of course, it would be the one person he didn't want to be there. The boy was staring at him, his eyebrows raised and his lips parted. He was dressed like a reject from that stupid aerobics craze in the eighties. His hair was pulled back with a headband that matched his hair color, and he wore blue yoga pants with a skin-tight white tank top. The new belly ring he'd gotten added a tiny bump in the middle of an otherwise flat, taut stomach. The human looked adorable, as always. *Lickable. Fuckable.*

"What are doing here?" Val demanded, his surprise and embarrassment coming out as temper.

That was the wrong tack to take with the brat. Mackie's expression changed to something between dismissiveness and allure. "I was going to work out. Good thing I wasn't planning on using that."

He pointed to where the punching bag lay in a heap on the floor with its stuffing spilling out. The wall where it had hit was buckled with plaster and wallboard hanging down. Val closed his eyes for a moment, partly to clear the last of his foggy state, partly because he didn't look forward to explaining that little repair to Alex.

"Don't let me stop you." Val tried for casual. Failed, apparently, because instead of turning away from him, Mackie stepped closer.

"Are you all right?"

Fan-fucking-tastic, as Duncan had so elegantly stated hours ago. Now Mackie was worried about him—or worse, feeling sorry for him. "I'm fine. Just working off some steam."

Mackie got within touching distance. "I know you guys are strong, but still… Seeing this makes me appreciate how much you were holding back when we, um…played. You could have taken off my head with one blow."

"I would never hurt you." It needed saying, even if Mackie hadn't intended his observation to convey worry.

The boy's lips turned down. "That's not true. You cut me to the quick."

The hurt his saw lurking in the boy's eyes was difficult to observe. *I had to, for your sake…and for mine.* He didn't express those thoughts out loud. He could never admit to Mackie how much it had pained him to do what he'd done, say those awful things that he hadn't meant. It was better this way, inevitable. Their relationship had been doomed from the start because he had nothing left to give the boy.

"I meant physically." He shifted his feet to leave.

With a deft move, the boy blocked him. "I know what you meant." He swept his gaze up and down Val's body. It was a visual caress that caused Val's heart to beat faster and his blood to course down to his cock. "Now that I know you're an alien, I understand why you never break a sweat."

Val started to respond, found his throat constricted and had to clear it. "We have an internal cooling system."

"You're an interesting species, I suppose. There's so much I don't know." Mackie reached out to place his palm against Val's pec before Val could stop him.

No, that was a lie. Val's reflexes were warp speed compared to the human's. He almost sighed at the familiar touch. It took more self-control than he thought he possessed at the moment not to react.

Mackie pursed his lips. "Your skin is warmer than usual, the same way it used to be after you fucked me." He flashed his eyes from under his lashes.

Val bit back a grunt and told his dick to chill out. But given that his core was dispersing the heat of his workout through his system, his cock was more than glad to accept some of it to harden. Thank God he wore tight enough jeans to contain it. Fixing his gaze past Mackie's head, he tried to wait out the boy by not reacting to the provocative statement.

Mackie slid his fingers to the middle of Val's chest and picked up the crucifix dangling there. "It's funny," the boy mused. "Our vampire legends say that you're repulsed by the cross."

"They're just that...legends. Your religions mean nothing to us, but we adopted the one practiced where we first made our home, to blend in more. This was supposed to make them feel safe around us. We simply got into the habit of wearing them. Then, when the schism occurred with Dracul, it became a symbol of how we differed."

"Huh, what would Jesus do?"

"If you like." He ground his molars while he waited for the brat to tire of the game.

Dropping the crucifix, Mackie tipped his head back. "What are you afraid of, Val?"

He looked down his nose at the boy, knowing that it wasn't going to work as an intimidation tactic. "Nothing." Another lie. *I'm afraid of caring again, of losing again.*

Mackie pursed his lips. "Liar. I don't believe you. It's not like you guys are Vulcans or something. You have feelings. I can see that in Alex's love for Quinn, Harry's for Lucien and Demi." He made a face at his mention of the boy. "No accounting for taste, I suppose. And, Emil is the biggest softy I've ever met."

"You didn't ask me if I had feelings. You asked what I was afraid of."

"Same dif."

Val furrowed his brows. "No. Fear is a subset of emotions. They are not the same thing, merely related."

Mackie rolled his eyes at that answer. "So analytical. So always in control." Rising on his toes, he steadied himself with both palms now pressed against Val's chest. "Except when you were drilling my ass and flooding it with your cum."

The boy licked his lips in a slow turn of his tongue. "You still want me, don't you?"

Val's gaze followed the provocative movement and stared at those pouty lips as they taunted him. But when Mackie snaked a hand down toward Val's crotch, he snatched it before it reached its obvious destination. He held the small wrist with a tight grip.

Mackie dropped down to the flat of his feet with a whoosh for breath. "No fair. You have the advantage of alien speed."

Val made his face go grim. "Don't bait me, Mackie."

The brat glared up at him and tried to tug his hand free. "You're hurting me," he whined when Val wouldn't let go.

"No, I'm not, and you'd like it regardless."

"No, I wouldn't."

"Now who's the liar?"

Mackie's eyes narrowed, then he stood straight, and looked right into Val's eyes without flinching. "Red."

Val dropped the boy's wrist before the 'd' had left his pretty lips. In all the times they'd played, Mackie had never given the pedestrian safeword that Val had insisted on. Stepping away, Val nodded once. "My apologies."

Mackie rubbed at his newly freed wrist and stared at the floor. His lashes fluttered wildly, as if he were holding back tears. That couldn't be. Val knew he hadn't held him tightly enough to truly be in pain.

"I need to go," Mackie blurted.

Waving at the door, Val said, "I'm not stopping you. I need to clean up my mess, anyway."

"Not the room. I mean, I need to leave the club."

"What?" The one-word question came out like a roar. Mackie flinched, making Val instantly regret his outburst. He didn't want the boy to fear him. "Please clarify," he said in a more modulated tone that nearly made his head burst with the strain of it.

"I-I need to find my own place again. Working here is one thing, but it's like I'm a prisoner. I can't stay here twenty-four-seven forever, living off Alex's charity, hiding from I don't know what."

"A stone-cold mass murderer who has no more regard for you than you do an ant you might step on. That's what you're hiding from."

"I don't see why he'd care about me."

"Because you're part of our faction now." He didn't add that it was because Dracul would see Mackie as being Val's, and that belief would be more than enough reason to rip the boy to shreds. The very thought sent Val's system into overdrive. His fangs punched down, and he had to force them back.

"I can take care of myself. I was doing a fine job of it when we met. If I have to, I know how to get lost and stay off the grid."

Val scoffed. "You were not and you do not. You were on the verge of starvation and freezing to death when I picked you up."

"You *would* throw that in my face," Mackie said back.

"I'm trying to keep you alive. Dracul and his boys are more cunning and deadly than you can imagine. You of anyone should know that."

Now Mackie rubbed at his arm where it had been broken. "I'll know what to watch out for this time around. You kept me in the dark before." The bitterness came through.

Val knew shame at how badly he'd failed the boy. "I'm sorry for that. We'll do better keeping you safe so long as you stay within our orbit of protection. It's for your own good."

Mackie folded his arms and now he was mad. Val knew that look, having seen it plenty. "*Am* I a prisoner?"

Val leaned down. "If necessary."

"You can't keep me here."

"Watch me."

"Red!"

"No." Val shook his head once. "This isn't a game we're playing. You stay put. If you try to run, I swear I'll track you down and strap you to the St. Andrew's Cross if I have to."

Mackie's eyes flared with anger and his chest rose and fell on a harsh breath. "I hate you!"

"Good."

The boy whirled and stomped his way out.

"Good," Val said again to an empty room. "It's safer for both of us that way."

* * * *

Mackie kept it together until he reached his room. He slammed the door behind him before letting the tears flow. God, he hated how emotional he'd gotten. Val wasn't worth it, yet there was no stopping the crying. With his arms wrapped around his waist, he shuddered alone in the middle of the pretty space. It wasn't his bedroom, not really. It was merely the place they had put him while he'd recovered from his broken arm.

For all its warm colors and expensive furniture, he hated it. It was decorated for human tastes, and he longed for what had become familiar to him. He wanted the alien bedroom that he'd shared with Val. He understood now the heavy, dark drapes and the large, sturdy bed. The black and silver were remnants from their home world décor, or so Quinn had said. The red accents were for blood, their delicacy. It all made sense now, and he missed it.

He missed Val. *Damn it.*

Mackie sat on the edge of his soft bed, sniffling like a baby. He couldn't stand looking around at all his stuff boxed up from his apartment. Val had moved everything over without telling Mackie first and had paid off the lease, as well. Mackie would be safer at the club. That's what he'd been told. And, of course, it made sense, except now Mackie was essentially once again homeless.

He hated that and hated being under some else's thumb. That had been his miserable life for the first sixteen years. Then, he'd been at the mercy of the streets and strange men who wanted what his body could give them. Val had been the first man to treat him with respect and dignity, and wouldn't you know? The guy wasn't really a man at all. Being with him, playing with him, had been Mackie's choice. The apartment that Alex's generous wages and the club members' even-more-generous tips had given Mackie had been where he could escape to any time he wanted.

Now that was gone. The only difference was that Mackie had money. That hadn't been taken away from him. There was enough there for him to leave and start fresh, except that Val had made it clear Mackie wasn't free to do so. Val would hunt him down, and it didn't matter if the reason was sensible or protective. Mackie still felt trapped.

He swiped impatiently at his tears and tried to stop feeling sorry for himself and start thinking of a way out of the mess he was in. A knock on the door startled him. He was about to tell whoever it was to leave him alone when it opened, uninvited.

Quinn stuck his head around it. "Can I come in?"

Mackie sniffed, wiped and nodded. "Sure." Quinn was his only real friend. Of all the boys he worked with, it was this newcomer who he felt a bond with. It might have been their shared terrorizing experience, but really, it was more about how sweet the Midwestern boy was. He'd stuck to Mackie's side like a personal nursemaid, keeping him fed, helping him bathe. Hell, wiping his ass, and hadn't that been a fun time for both of them?

He'd turned out to be good company, too. They spent most of their days watching trashy reality shows and gossiping about the aliens they lived among.

Quinn shut the door behind him. "Are you okay?"

"Sure. Why shouldn't I be?" Mackie's mother had always told him he was prideful. She hadn't been wrong. Even with tears streaking down his cheeks, he hated admitting how unhappy he was.

Quinn gave him a pointed look before settling down beside him. "Well, aside from the fact that you are crying, there's the little matter of how I saw you run out of the gym. Which, by the way, is going to be out of commission for a few days while mysterious wall damage is fixed."

"That's Val's doing."

"I know, sweetie," Quinn replied with a pat to Mackie's knee. "He was in extra-grim mode when I stepped inside to check out what had happened. I assume you two had a fight."

Mackie rolled his eyes and wiped his face again. "If you can call it that." He picked at the hem of his tank top. "He mostly told me what to do, as usual." He left out the way he'd deliberately baited the guy with his teasing flirtation.

"They're a bossy breed for sure. Plus, this new twist with the weird-eyed dead guy has put them all on edge. I can't blame them for that. Can you imagine fighting a war off and on for a thousand years? And, on the down-low because you don't want humans to catch on? I don't know how they've managed it."

"That was their choice, and yeah, I get that our species has been pretty unstable. But, at this point, why not reveal themselves?"

Quinn gave him the stink-eye. "What do you think would happen? Half the world would want to kill them out of fear, and the other half would want to weaponize them. Alex says there are fewer than fifty of them worldwide, and about half of those are Dracul's goons. They're not invincible, and I want Alex to stay safe. I love him," he added, quite unnecessarily.

"I know you do. I can't blame you. Alex is like the perfect man, which is hysterical given that he's an alien."

Quinn's cheeks pinked up. "I wouldn't say perfect. He has his faults."

Mackie showed his dubiousness. "Name one."

"Well. Um…" Quinn gnawed at his lower lip. "He's overprotective. He won't let me leave the club without him."

Mackie dismissed that 'fault' with a wave of his hand. "That's because he's worried about you. You're probably at the top of Dracul's list of people to kill, not to freak you out or anything."

"That's okay. You're not telling me anything I don't already know. I'm plenty freaked out as it is. I do feel safe here at the club, though."

"You should. It's like Fort Knox now with the extra security Val installed. And we have a small team of linebacker-sized bodyguards."

Quinn nudged him with his shoulder. "You should feel the same way. This is a good place to be, so how come you haven't unpacked? You wouldn't let me do it for you because you said you wanted to do it yourself, remember?"

Of course Mackie remembered. It had been a stalling tactic. He hadn't been able to face it then and couldn't now. He wasn't sure where all his furniture had gone.

It had all been second-hand and there hadn't been much of it. Still… "It seems pointless," he replied. "I'm not staying here forever."

"Well, not forever, but for the foreseeable future, right? I'm sure Alex won't mind, even after Dracul is dealt with."

"I can't!" Jumping to his feet, Mackie paced away, fighting back more tears. "Being here and not being with Val is too hard. I can't keep doing this."

"Oh, Mackie." Quinn joined him and wrapped him in a hug from behind. "I'm sorry. I know it must be horrible for you. He was such a dick, regardless of his motives."

"I want to hate him," Mackie confessed in a quiet voice. "I tell myself that I do, but it's a lie. Much as I try, I can't. I'm such a dope that I can't put him aside and ignore him."

"You love him."

Mackie's heart tripped. "No, I don't. He's hot, that's all — and a great Dom. I miss that."

"There are plenty of drool-worthy club members who like to play. It's Val that you want. You can talk to me, you know. I won't say anything to him."

Patting his friends arm, Mackie pulled out of the hug and walked over to the window. His drapes where open, exposing the sheer white curtain underneath. He parted it and peered down. It was a nice-enough view. People scurried down the sidewalk, bundled against the growing chill. Most people would be thrilled to have what he did. Then again, most people didn't know what it was like to have and lose someone like Val.

"I do want him, which is pathetic and pointless. He doesn't want me anymore."

"That's not true. He does. Anyone can see that."

"Well, I can make him hard, if that's what you mean." Twirling around, he swept his hand in a display of his body. "Come on… Who doesn't want a piece of this?" He batted his eyes at his friend, falling back on his old habits of making light of everyone and everything.

Quinn snorted. "Other than me and Alex? No one can resist you, Mackie. I think Val's scared of you."

"Huh! Val's not afraid of anything."

"He is of getting hurt. I know that much." Quinn dropped his gaze to the floor. "Alex told me something a few days ago when he was in his post-blood-drinking fog. Something happened with Val involving a human that devastated him. That's what scares him, I think — getting too close to another boy."

The news caused an embarrassing spurt of jealousy to course though Mackie. Who was this boy who'd what? Captured Val's heart? He wasn't sure the guy had one. A huge cock, yes, an endless libido, sure, and a keen aim when inflicting punishment, naturally, but, Mackie had only seen two emotions from him — indifference and anger. At least, that's all Val had let him see. The idea that a hidden softer side existed was intriguing.

Mackie tapped his fingers on his thigh. "You think that's why he hasn't bothered to apologize for dumping me so hard and try to win me back, now that I know his secret?"

Quinn shrugged. "I honestly don't know, but it makes sense. Alex had the same problem. I'm lucky he got over it, otherwise I'd be as miserable as you are. These guys can be awfully stubborn and surprisingly vulnerable. The only way to know for sure how Val feels is for you to stop allowing him to dictate the terms of your relationship."

Mackie's heart lightened at the suggestion. "You mean I go after him? It's risky," he observed, remembering how quickly things had gone south on him in the gym. "He's no pushover, although I already know I can make his dick take notice. I just have to bring the rest of him around to the idea that we should be together."

Quinn grinned broadly. "Yeah, that's a plan." His face fell. "Although, you're right about Val's being a tough nut to crack. You might end up being more heartbroken than you are now."

"I'm not sure that's possible. I feel trapped and hopeless. I really don't have anything to lose."

* * * *

"Go around the side and head him off at the end of the alley." Trey shouted the order at Karl, then poured on the speed.

He closed the gap between himself and his quarry and reached out to snag the asshole's hoodie. Closing his fingers around it, he tugged to bring the guy down. The slippery bastard wiggled out of the jacket instead and dashed forward.

"Sullivan, you snake, hold it right there!"

Words were useless. The small-time drug dealer was not going to listen. Trey had to stop using his voice and start using his legs. He pumped harder and caught a break when Karl loomed at the end of the alley. The sight of him gave Sullivan's momentum just enough pause that Trey was able to catch up.

This time, he grabbed arms, not clothing, and swung Sullivan up against the brick wall on one side. There was a quick struggle that ended with Trey's arm pressed against the back of the man's neck.

"Knock it the fuck off, Sully. We only want to have a chat. You keep resisting and it's going to earn you an arrest."

"You suck, Duncan."

Trey leaned on the man. "That's not helping your cause."

There was a wheezy cough. "Okay. I'll talk so long as you stop mashing my face into the wall."

Cautiously, Trey loosened the pressure and stepped back to give the guy room to turn around. Karl came loping up and stood to one side, ready to snatch Sullivan if he tried to dodge Trey. The dealer faced them slowly, experience no doubt telling him not to make any quick moves that could be wrongly interpreted. He breathed heavily and was sweating, despite the chill of the day.

Trey gave him a tight smile. "Been a while, Sully."

"I was out of town, visiting relatives down south." When Trey gave him a dubious look, the man added, "Hey, they've got Irish there. Haven't you ever read *Gone with the Wind*?"

"Sure. It seems odd, though, that you'd be away from your home turf for so long. You missed Murphy's funeral. Why didn't you come back for it? Didn't you know he was dead?"

Sully sniffed and ran his hand across the end of his nose. "I heard. I was tied up, that's all."

"That's not what we heard. Is it, Karl?"

"Nope. Willy Flanagan said you and his cousin were on the outs when you left." It was the only remotely useful information the bar owner had given them.

"That pussy don't know nothin'," Sully sneered.

Shoving his hands in his pocket, Trey took a relaxed stance. Sullivan seemed in a talkative enough mood. "He knew enough to tell us you were back in town."

"I had to see my ma, didn't I? She had the flu real bad. The sisters at her nursing home called to tell me to come back."

"We're sorry to hear that. Is she doing better?" This small-time dealer had always been better coaxed than threatened.

Sully smiled. "Yeah, she is. Tough old bird will probably outlast us all."

"She certainly outlasted Murphy."

"She never liked him. Even when we was boys, she told me to stay away from Brian. Said he'd come to a bad end, and, boy, was she right about that."

Karl leaned in. "Is it scaring you straight, Sully?"

"Yeah, as a matter of fact, it is."

"Seriously, Sully?" Trey asked.

The man thumbed out his crucifix from under his shirt and kissed the cross. "I swear on the little baby Jesus that I'm done with the drugs. It ain't like the old days. You knew the sources and the dealers because they were all from your own neighborhood. They might have been stone-cold killers, but at least you knew where you stood."

Trey shared a glance with Karl. "What's changed?"

Sully's eyes shifted left and right. He clamped his lips shut as if trying to keep in words that wanted to come out.

Trey sighed. "Come on, Sully. I can still haul you in on charges of resisting arrest, assaulting an officer…"

"I never touched you."

Trey took his hands out of his pockets and rubbed his arm. "I don't know. I'm feeling a bit sore."

"Yup," Karl chimed in. "Looked to me like you put up quite a struggle, Sully."

"You guys suck."

"So you've said. Come on now. What was Murphy into and why did you leave town?"

"Because I didn't want any part of this new 'opportunity' Murphy had going." He put the word in air quotes and made a face like he'd smelled something bad. "It stunk to high heaven. I ain't surprised Brian got his throat slit. I knew the guys he was dealing with were bad news."

"Where did they come from?" Trey pressed.

"Hell if I know. They were foreign."

"Why do you say that?" *And why are the hairs on the back of my neck standing up?*

"They talked funny. You know…had accents and such."

"What kind of accent, Sully?" Trey could feel his blood pressure rising and his patience ebbing.

The man shrugged. "Can't say for sure. Sort of Irish. Welsh maybe, except there was something else mixed in there. Funny and foreign, that's all I can tell you. They scared the shit out of me, too. I didn't want to play, no matter how much dough they were throwing around. Those big bastards couldn't be trusted. They had dead eyes, you know? Like killing you would be nothing more than squashing a bug."

Okay, now the alarm bells were ringing in Trey's ears. Karl stiffened slightly. Trey didn't dare look at his partner. "Describe them."

Sully's shoulders went up and down. "Wicked big. Huge. Pale motherfuckers with long, black hair that was shaved on the sides."

Karl coughed. Trey ignored him, although sweat began to trickle down the back of his neck. "So, what was their deal with Murphy?"

Once more, Sullivan's lips thinned and his gaze darted around. "I don't fancy getting my own throat slit."

"We'll keep you out of it."

"Sure you will, Duncan. That makes me feel so much better."

"Sully, tell us here or at the station. Your choice. If we bring you in, everyone will hear about it."

"Have I told you how much you suck?" He huffed. "Okay, so these two mofos contact Murphy about dealing some new drug. They approached him at Brigid's one night when Murphy and I were hanging around, having a few rounds.

"They buttered him up, saying how they heard he was the guy in Boston to see about getting this new stuff out." Sully rolled his eyes. "Brian was like a brother to me, but he was no big-time dealer. He lapped up what they were laying down with a spoon."

"Did they say what this new drug was?" Karl interjected.

"They called it 'vamp', which is a stupid name, but stupid people do drugs, so...."

"Fuck." Trey muttered the word under his breath, although, in the alley, it was like a shout. "What's its selling point?"

"Better than E and crack and anything else you can get out there, according to Frick and Frack. Users will feel invisible, masters of the universe, a high that lasts for hours and makes them want to come back for more."

"Is it a tablet or a powder? Do you snort it or inject it?"

"No idea. Didn't want to know. I told Murphy those guys were bogus. Whatever shit they were into, I didn't want any part of it." Turning his head, he spit onto the ground. "Damn foreigners muscling into our territory with questionable goods."

"But Murphy was hooked."

"They paid him five Bennies just for listening. Of course he was hooked. They gave him an address and said if he came there the following week, they'd give him samples as freebies for his best customers. That was to get them *hooked* on the junk then start peddling it. You know the drill."

Trey rubbed a hand down his face. "Yeah, we do. Did you go with Murphy when he met them again?"

"Nah. We had words the second they left. I told him they couldn't be trusted and dealing with them would piss off our current suppliers. Either way, I figured it was the kind of thing that would get a person dead. He said it might be the chance of a lifetime to score big.

"I took off the next day in case things blew up in his face right away." He grimaced and looked away. "I heard about Murphy and the guy who took the swan-dive off the balcony at Copley. I put two and two together, 'cause that math wasn't hard. If it hadn't been for Ma needing me, I'd have stayed away longer."

"Was the dead man a customer of Murphy's?" Even as he asked the question, Trey knew the answer.

"Yeah. I recognized him as one of the regulars. Some guy who washed out of MIT and spent his days panhandling and getting high. Not exactly the crème de la crème, but I guess as good a test case as any. Maybe that means he started dealing this shit across the river." He shrugged. "I'm guessing here. I don't know what went wrong with Murphy and the suppliers, either, but as much as I loved him like a brother, Murphy was an idiot. He must have done something to piss them off."

"Maybe it was one of his old suppliers making a point with him about loyalty," Karl ventured.

"Nah, I don't think so. More like they would have used him to maybe muscle in on the new action. Bet they're staying far away from this shit now, though. This kind of spotlight ain't good for business."

It is if chaos is your goal. Trey hated the thought, except it was obvious that the aliens were involved. Sully's description had driven that point home. "Okay, one more question."

"Sure thing, because this little chat isn't making me nervous or anything."

"Who besides you would Murphy have trusted with this new venture?"

"That I can't tell you. Brian knew I wouldn't rat him out to the other suppliers. There was no one else I know of he trusted like that."

"Okay," Trey said again, already trying to figure out how he was going to steer Karl away from the Stelalux clan. "Thanks, Sully. If you hear anything else about these foreign suppliers, contact me."

"Not on your life, Duncan. It's a fucking shame what happened to Brian. I'm going to miss the son of a bitch, but I'm not sticking around to find out if I'm on someone's shit list."

Trey considered taking the guy in after all, but that would only endanger his life and not help Trey's investigation anyway. Stepping back, he jerked his head. "Get lost, Sully."

"My thoughts exactly." With that parting shot, the man took off at a brisk pace.

Two seconds later, Karl had planted himself in front of Trey. "Those guys he described sound familiar. We should head over to Lux. Damn," he added. "I was hoping the Stelalux family was on the up-and-up after all. I don't like owing my life to mobsters."

"We don't know that they are," Trey was quick to point out. "They may or may not be related to these new suppliers. We can't go by a physical description. You know we can't. That's profiling."

Karl furrowed his brows. "Yeah, but sometimes what looks like a duck and quacks like a duck is actually a motherfucking duck."

Trey took a deep breath to steady his nerves. He really wasn't cut out for all the subterfuge. "Okay, so maybe they are involved. If so, I don't want to tip our hand too soon. Let's see if we can tug some other lines before we question the Stelalux boys. If Sully thinks maybe Cambridge is where this is centered, we start there. I know someone in vice over there. We can see what he's heard."

Karl scratched his head. "You think that's the right way to play this?"

"Absolutely." Jesus, Trey hated treating his partner like the enemy. He was also going to have to bring this new information to his alien allies just as soon as he managed to lose Karl for the day.

Sully was right — at that moment, Trey did suck.

Chapter Five

"Come on, honey. The club's so quiet tonight. Why don't we go up to one of the private rooms?" Warren's warm breath tickled the back of Mackie's neck while the man snaked his hand around to cup Mackie's package.

The touch was light and not the least bit erotic. However, as he'd decided to begin Operation Seduce Val that night, Mackie leaned against his would-be suitor and moaned. "You make a tempting offer, sir, but I'm due on stage in a few minutes."

"Oh, come on. Can't you get someone to fill in for you?" He gave Mackie's dick a squeeze. "I can see your pretty cock through that sheer thong you have on. Such a naughty look."

Slipping out of the hold, Mackie shimmied away, trying not to hurt the man's feelings. It wasn't Warren's fault, after all, that Mackie only wanted Val and was desperate enough to use what ammunition there was.

"Sorry." He blew a kiss and sauntered over to where Shawn was finishing up his set.

The other boy made a face. "It's a slow night. Hardly worth slipping into a G-string for." His gaze dipped. "Not even one that's see-through. Damn, girl, you are looking fierce."

"Thanks. It's a new look I'm trying out."

"Uh-huh. Well, try not to give any of these geezers a heart attack."

With a laugh, Mackie patted Shawn's shoulder then he hopped up onto the stage. He'd already had a talk with Kitty, the mistress of the music. He nodded at her from where she stood behind her bar. When the current song stopped, the haunting strains and driving beat of Linkin Park's *Faint* commenced. It was a good thing the club wasn't filled with members. This song was an edgy choice for the usual crowd. It didn't matter. The lyrics conveyed his feelings perfectly, and now that he'd admitted to himself how much he wanted Val back, he was prepared to do anything to get the man to sit up and take notice.

As he grabbed the pole by both hands, he began to twist around it. This show he put on was for only one man in the room. He'd already scoped out Val's location. No matter how many rotations Mackie made or poses he struck, he made sure to orient his gaze in that direction. He got a jolt of satisfaction when saw that he already had caught Val's attention. He had no doubt he could hold it.

Seduction was an art, a thing that required finesse — at least at first. He gave himself time while the song ramped up to reconnect with the slick metal he grasped. When he was in the groove, it became an extension of him — or he of it. It didn't matter. All he knew was that it was natural for him to turn it into a partner of sorts. The pole was an ally in his scheme, a temporary lover to help entice the real one he sought.

He climbed up it using only his arms and, spreading his legs wide, swung around it all the way back to the ground. The moment his feet touched the stage once more, he arched his back, tipped his head and winked at Val. When the chorus of the song kicked in, he humped the pole with heavy-lidded eyes. He lip-synced the lyrics, letting the late, great Chester Bennington's raw voice convey his demands.

Val stood like a pissed-off statue by the bar. There wasn't much distance between them, so it was easy to see how the man's gaze was homed in on his every move. Buoyed by the knowledge that his plan was working so far, Mackie picked up his routine. Doing gymnastics had always been a dream of his. As a boy, he'd begged his mother to allow him to take lessons. The answer had been no. It wasn't a boy's sport. Neither was dancing. Asking for either had only set off a string of punishment and abuse, proof that he was unnatural. Still, he'd watched the Olympics and dancing contests and had practiced what he'd seen wherever he could find a spot to do so. Pole dancing was the perfect way to show off his passion for both.

After climbing the pole again, he hooked one leg around it to descend once more, slowly this time. With each rotation, Mackie blew a kiss in Val's direction as their gazes met. The man's eyes narrowed, the only movement visible. It was enough, though, to encourage Mackie further. When his feet landed on the stage, he rubbed his ass against the pole and ran his palm down the front of his body. He lingered at his package, cupping himself and giving Val the 'O' face. He held the man's gaze for a second before twirling around, climbing the pole yet again and doing an upside-down split. His cock was already half-hard, and he knew it was visible through the confines of the lacy G-string he'd donned.

With the lyrics of the song voicing his feelings perfectly, he fell into the tempo. He let it drive him into a frenzy of movement. He swooped and dipped and swung, making love to the pole with the acrobatic agility that he prided himself on. He put in every sensuous move he had. His arm twinged in protest when he held his body perpendicular to the pole. He ignored it and tightened his core to compensate for the weakness. He wanted to show off his strength as well as his grace.

Do you see me, Val? This is who I am. This is what I can do for you. I'm tough. I can handle anything. The only thing I fear is losing you.

As the song came to an end, Mackie tangled his legs high up around the pole, and flung himself upside down. He held his arms out wide in a reverse crucifix move he'd learned from Demi, of all people. Maybe the martyrdom imagery was a bit over the top, but he was desperate for his efforts to work. He was offering himself up as a sacrifice to Val's power and need.

He instinctively shifted his gaze to Val's spot by the bar. It was empty, and his heart sank at the notion that all he'd managed to do was chase the man away. Then his view became obscured by thick legs clad in black. Mackie blinked in surprise, then he smirked in understanding. Val must have used his alien speed to arrive at the stage in record time. That lapse in judgment told Mackie more than anything else that his plan had succeeded.

Of course, it was also like poking a tiger with a stick. In the blink of an eye, Mackie was being pried off the pole. He squeaked when he was yanked away and his world spun in a dizzying rush. He landed with his head still down, but now flopping against Val's broad back. He struggled in an automatic response until a stinging smack on his bare ass made him gasp. It also made him smile.

To his growing delight, he watched the main room pass by in a blur as Val carried him up to the second floor. There was no way he'd give Val the satisfaction of any easy conquest, however. Mackie had cultivated his brat persona because it suited them both for him to do so. He wanted to restart their relationship the way he intended for them to go on.

When he was once more twirled like a rag doll and set on his feet, he hissed. "How dare you! I'm in the middle of my set." He put his hands on his waist and flashed his eyes in a manner that was guaranteed to get a rise out of the guy.

Leaning down, Val scowled into Mackie's face. "Don't act so outraged when you're getting exactly what you asked for." Val's admonishment came out sharp like a slap.

The man's sternness turned Mackie on. This was what he'd missed, being admonished, then disciplined, by a commanding man. He hadn't understood until he'd met Val that his whole life had been a quest to find this kind of relationship. Val's aloofness and seeming indifference to him these last few months had left Mackie adrift. He needed a Dominant. He needed Val. Still, he wasn't going to make it easy on the guy. There was no fun in that.

He folded his arms and tapped one foot. "What exactly do you think it is I'm asking for?"

"My attention."

Mackie tsked. "As if. You made it quite clear you want nothing more to do with me. I have no interest in anyone stupid enough to toss me away. I was trying to entice Mr. Warren, if you must know. I figured if I pretended to be flirting with you, it would make him jealous."

"You lying little brat," Val spit out, showing more anger than Mackie had ever seen before. "That letch had his hand on your dick before you stepped foot on the stage. You had him with that frilly 'see me, touch me' thong." Val's gaze shifted down to Mackie's crotch. "He didn't need a show to spur his cock on. And, it looks like you didn't need anything more than your own performance to get hard yourself."

Those violet eyes made Mackie feel as if a hand had grabbed him. Unlike with Warren's actual touch, this look caused blood to pool in his cock. If he hadn't been hard already, Val's gaze certainly did the trick. The tiny bit of fabric trying to contain his cock and balls strained under the pressure of his fattening dick. An ache between his legs told him that his own need had reached a point of no return. If he didn't get some relief from Val soon, his balls were going to hurt like a bitch.

Val's nostrils flared. With what Mackie now knew about the man's alien nature, he dared to hope it was a sign that his arousal could be scented as well as seen.

"What do you care who touches me?" Mackie's voice came out breathy, testament to how quickly he was losing control of the situation. "Or who and what turns me on?"

"I don't." Val's voice sounded strained. Thank God, Mackie wasn't the only one spiraling. "I simply don't appreciate being teased."

"You're a head case. I barely noticed you, and only did so because you're like the specter of doom out on the floor. Honestly, a complete buzzkill." He was babbling at this point, stringing inflammatory words together to push Val into action. The mixture of fear and excitement he felt was a comfort, old times made new again. It gave him hope, even as it scared him witless.

Mackie squeaked again when he found himself eyeball to eyeball with Val, the fear edging out the excitement for a moment. The man had Mackie in a tight grip around his waist, with his feet dangling about a foot off the floor. Mackie grabbed Val's biceps, catching a fistful of his silk shirt in suddenly sweaty palms. Mackie's heart beat wildly and he could barely catch his breath. The familiar sensations were already sending him to subspace.

Val's touch was cool, as usual, but his gaze was red hot. His pupils had turned from violet to almost black. That was something Mackie had never seen before. Then again, he'd never known Val to be on the edge of losing control, nor had they ever fucked face-to-face. Val had always taken him from behind after he'd paddled or whipped Mackie's ass. The heated gaze was fixed on a point below Mackie's face. He realized with a jolt that pulled him back from bliss that Val was staring at his pulse point.

Blood. Val wanted to suck Mackie's blood. He needed to, maybe. Mackie had a sudden image of Val as a vampire, fangs down, striking at his neck and drinking him dry. If that happened, it wouldn't be like before with Mackie still floating in subspace, barely aware of what was happening. This would be different. This would be terrifying.

Mackie's bravado deserted him. He'd remembered a little too late that he was messing with a frighteningly strong alien being. *What if I've pushed him too hard too fast?* He allowed himself only a moment of worry and regret before shoving both aside. This was what he wanted, Val back in his life the way he used to be. The man had never abused the trust Mackie had given him. There was no reason for him to do so now. Mackie had to give that trust again, or there was no hope for them. And, he wanted there to be. He might not ever forgive Val for the way he'd treated him, but he did still crave his attention and his touch.

"Careful, boy," Val warned. "You know better than to challenge me."

Oh, thank God. Here was the familiar, the Dominant chastising the submissive for getting above his station. Mackie licked his lips, appreciating how Val's gaze tracked the movement. "So, what are you going to do about it?"

Val bared his teeth, his pointy canines shining in the muted light. The sight, another first, caused Mackie's lungs to freeze. "I'm going to give you exactly what you want, *boy*."

Mackie's world tilted yet again as Val whisked him over to one of the lap-dance chairs. Mackie had a quick second to scan the area and was relieved to see they were alone. If the choice had been up to him, he would have preferred to do this in private. But, it wasn't his decision, and that was the whole point. Val could do the thinking and planning for the both of them, and knowing that he could rely on a strong, intelligent, reliable man to fill that role caused Mackie a peace of mind that had been missing for his entire life before meeting Val.

The second-floor balcony area was familiar territory, although not in the usual way. Instead of straddling a lap, Mackie was lying across one — Val's, to be exact. Instead of leading a club member in a hot pantomime of sex, Mackie only had to lie there and take whatever Val decided to give him.

Mackie's position was awkward until he stopped tensing against it and went boneless. His face was mashed into the velvet of the seat, a cozy spot that also made it impossible for him to see exactly what Val was doing. His bare ass was unguarded, and his stiff cock pressed against both the front of his thong and Val's pants.

He felt both trapped and exposed — and thrilled.

"You need discipline, boy, like you always have." Val palmed Mackie's ass, his hand large enough to cover the entire expanse. For the moment, it merely rested there.

Mackie knew it was the lull before the storm. "Don't you dare," he threatened in a voice muffled by the chair cushion and the music floating up from downstairs.

"I don't recognize that order. There's only one word I do listen to. Are you saying that?"

"No," Mackie ground out. He knew that he ultimately held the reins in all of this. The simple fact was that he wanted what Val was about to mete out.

The first blow was more of a warning shot. Not much more than a tap and merely a warm-up. The next came quickly and it was harder, a sharper discomfort. Then, there was a soothing circle as if to say 'just kidding', except it was followed by a blow that robbed Mackie of his complacent breath.

The spanking ramped up to a string of strong slaps against his entire ass each time. Val's hand was so big compared to Mackie's backside that there was no need to focus on only one cheek at a time. Val pitched his smacks with an upward curve that started with the slope where ass met thigh and ended with the fleshier parts. Closing his eyes, Mackie pictured how they looked. The playroom walls were covered in mirrors. Val had often forced Mackie to watch his own punishment to keep him in the present and away from the escape of subspace.

There was no such possibility now, nor did Val make him count the blows. Mackie was free to simply experience the exquisite relief that came from a good spanking. It was nothing like the beatings he'd received as a child, and the soothing nature of Val's ministrations had long-ago helped Mackie let go of his childhood traumas.

Against all sense, here was peace. With Val's smacks setting a steady rhythm, Mackie had no trouble descending into the subspace that he craved. Oh, how he'd missed this for these last two months. All the stress and fear he'd held inside melted away in the face of his punishment. Like rubber bands snapping, his body shed, one-by-one, the tensions that had enveloped him since that horrible night when his world had come crashing down.

There went his heartbreak. There went the horror of a nightmarish monster made real. The pain of his arm snapping — gone. The fear of being out in the world alone again, rudderless and without a visible future, melted away as he gave himself over to Val's stern care.

He hadn't quite descended all the way to that floaty plain where all was a perfect haze of happiness when a sharp pinch of his ass cheek snatched him back to reality. He whined and wiggled. Another pinch made him stop.

"You were humping my leg. I didn't give you permission to come, boy."

"Sorry, Sir." He hadn't been aware of doing that, of course. The idea had merit, however. His cock had come loose of the thong and pressed against the soft fabric of Val's pants. Mackie wasn't the only one hard, either. The rigid length of Val's cock jutted against Mackie's hip. It made him wonder if the evening would end in a good fuck, not that he should get ahead of himself. The spanking would have to be enough for one night if that was all Val gave him. The man was prideful and stubborn. He wouldn't capitulate to Mackie's onslaught easily.

Val landed a blow that had Mackie rearing up in shock. "Stop thinking." Val's order brooked no argument.

Damn the man. He'd always been able to read Mackie's mind. *Is that an alien thing?* Swallowing hard, Mackie said, "Yes, Sir. Sorry, Sir."

The spanking recommenced. This time, Mackie was aware of how his dick was being stroked by the rocking movement caused by the blows. He bit his lip to fight against the rising orgasm. He might have been out of practice, but he knew how to be a good sub. He had mastered the control to hold back his climax until given permission. And, when it was given, the pleasure was all the greater for the waiting.

It had been too long, though. Not having come in months, his body was primed for an orgasm. He fought to keep himself in check, and when he feared he was losing the battle, he did what a good sub would do—he asked his Dom for help.

"Please, Sir. I can't hold it back. I'm too weak."

"No, you're not. You can do it. You're a good boy, Mackie, when you give yourself to me. Strong. Capable. Don't come, not yet."

The words of praise warmed him. He'd missed this simple affirmation, too. He wasn't the worthless boy he'd been taunted as in childhood. Val saw more in him. Val trusted him. With gritted teeth, he kept his dick in check.

He knew the moment when he was lost. "Sir!"

"Come now." The command was issued in a cool voice that barely rose above the music. As he gave it, Val slipped a finger past the thread of the thong and slid it up Mackie's ass.

The pressure of being invaded set him off like a rocket. With a keening cry, he arched his back and watched the explosion of white behind his eyelids. He clawed at the seat cushion as if trying to drag himself away from the intrusion and the climax. He humped Val's lap, the rasping against his sensitive dick goosing another spurt of cum out of him. His head spun and his hearing dimmed as he slumped back down in a mindless heap.

* * * *

This was duty.

Val reassured himself on that point as he carried a boneless Mackie to the boy's room. He weighed almost nothing, like he always had, except it seemed as if he were lighter than usual. He'd looked thinner to Val since his recovery from the broken arm. Emil had been right about fattening the boy up.

Mackie had obviously needed the spanking, as well. Physical discipline had always chased the stress out of the boy, and given their current situation, Val should have been more attentive to that. His job had always included looking out for others. It was his role within the hive. Being human notwithstanding, Mackie was part of the loose familial group Alex had formed since being marooned. Val had let his own worries keep him from tending to Mackie's needs. That stopped *now*. Helping Mackie didn't have to mean becoming personally involved again. Val could separate the physical from the emotional.

Mackie barely stirred when Val laid him on the bed. The boy simply curled onto his side, facing Val, with his eyes shut and his lips slightly parted. He tucked his fists under his chin while Val drew the covers around his slight body. Mackie uttered a sigh of contentment before his breath evened out. He looked impossibly young and completely relaxed.

Sleep hadn't always brought Mackie peace. For the first few months after Val had taken him as a lover, Mackie had been tense and wary all the time, in bed and out. And, he'd suffered from nightmares that had him bolting up and cowering. It was only when Val had cautiously introduced the bondage and discipline that Mackie had begun to lose the almost-feral quality that had undoubtedly served him well out in the world.

Val had taken pride in making a difference in the boy's life. It was the emotional intimacy that had been the problem. Val hadn't intended to take things with the human that far. He still didn't. There was no denying, however, that he was responsible for Mackie.

There was no turning away from him completely. Not yet, anyway.

He certainly couldn't leave the boy at the moment. Even a spanking required aftercare, especially given how Mackie had responded. That orgasm had drained the boy with a force that told Val that Mackie had been without a release for probably the entire time he'd been recuperating. There was no telling how he might feel in the next few hours. Leaving him unattended was out of the question. His care was Val's duty, as well, so that meant one thing.

With only a moment's hesitation, he kicked off his shoes and slid onto the bed beside Mackie. He propped himself up against the headboard, determined to stay the night without sleeping. Lying by Mackie would provide too much temptation. His presence didn't disturb the boy, either. Far from it. With a breathy little murmur, Mackie rolled closer to Val, so that their bodies touched. Val couldn't resist petting the boy's head a few times before pulling out his phone and texting Alex that he needed to take the rest of the night off.

Alex acknowledged the text without asking any follow-up questions. Not surprising. The man knew that Val never shirked his duty, and there had to be a good reason for his clocking off so early. He probably suspected it was Mackie-related, given how Val had swept the boy up from his stage time. That probably meant there were too few boys dancing for the night to keep the club members happy. Val didn't care, nor did he regret his actions. He told himself it was because it was good for Mackie. The truth was not something he wanted to face, not at the moment.

There was nothing to do except play with his phone. The Internet held an endless amount of entertaining choices. He tried not to watch Mackie sleep, although he was tempted. He also avoided looking at the room. It was filled with the boxes Val had packed himself from Mackie's old apartment. The boy had done nothing to unpack and make the former guest room into his own personal space.

Because he doesn't intend to stay.

That thought irritated him for reasons he was unwilling to explore. So, he kept his head down and his hands to himself. The sound of Mackie's deep, even breathing lulled Val. The erection he'd suffered while he'd spanked Mackie's taut ass had subsided. He had no intention of indulging it, either.

About an hour later, his phone pinged with a text.

My office, now!

Val sat up. Alex's urgency came through loud and clear through the brief message. But Val was immobile with indecision. His duty required him to shoot down to Alex, yet he couldn't leave Mackie unattended. Subs coming down from the endorphin flood created by the discipline were vulnerable. There was no one he trusted to come watch the boy, and it was his responsibility to look after him, regardless.

"Mackie, wake up." He issued the order in a low voice so as to not startle him.

At the same time, he left the bed and went over to the dresser. He pulled out socks and clean underwear. In the bottom drawer, he found yoga pants and a sweatshirt. The last item surprised him. It was his, a ratty old thing he'd forgotten about. Mackie must have put it on at some point during their relationship and had still kept it. He almost put it back and found something else, but some primitive part of his brain stopped him.

Turning, he saw that Mackie was propped up on his elbow with sleepy eyes. "What's up?" The boy's voice was sweetly childlike, unconcerned and merely perplexed.

Val returned to him and stripped back the covers. "Alex needs me and I can't leave you alone. Come on. Let's get you dressed."

"Okay." Mackie was docile, letting Val do whatever he wanted.

The first thing was to strip off that silly lace thong crusted with Mackie's cum. Val tossed it on the floor and wrestled the clothing he had onto Mackie's pliant form. The boy yawned loudly and blinked up at him owlishly. Devoid for the moment of his usual snarky demeanor, he appeared sweet and biddable. Val told himself he liked him better this way, but that wasn't entirely true. There was something perversely appealing about Mackie the Brat.

When he was done dressing the boy, he scooped him up in his arms once more and strode for the door.

"I can walk." Even as he made that declaration, he wrapped his arms around Val's neck and lay his head on Val's shoulder.

Val used the back stairs to whisk them both to their destination with his natural speed. He took the risk that none of the club's human employees would be lurking about to see it. When he entered Alex's office, he found Alex sitting at his desk with Quinn perched on his lap. Harry and Emil stood nearby, staring at the large flat-screen on the far wall, as did Duncan, of all people. The room's occupants swung their collective gazes in his direction.

Jerking his head at Mackie, Alex asked, "Is everything all right?"

"Yeah." Val craned his neck to see what had captured everyone's attention. "Mackie needs aftercare. That's all."

He didn't bother to explain exactly what had transpired for the boy to require monitoring. He figured it was self-evident, and besides, he wanted to know what was going on. There was a lot of yelling coming from the TV. Getting closer, he focused on the scene being covered by a clearly wavering videographer.

Two men, one naked and one in tattered remnants of clothing, were shrieking as they ran down a sidewalk. They were smashing store windows with their fists and terrorizing anyone in their path. People scattered, screaming. Cars started and stopped as the men wove among the traffic. They attacked any vehicle they passed, as well, rocking cars and banging on hoods. One managed to rip a windshield wiper off and whipped at the windshield with it.

"What the fuck?" Val crowded out Duncan to get a closer look.

"It's from an hour ago," the cop said, "on Newbury Street. A pedestrian took the video."

Now cops came screaming up, people in uniform jumping out of their vehicles and shouting at the men to stop. They both ran toward the officers instead. Tasering didn't stop them, barely slowed them down. And, when the man with the wiper charged a cop with it raised up like a weapon, the cop dropped him with a couple of rounds.

Mackie whimpered and buried his face in the crook of Val's neck. *Damn.* He'd been so caught up in the drama, he'd forgotten about the boy.

"Shh, it's all right." He cupped Mackie's cheek and held him firm.

The remaining man was overwhelmed by a few officers, but he put up a hell of a fight. It took all three of them to get him on the ground and cuffed. The videographer managed to get in close as they were raising the crazy guy to his feet. There was a moment when he looked right at what was undoubtedly a phone. His red eyes stared at the lens before rolling back into the man's head. He collapsed into the firm grips of the cops. That's when the screen changed to two people sitting behind a desk explaining what the viewers had just witnessed.

Alex switched off the TV. "Well, that didn't take long to escalate."

Val headed for the couch and sat with Mackie still cradled in his arms. Emil joined them, sitting at the other end. He shot Val a knowing smile. The man was a real soft touch when it came to relationships, although he'd never formed an attachment to a human that Val knew of. Not wanting to give his compatriot any encouragement, Val focused on Duncan.

"Did you come here because of that?" he asked with a nod to the television.

The cop sat on one of the visitor chairs, while Harry took the other. "I was actually on my way to see you already. I have information to share and couldn't get away until now. What went down on Newbury Street is pure happenstance." He sighed and ran a hand down his face. "I'm going to have to go back into the station.

What we just witnessed is obviously connected to my murder case."

"How so?" It was Mackie who posed the question before anyone else could.

Val frowned down at him. "You don't need to worry about this. Go back to sleep."

Sitting up, Mackie rolled his eyes. "Like I could, through all this commotion."

"Right." Val should have left him in his room after all or handed him over to Kitty, perhaps. This new trouble was surely pulling Mackie away from whatever relief the spanking had provided.

"I'm okay." He gave Val a shy smile. "I feel pretty good actually." Now his cheeks pinked in that cute way of human capillary functioning.

"Okay." His lips twitched in a desire to return the expression. He resisted the impulse and eyed Duncan instead. "So, what gives?"

The cop took a deep breath, signaling that whatever he'd come to say was going to be long and irritating. Val's suspicions were confirmed once the man launched into his story about some kind of new and dangerous drug entering Boston via Cambridge, perhaps. It didn't take much for everyone to realize that what he was describing explained the scene they'd all witnessed on the television.

It was Mackie, again, who voiced the thought they were all having. "They actually named it *vamp*?" Giving Val a sideways glance, he added, "Does this Dracul guy have a sense of humor or something?"

Val's gaze landed quite against his will on the boy's lips. He'd always found them to be far too sensuous for anybody's good. They appeared perfectly suited for wrapping around a guy's dick. That thought, coupled with the way the boy's bottom already fit perfectly against Val's lap, sent blood rushing to his cock. It rose, pressing against Val's slacks and Mackie's pert ass. Val could tell the exact moment the boy felt the reaction by the way those lips of his curled up a bit at the corner.

Damn, I should have relieved myself back in Mackie's room after all. Although who was he kidding? When had one orgasm ever been enough where this human was concerned?

Val shifted his gaze and resisted the urge to squirm. "In his own sick way, yes."

"Dracul proved to be more adept at understanding humans than the rest of us, too, I'm afraid," Alex added. "He knows what makes you all tick—your needs and wants and weaknesses. He found your 'buttons', as you would say and learned to push them early and often."

"I don't get what he hopes to accomplish." This from Quinn, who rested his head against Alex's chest in an act of obvious comfort.

Alex ran a soothing hand down the boy's arm. "Sometimes it's enough for him to cause chaos. Humans running riot across the city, hurting themselves and others, is a kind of real world theater that amuses him."

Val nodded. "He also learned early that when humans are faced with the unknown and the frightening, they become much easier to manipulate. It gives him an opening to lead them in a direction that benefits him. Demagogues of his choosing rise up and become a bigger threat to the very people whose fears he exploits."

Tightening his grip on Mackie in an automatic gesture of protection, he added, "It all feeds into his overarching plan to take control of this world and subjugate the human race. He can be patient. I expect Boston is his test case. If this drug of his works here, he'll distribute it globally in no time."

"Agreed," Alex replied. "Harry, this is your area. What do you suggest?"

The older man leaned forward with his hands clasped between his legs. He looked tired and more concerned than anyone else in the room. No surprise there, given he had a husband and a son to worry about. Demi, in particular, was at risk of breaking away from his fathers' influence and getting into trouble. "I need a sample of that blood to test." He turned his gaze toward Duncan. "I have to take it from the man still alive. The dead one's blood might already be decomposing inside the body."

The cop pursed his lips and cracked his neck. "I'm going to have to tag my partner and get down to the morgue. Now that it's clearer that we've got a connection with our homicide case, I have a legitimate reason to be in on the autopsy."

"How does that help me?" Harry asked in his mild-mannered way.

"It doesn't. You're going to have to find a way to get past whatever security they put in place for the prisoner. My guess is that he'll be at the hospital for observation at least for a few hours, maybe more. There should be one officer guarding his door. I can eventually get a crack at questioning him, but it will be after he's lucid enough for Miranda-ing, then vice will have at him." He shrugged. "I probably won't see him until after he's been processed into a cell. Sorry."

"Not to worry, Sergeant," Alex said. "We'll figure something out."

Mackie sat up straighter. "I can help."

Val tightened his grip around the boy's waist. "No, you can't." The words tumbled out in a short, barking order.

Slowly, Mackie shifted to stare at him face-to-face and practically nose-to-nose. "Yes. I can." He lifted his eyebrows in a way that challenged Val to disagree. The brat was back. "I've watched plenty of TV shows and movies, enough to know that you simply need a distraction." He switched his attention to the room at large. "I only have to take the cop's attention away from the room for…like a minute, right? Harry can race in, take the blood and book out before the cop can see anything."

Harry chuckled. "I'm not that fast, Mackie. I'll need more like two minutes."

Mackie tossed his head. "Easy-peasy. Give me an hour to make myself fabulous and we can go."

Val shot his gaze over to Alex, ready to argue against the idea. It was too late. His boss was already nodding in agreement. "Will that give you enough time, Harry, for what you need to do to prepare for taking the sample?"

"Yes, sir. Ample."

Now everyone in the room was stirring, getting up to implement the plan. *Fuck*. There was nothing he could do except go along with it, too, and keep Mackie safe.

"I'll be in touch," Duncan said as he left. Harry and Emil followed in his wake.

"*Val*."

"What?"

Mackie's answer was another bratty look. That's when Val realized the boy had been trying to get up and Val had been holding him in place.

"Oh." Instead of releasing the boy, he stood with him in his arms.

Mackie chuckled. "I can walk."

"No." Val issued the terse reply while leaving the room. He knew he was being ridiculous yet couldn't quite bring himself to set the boy down. The hard-on he still sported was the least of it, although he decided to switch over to jeans at the first opportunity. Fine cotton slacks left nothing to the imagination. It wasn't embarrassment that drove his actions. It was pure, animalistic need to keep control over Mackie. Their breakup notwithstanding, the impulse currently ruled his actions.

Mackie wrapped his arms around Val's neck and snuggled up close. "Whatever you say, *Sir*."

Shit. Despite his carefully considered plans and successful discipline for the last few months, he was back in it with the submissive boy — deep. Worse, he was no longer sure he wanted to climb back out again.

Chapter Six

Mackie checked himself out one more time in the shiny doors of the elevator before stepping out. He'd dressed carefully for this 'op', as he'd come to think of it—a combination of street-rat shabby, little boy lost and sex on two legs. Although he walked off alone, he didn't feel exposed. Having taken the stairs, Val was already lurking somewhere nearby, ready to step in to protect Mackie should it become necessary.

He tried not to get excited or optimistic about how the last few hours or so had gone. Sure, Val had given him the discipline he'd needed to calm his frayed nerves. Of course, the man had provided the necessary aftercare, as well. Val made an excellent Dom because he took the role of protector seriously. No one could argue with the guy's dedication and selflessness. It was the way he'd held on to Mackie right up until he'd been forced to let him go for a shower and to dress that had bolstered Mackie's spirits.

Plus, the man's raging erection was another telling sign. Regardless of how Val had failed to fuck Mackie or allow him to give him a blow job, the guy was obviously affected by their experience. If he really saw Mackie as nothing more than a nuisance or duty, would he get aroused like that? The guy might be an alien, but everything Mackie had ever experienced with him said that their species was just like humans when it came to sex. Val got hard because he wanted him. The numbers added up just fine, for the moment anyway.

Who could blame him if he dared to see a bit of hope on the horizon?

While acting had never been a passion of his, he fancied that he'd gotten good at it. You had to in order to convince some skeevy john that you really did want to suck his stinking dick. Mackie plastered a concerned expression on his face and hurried down the hallway, scanning the doors as if he were looking for the right one. He already knew what room the latest victim of Dracul's drug had been given because Duncan had managed to relay that much information.

What Mackie didn't know was the gender of the officer assigned with guarding the door. No matter. He had a plan for either possibility. Men and women both tended to see him as younger and more vulnerable than he was. He would play up that angle regardless. He was also going to throw in a bit of the 'sexy', in case it was a gay man or a straight woman. His crop top showed enough torso to catch just about anyone's eye, regardless. He'd switched over to a very blinged-out belly ring, too. Distraction was the point, however he might accomplish it.

He rounded the corner and saw a young, reasonably hot male cop standing beside a closed door with his thumbs stuck in his waistband. Mackie put a swing in his hips and called up a few tears as he rushed forward. "Is that his room?" he shouted out.

The cop turned in Mackie's direction and actually held his hand up like he was directly traffic. "Stop right there...sir," the man tacked on, although the way his eyebrows winged up indicated he wasn't sure he'd used the right honorific.

Mackie widened his eyes, put a palm to his mouth and skidded to a halt a few feet away from the cop. "I'm sorry." He hitched his breath noisily. "I heard he'd been brought here, and" — he bit back a sob—"I just had to see for myself if he's okay."

"You know this man?" The cop jerked a thumb toward the room. Behind him, a blur of black swept up and in.

Mackie was careful to keep his focus on the man in front of him and not the startling sight of Harry moving like The Flash. "Um..." Now he shifted to coy. "We kind of hook up now and again." He ran a suggestive hand down his front, running his finger around the ring. He stopped right before he reached his crotch.

Reasonably Hot Cop tracked the movement with his gaze. "You mean he's your boyfriend?"

Mackie let his palm linger, flicking his belly ring with his thumb. "Not exactly, sir." He used the same tone he would while playing with Val. Even a straight guy would appreciate a pretty boy being submissive. "We just, you know...keep each other warm some nights." He made his cheeks go pink, another trick he'd mastered while on the streets.

The cop cleared his throat. "Oh. But you can give us a name? He didn't have any ID on him."

No shit, given that he was practically naked when he'd been arrested. Mackie lowered his gaze. "I'm sorry, sir. I only know him as Steele." From what he'd glimpsed on the television, that nickname suited the guy well enough on all fronts. Mackie threw in a bashful look for good measure.

"He made me feel safe. There are some nasty guys out there and I'm not very big." He swayed back and forth. "Steele kept them away and I showed him how much I appreciated him for it." Mackie bit his lip. "I hate the idea of him being sick and alone. Could I see him? Please?"

The cop coughed again and started to turn away. "Well, I've got to call this in. The detectives on the case will want to interview you. Anything you can tell them might prove useful. The guy is out of his skull anyway. He won't know you're there."

"Wait!" Mackie lurched forward, forcing the man to once again focus on him. Mackie held out a hand as if trying to touch the cop.

The guy stiffened and gave him a stern look. That was fine because the whole point was to keep him from seeing the second blur of movement. This time it was to leave the patient's room. "Please stand back...sir." *Boy, does the guy hate using the term.* He didn't look very happy with Mackie, either.

So, straight guy — or maybe someone fighting his own impulses that he didn't like. Either way, it was time for Mackie to retreat.

Snatching his hand back, he said, "I'm sorry. I just wanted to see my friend. If he's not awake, I could maybe hold his hand. He might know I'm there." He laid it on thick, even as he poised to leave.

"No visitors allowed," was the terse reply. "But, my superiors are still going to want to interview you, so stay right there." The cop reached for his radio.

Mackie took a step back. "That's okay. I really don't have anything useful to tell them. I, um, haven't even seen Steele for a couple of weeks. I saw him on the TV when I was at a bar and was worried."

He kept backing away before turning and running. The cop yelled at him to stop but wasn't stupid enough to leave his post, thank God. As he rounded the hallway corner, Mackie saw Val standing by the exit stairs. The sight sent a thrill down his spine. He headed straight for him and another spurt of joyful adrenaline hit him when the guy swept him up and punched through the door.

Then Mackie's breath froze, his heart skipped a beat and his stomach dropped down to his toes. Without hesitation, Val had jumped up and over the stair railing. He clasped Mackie tightly to him as they dropped five floors straight down. Mackie shut his eyes tightly and pressed into the hard wall that was Val's chest. It was like riding the best and worst carnival ride ever. They hit the concrete with a jarring thud that was mostly absorbed by Val's alien body. It still rattled Mackie's teeth.

There was no time to even register what had just happened before Val had set him on his feet again and was dragging him by his arm. They slammed out of a door that led to the hospital's parking garage. The Escalade they'd arrived in was idling nearby with Emil behind the wheel and Harry sitting in the passenger's seat. Val opened the back door and shoved Mackie in.

A second later, Emil hit the gas, although he went slowly around the garage's lanes. Val didn't have to tell

Mackie to get down on the floor. That had already been part of the plan. On the assumption that the cop at the door would have alerted others to look for a redheaded boy, Mackie had to become invisible until they left the hospital's grounds.

He tucked himself into the footwell and tried to make himself as small as possible. He struggled not to freak out when Val settled a heavy blanket over him. A knee got shoved past the edge of it. Mackie would have recognized Val's Tom Ford jeans even if he hadn't known the guy was right next to him. He pressed his cheek against the hard cap of bone and immediately felt better.

If there was any trouble getting out, he wasn't aware of it. His entire focus had been on the simple contact with Val, his Dom, as far as he was concerned. That was the great attraction to the BDSM lifestyle for him. It gave him a safe zone to retreat into. It was a concept that he hadn't known existed, hadn't dared dream about, until Val had shown him the way. The irony of a scary alien giving him a sense of safety for the first time in his life wasn't lost on him. Oh, if his shitty family could only see him now! What would they think?

He didn't care, not anymore. That was another thing Val had done for him. He'd finally been able to let go of the anger and resentment and fear his supposed family had infused in him from toddlerhood.

It was almost disappointing when Val pulled the blanket back and helped Mackie sit up on the seat. The man gave him an approving nod. "You did great." The simple praise warmed Mackie. He liked pleasing this man, even when he was mad at him, which he still was on some level.

Harry craned his neck around. "Yes, indeed. I have what will hopefully give us some answers, and if we're really lucky, a way to counteract the drug." Turning back to stare out of the windshield, the older man shook his head. "That poor boy in the hospital is out of his mind, even unconscious. He's thrashing and moaning terribly. They have him in restraints."

"You'll figure out what to do about it," Emil said with his characteristically optimistic attitude.

"One can only hope," Val said. "Put on your seatbelt, Mackie," he added.

Before Mackie could comply with the order, Val reached across his body and did it for him. The way his arm brushed against Mackie's exposed stomach made him shiver. "Thank you, Sir." He couldn't hold back a grin.

* * * *

Hours later, Mackie's nerves hadn't settled from the exhilarating high of his cloak-and-dagger mission, as well as the taste Val had given of what it meant to be one of his kind. Restless, he went to the playroom where he'd spent so much time with his Dom. He could have worked out at the in-house gym. Val hadn't destroyed the entire room, after all, only one corner of it. But it wasn't exercise he needed. He recognized his feelings as being a jumpiness that required the type of attention only a Dom could give, not that he had any expectations about that. Val had kept his distance since they'd come back to the club, meeting behind closed doors with Alex and the other family members.

He closed himself inside the playroom and took a deep breath. The smell of leather from the equipment was enough to settle a small part of his tension. He roamed around, running his fingertips along the various pieces, soaking in the sensations of smooth wood, soft suede and cool cowhide. There was nothing in the room that he didn't like, it having been populated with items by Val that he and Mackie both enjoyed. From the beginning, Val had let Mackie lead the way, never pressuring him into anything he couldn't handle. No one had ever given Mackie that much power or consideration before.

There was the revolving wheel against the far wall that allowed Val to keep Mackie upside down and disoriented, especially when he was hooded, as well. The punishment chair sat in one corner with the built-in dildo that would stretch Mackie's hole almost as wide as Val's huge dick did. With a cock cage keeping Mackie's own dick in check, that was always a particularly hard place for Mackie to stay while 'he considered how much of a bad boy he'd been' in Val's estimation.

The mere thought of it caused Mackie to harden in his yoga pants. He couldn't resist pressing the heel of his palm against the shaft for a brief second. He resisted the temptation to relieve himself in any other way. Although they weren't officially back together, Mackie considered his body to belong to Val. That meant no coming without permission. Even during his recovery, some part of him had thought that way. How else could he explain why he hadn't jerked off? Broken arm or not, he was a young guy with a healthy libido. He woke up every morning with an erection, but he hadn't touched himself, regardless. Handing your orgasms over to someone else made them that much more amazing when you did have them.

Like last night. His attempt to seduce Val had worked. The spanking and the climax had allowed Mackie to sleep, at least for a little while, more peacefully that he had in months. But he hadn't been able to get more rest when they'd returned from the hospital. All he'd managed was to toss and turn until he'd finally gotten back up. Here he was, wandering around his favorite place in the world, feeling lost again and lonely—and horny.

He ran his fingers through the strands of his favorite flogger and sighed wistfully. Another circuit of the room had him edging closer to the spanking bench. Of all the equipment and instruments in the room, this was his favorite. He especially loved it when Val laid his bare hand across his upturned ass. The cool touch warming his flesh in a steady rhythm that sent him flying through subspace was the ultimate high.

I miss this. I need this!

Mackie indulged himself by climbing onto the bench and settling down into position. With another sigh, he rested his face against the worn leather and closed his eyes. He slipped his hand through the cuffs and pretended that they were tight and he couldn't remove them. If he tried, he might actually fall asleep in this position.

"Such a pretty picture."

Mackie's eyes flew open and his heartbeat sped up. He hadn't heard Val come in. Then again, these aliens could move as quietly as they did quickly.

"I didn't give you permission to get up there, however. Get off."

The whip-crack order had Mackie jumping to obey. He stood staring at Val with a renewed hope. The man's expression remained cool and detached, of course. Val was the consummate Dom, always in control.

He stared down his nose at Mackie with that stern look that made Mackie's guts loose and his dick hard. "On your knees, boy."

Mackie dropped before the last word had passed Val's lips. He knelt with his hands clasped behind his back, his back straight and his head bowed. Blood pounded in his ears and his breath quickened.

Val began to circle him. "Sloppy. You know better than this." Using his foot, he nudged Mackie's legs wider apart.

Mackie hid a smile. He'd deliberately held his pose badly for correction. "I'm sorry, sir. I'm out of practice."

"Your opinion wasn't requested." Val punctuated his admonishment with a flick of his finger against one of Mackie's ears. The sting wiped the smile off his face. It also goosed his dick.

"You obviously can't be trusted to take care of yourself. You are supposed to be sleeping. Why aren't you in bed?"

"I was restless, sir. The trip to the hospital wound me up." The truth was always useful when it could lead to what one wanted.

Val was quiet for a few seconds, circling Mackie once more. "I can fix that problem. On your feet." Once Mackie was vertical, Val issued his next order. "Strip."

Mackie tore off his sneakers and socks, T-shirt and yoga pants. He wasn't wearing anything else, so he stood naked within seconds. He'd deliberately dropped everything on the floor instead of folding his clothes and putting them on the nearby chair as he knew Val expected, the way he'd trained Mackie to do.

"Very sloppy boy," Val admonished in a harsh tone that caused Mackie to stiffen to full mast. "You know better than that."

Val punctuated his critique by grabbing Mackie by the waist and bending him over with a speed that made him dizzy. A few hard slaps administered to Mackie's ass highlighted the critique more severely before Mackie was once again vertical. His dick stood out from his crotch, bobbing with his abrupt movement.

"Do it right." Val's order was issued in his typical modulated tone. It was nevertheless a forceful command.

Mackie slowly obeyed, taking his time, picking up each article of clothing and painstakingly folding it. He placed each one carefully on the chair. He sauntered back and forth, giving Val a good show. Mackie knew how sexy he was. God knew he'd worked to hone his body, making himself attractive to the men who frequented the club. It took hours of hard work keeping his ass high and tight. It was his best feature. Val had certainly loved beating and plowing it in the past.

When he was finished, he shot Val an insolent look. "Is that what you wanted, Sir?"

Val regarded him with hooded eyes. "Back on the bench, brat."

Mackie was careful to hide his glee as he did as he'd been told. Once again, he placed himself into position. This time, however, Val buckled both Mackie's wrists and his ankles into the attached cuffs so that he truly couldn't move. The restraint caused the tension within him to start to drain.

"And, I don't like this." Val reached under Mackie and squeezed his cock. "You're getting ahead of yourself, as usual, boy."

"Sorry, sir." *Not sorry.* "Being near you makes me hard, Sir."

The wallop Val delivered made Mackie yelp and jerk. "You're still mouthy, too, I see. Keep your bratty lips shut unless I demand words from you."

Val moved away. Mackie could hear him but had no idea what he was doing. The anticipation of the unknown was arousing in itself. He shifted slightly, testing the strength of his bonds. He was tightly trapped, as he knew he would be. Val didn't make mistakes.

"This ought to do the trick." That was all the warning Val gave him before pressing an ice cube against Mackie's shaft.

The cold had him sucking in a ragged breath before shrieking in outrage. In the next instant, Val trapped the withering dick in a plastic cock cage. The familiar hard and smooth device settled Mackie down again. He hated the thing — and loved it.

"You've had enough of climaxing for the moment. I'll let you have another at some point, so long as you behave yourself. You have to earn your release."

Mackie opened his mouth to agree, before remembering that he wasn't supposed to speak.

Val patted his butt. "So, you have retained some of your training. Good boy."

Mackie melted from the praise. He kept his ears open for signs of what Val intended to do next but otherwise stayed loose and as relaxed as he could. Something was going to start hitting his ass, and it really didn't matter what. It was all good, all pleasurable, and he desperately needed it.

Softness brushed across his ass. A flogger, his favorite instrument for a beating. That made everything better, and Val had known it would. The man was more inside Mackie's head than Mackie was himself.

The discipline started off slowly and gently, every pass of the suede strands more a caress than a punishment. It lulled Mackie into a sleepy complacency he knew wouldn't last—and it didn't. Landing on one cheek, then the other, the strokes picked up speed. They became hits and the impact grew in intensity.

It didn't matter. The rhythm was the thing. The way Val wove the flogger in a figure eight soon left Mackie panting without more than a second of relief. Mackie knew better than to fight the assault. Instead, he embraced it, allowing the flogging to send him once more into the blessed pleasure of subspace.

Soon, he flew, absorbing a high that sent him spiraling up more than the adrenaline-rushed experience at the hospital. Endorphins made him soar, chasing away the negative effects of stress and worry. He was safe. He was free. He was Val's.

The bloom of red spread across the taut globes of Mackie's ass. The boy was already lost to subspace, in total thrall to Val's beating. Val was, as well, truth be told. He'd been surprised to learn years ago that being a Dom relieved him of the stress of his own existence on Earth. It was so unlike the boredom of daily life or the terror of the battlefield. It allowed him to expend nervous energy without losing his natural duty to protect. It was perfect in its own little way.

Mackie is perfect.

He turned away from that thought. Nothing had changed since that night when Alex had defeated Adrian and Mackie had been badly injured and almost killed, really. It was still unacceptable that Val give his heart to another human. That way led to madness, something that afflicted humans and not normally his species. After so many centuries on this planet, Val feared he was becoming more human himself.

Picking up speed, he tried to focus on the task and not his wayward thoughts and feelings. He ignored the rigid cock encased in its cage mashed against his jeans and refused to allow himself to zero in on the pulsing beats of Mackie's pressure points. The one in the boy's groin had always been Val's go-to place to drink freely. It had kept his fangs away from Mackie's prying eyes and allowed Val to feast on the succulent blood in peace.

Even now, if he inhaled deeply, he could smell the boy's unique scent. It took nothing to recall the sweet taste of Mackie's blood, to remember the way it flowed down Val's throat. His stomach rumbled at the memory, reminding him he hadn't eaten since the night before. He was hungry and not for any of Emil's excellent food. He knew that all he had to do was drop the flogger, kneel and latch on to Mackie's inner thigh.

The boy wouldn't mind. He knew that. Mackie had made it quite clear that he wanted Val back as his full-time Dom—and that was despite knowing Val's true nature. It didn't have to mean anything. A little drink and he could let the boy rest. Val's fangs descended and his breath quickened. His head nodded down and forward without his consent. Jerking it back, he delivered a vicious blow against Mackie's ass. The boy gasped and raised his head.

Dropping the flogger, Val rushed forward and put his hand on the back of Mackie's neck. "Easy." He struggled to regain control of himself, forcing his fangs back and his breathing to slow.

He touched sweat and, with a frown, felt Mackie's palms. Damn, he'd pushed the boy too far. Subs couldn't be trusted to put on the brakes once they were deep in subspace. It was Val's job to know when the boy had had enough.

"Good boy. You did well." The praise mattered. It was what a sub needed to hear from his Dom. *Nothing personal in it.*

Scooping the flogger up from the floor, he returned it to its place among the instruments of play. He grabbed a bottle of water from the mini-fridge, a cloth and, at the last moment, a butt plug and lube. He put everything but the water on the bench next to Mackie.

"Drink." He held the now-open bottle to Mackie's lips and helped him lift his head to take a few sips. "That's it," he encouraged, before taking it away. "More later."

He used the cloth to wipe the boy down, removing sweat so that Mackie wouldn't get chilled. When he was satisfied that enough had been done, he tossed that and picked up the plug and the lube. He slathered the one on the other before positioning himself behind Mackie. He laid his free hand on the small of the boy's back.

"One more thing to remind you of your place, boy."

He positioned the end of the plug against Mackie's hole. Val's dick pulsed with need. The temptation to free it and slide it instead of the plug into Mackie's tight heat was almost something Val couldn't resist. But if he fucked the human now, he feared there would be no going back. Mackie would certainly see it as confirmation that they were a couple again. Val didn't want to hurt the boy's feelings any more than he already had. Plus, he didn't trust his own discipline to back off again.

Hardening his resolve, he shoved the plug in with a long, fast stroke that spread the boy's puckered ring obscenely until the wide part disappeared entirely inside. Mackie bucked against the invasion and gasped. Val held the plug in place and ran circles around his back with slow strokes of his palm.

"Steady. Deep breaths. It's been a while, but I know you can take it." He held it in place until he felt Mackie relax again. "That's it. You know to keep it in until I say otherwise, yes?"

Mackie nodded slowly. "Yes, Sir."

He patted his back. "Good boy."

With hands less steady than he would have liked, Val unbuckled the cuffs and picked Mackie up off the bench. The human curled around him in a gesture of utter trust. Mackie's strength never ceased to amaze Val. He was so young, even by human standards, and had weathered a hard life. And yet he was capable of trying something like this lifestyle that would frighten many people. He also was able to believe in Val, despite so many other people having hurt Mackie — people that Val would gladly hunt down and punish in ways that wouldn't bring any kind of pleasure. That wasn't anything to do with sentiment, either. It was justice. That was all.

Val set Mackie on the couch as he always did. He wrapped him in a large fleece blanket kept in the room for the purpose of warming a sub coming down from subspace. He settled himself at the end, cradling the boy's head in his lap. He carded a few wet strands of hair that had flopped over one of Mackie's eyes.

Mackie wiggled back, which had the effect of rubbing the back of his head against Val's hard dick. A hiss escaped Val before he could shift away. But Mackie, the little brat, hadn't been beaten completely into submission, apparently. He moved with Val to maintain the contact, proof that it had been no accident.

"Stop it." Val's order came out in an embarrassing croak. He grimaced at the pressure on his aching cock.

Far from stopping the sweet torture, Mackie turned his head so that now his face was mashed against Val's bulge. The boy moaned and rubbed his lips along the stretched denim. Val grimaced and mourned the loss of the days when his lower half had been encased in leather. Even jeans were soft and thin enough for the feel of Mackie's mouth to raise up Val's arousal another few thousand degrees.

"Stop!" he tried again, this time, snaring strands of hair and pulling them away.

But Mackie was done with being a 'good boy' apparently because he resisted the effort and doubled down on delivering a semi-blow job. The boy moaned again, the vibrations penetrating the fabric and dancing along Val's shaft.

I can end this. Any time he liked, all he had to do was tug strongly on the boy's hair and put him back in his place. *I should end it.* Except Mackie wasn't the only one who was stressed out from the night's events. It had been difficult hanging back and allowing the boy to distract the cop. Logic had told Val that Mackie was perfectly safe. The more primitive part of him had sweated it out, anyway. He couldn't shake the feeling that Dracul's boys were somewhere close. It had to be Dracul's sons distributing this new drug. The description Duncan had given dictated as much. Dracul had produced two copies of himself, only with more viciousness and fewer brains. Always a bad combination.

So, instead of doing the right thing, Val took control of the situation in the opposite way. He used his grip to leverage Mackie's head up, but only so he could unzip his jeans and free his dick. The second the thing sprang out, he pushed Mackie's head back down. The boy knew what to do. He greedily sucked Val's cock into that warm, sweet mouth. Having been teased too much already, Val was in no mood for a slow blow job. He needed fast and hard. He forced Mackie to take the shaft down as far as he could. The small human had no gag reflex anymore and his tight, narrow throat encased Val's cock with a grip that made him come immediately.

He bucked his hips to send the dick down another inch as he climaxed. Mackie coughed and wrestled against the hold as Val's cum overloaded the human's mouth. With his control snapped, Val didn't let up, not the hold or the coming. A second orgasm released before the first one had finished. The sound of Mackie gagging actually gave him a sense of satisfaction. *That's what happens to brats who push their Doms too much.*

But when a small fist pounded on his chest, he knew Mackie had reached his limit. Val yanked his head back fast enough to cause Mackie's teeth to graze Val's still-hard shaft. The bite of pain sent another spurt of cum out, so that it hit Mackie's swollen lips. The boy sputtered and panted with strings of cum dripping down his chin. The sight of the boy coated with Val's semen gave Val a strange feeling in the middle of his chest. It felt as if he'd taken a punch to his breastbone. His own breath labored, and he had to look away to regain his calm.

"Thank you, Sir." Mackie's sleepy appreciation forced Val to refocus on him.

The boy's eyes were closed and his breathing had slowed. Taking a corner of the blanket, Val carefully wiped the boy's face clean. The pulse at the base of Mackie's throat caught and captured Val's attention. He watched it, hungry and needy, while the boy slept.

He would not touch Mackie anymore. He'd done enough, had earned his reward, while Val had earned this penance for his failure at being able to let the boy fully go.

Chapter Seven

Wales, Dracul's Castle

Dracul wiped the remnants of the fucking from his dick, grimacing in disgust at the retching sounds behind him. "Must he keep doing that?"

"It's a good sign, sir. Not only does it indicate he has a viable pregnancy, but the extreme nausea may mean he's carrying twins again." The doctor sound quite pleased, and as well he should. Dracul had been losing patience with the man before he'd announced that Dafydd was finally breeding.

"Well, I'm not into vomit sex, so make him stop." Dracul dragged on his favorite silk dressing gown and sauntered over to the fireplace. A knock on his door caught his attention as he poured a glass of wine. "Enter."

Petru glanced in the direction of the bed, wrinkled his nose in disgust before approaching Dracul. "Sir." He bowed and stood waiting for permission to speak.

Dracul took a sip of his wine before settling into his favorite chair. "You have good news for me, I trust."

"Yes, sir. Your sons have succeeded in introducing the drug to the human population. There have been two public incidents. The second one caused significant damage to property and involved the local police killing a user. It's all over the Internet, as well as international news." The man paused. "I was wrong in my advice earlier. Your sons have done you proud, sir."

Dracul flicked his gaze at his lieutenant. "Don't try to flatter me, Petru. You're terrible at it, plus I value your honesty more than your loyalty. When you cautioned me against giving in to Cadoc and using the boys for this next round of war, I did consider it. Your instincts are often right. They might still be. We both know this little exercise is more a trial balloon for them. It's almost impossible to fuck this up unless they get stupid." He took another sip and shrugged. "A possibility I don't discount, either, given the weak genes they carry of necessity." He gestured in the direction of the bed where the physician was giving Dafydd something to hopefully soothe the little puke's stomach.

"I will continue to monitor the situation carefully, sir."

"No. Not necessary. They will either succeed or fail on their own. You're to give them no help or guidance. I have another job for you."

"Anything, sir."

Good old Petru, such a suck-up. And not a surprise, given that he'd been a lowly technician onboard ship with little chance of advancement beyond his status in the hive. Being stranded had opened up new possibilities for the man. Dracul had opened them up, that is.

"As you can see, my seed incubator is not in the best of shape. Fucking him has become a bore. I need someone new — a nice, fresh hole to fuck and a different source of blood. Find me one. As young and unattached as possible, if you please. I don't want any legal alarm bells going off if it can be avoided."

He drained his glass and refilled it. "Humans have become so tiresome with their modern morality. It used to be easy to pick a boy who was barely ripe. A few coins and a father would hand one over without a qualm." He sighed. No use lamenting what he couldn't have. Whining was not his style.

"I will find someone suitable at once, sir."

"Yes, yes." Dracul waved the man away. The sound of Dafydd vomiting again made him grimace. "Oh, do shut up!"

The Welsh boy's eyes showed through his curtain of hair. His hatred was visible. Dracul smiled back. He was going to miss the boy's spirit, but it was time to start in on someone new. Once Dafydd gave birth, Dracul would make a feast of his sweet body.

He would drain it of every last drop of blood.

* * * *

They could hear the patient hollering before the elevator doors opened. Trey stepped onto the hospital floor with Karl at his side. Bronner and Diaz were a short way ahead of them. The four were now officially working the case together because of the information Sullivan and the Cambridge police had given them about vamp. The Newbury Street rampage had put everyone on edge and a lot of weight was crashing down from the top. The problem was now officially global Internet fodder and that kind of publicity wasn't good for the city. Either of them.

They'd finished with the autopsy, although nothing new had come of it any more than it had for the jumper, except that Almadeo now accepted that the red pupil issue was drug related. The latest two victims hadn't gone splat on the ground from a high fall, so it was no longer thought to be trauma-induced. That wasn't necessarily good news for Duncan. He vacillated hourly between hoping someone would notice that aliens walked among them and dreading it.

"Jesus, what's up with the guy?" This from Karl.

Bronner glanced over her shoulder. "The doctors say he's been like that since waking up. It's not good. They've had to strap him down."

The young cop on the door looked like she was really reconsidering her career choice. She straightened at their approach then jerked when a loud howl came out of the room. "Sorry, ma'ams, sirs. It's been like that for hours."

"It's okay, officer," Diaz said. "Take fifteen. We're here for that long at least."

"Thanks, ma'am."

"Oh, any more sign of that boy?"

Trey hid his wince. A report of a redheaded boy trying to see the patient had come in hours before. There was a BOLO out on him for questioning but no luck so far. And, there wouldn't be any, because Mackie was safely tucked into the club for the duration, no doubt. It had taken some fast talking to convince Karl that redheaded males were a dime a dozen in Boston and that there was no way Mackie would be slumming it with a druggie. His partner was getting suspicious, though, no doubt about it. It was only a matter of time before Karl wised up to the double life Trey was leading. He was too good a cop not to. There was nothing to be done about it, however, so he turned his attention back to what was playing out in front of him.

"No, ma'am," the officer said before she took off.

"Too bad," Bronner observed. "We could use a break on this one."

Trey scratched the back of his head. "I don't know. Unless the kid was freaking out, he probably wasn't taking whatever the hell this is. He probably doesn't know anything useful."

"We only need the name of the dealer," Bronner pointed out. "The kid might know that much."

Before Trey could think of a suitable follow-up to get them off Mackie's scent, a tired-looking doctor came out of the patient's room. His warm brown eyes were bloodshot and bleary, testament to how he must have been on the end of a long shift.

He pulled up short at the sight of them. "Oh, hello."

Diaz held up her badge. "Sorry to disturb you, Dr...."

The man ran a hand down his face and blinked a few times. "Paz. Ricardo Paz. I'm the chief resident assigned to this case."

Diaz introduced them all. "We're working this case from different angles and were hoping to interview the patient." Before the last word was out of her mouth, another howl erupted from the room.

Dr. Paz winced. "I don't think that's likely. He may be awake, but as you can hear, he's hardly lucid and still very violent. Not only have we had to restrain him, we've also taken the risk of giving him a sedative while not knowing what's in his system. It hasn't made any difference, and we've maxed the dosage. We don't yet dare try anything else."

Trey shoved his hands in his pockets and let the women take the lead. It was still more their case than his. Besides, he was already compromised and didn't trust himself to ask the right questions. It was mostly routine, anyway. No one really expected to learn anything from this visit, not under the current circumstances. Then something that the doe-eyed doctor said caught his attention.

"I'm wondering if toxicology would produce useful information if we drew blood differently." The man's fatigue dropped away as he became more animated. "I think it's possible that the chemical composition of the drug is altered the moment it leaves the body. It might be better if we suspend it in an inert solution and observe it in a hermetic environment."

Fuck. Dr. Paz was proving to be smarter than the average medical bear. Trey shook off his own tiredness and racked his brains to come up with a persuasive argument against such a tack. Yeah, like he had anything useful to say to a doctor about bloodwork.

In the next instant, it didn't matter. A shriek, followed by a loud crash, caught everyone's attention. They rushed en masse into the hospital room in time to see the patient miraculously out of bed. His restraints lay in tatters and blood streaked down his arms where he'd torn tubes out of his skin. He was using the IV pole to smash his window.

"What the hell!" Paz rushed forward before Bronner or Diaz could stop him. The patient turned wild-and-red eyes on the man before punching him hard enough to send the doctor flying backward.

Paz landed against the women, knocking them down like a couple of split ten-pins. It would have been funny if not for the fact that Diaz cracked her head on the wall and the doctor flattened Bronner with his body onto the floor. Ever the gentleman, Karl reached to help the women first. The fact that he would have had to step over them to reach the patient was another factor.

Trey took a different route. He went over the bed, careful to stay out of swinging range of the pole. "Sir, please calm down." He felt like an idiot trying to reason with the man.

The man reared back and beat against the window again. This time, it cracked, the fissures running in all directions. Trey lunged for him but ended up ducking before the pole could smash against his head. By the time he came back up for another try, the patient had used his fists to break the glass completely, the same way he and his friend had done to storefronts.

It defied belief that he had that kind of strength, except Trey knew the truth. Some variation of alien blood surged through his body, giving him an inhuman amount of power. Jumping up on the sill, the drugged-out man turned his frightening red eyes in Trey's direction.

"I am God!" he yelled before jumping.

"Son of a bitch!" Karl leaped forward and peered down, catching his jacket on the jagged glass. He tore it while freeing himself. Vicious curses spewed out of him, even while he tried to look out of the window.

There was little point in the effort. They were on the fifth floor. Absent some miracle, the guy was dead. Karl's weary look when he turned said it all. The doctor was helping Bronner and Diaz, who appeared stunned.

"Let's get these women somewhere for examination," Trey offered, "then go down and start in on that mess."

"Fuck that," Diaz barked. "I'm going, too." She stumbled into Paz's waiting arms. "Well, maybe I could use a quick rest first. Jesus Christ, this is going to be a shitload of paperwork, and our case is going down the toilet."

There was nothing to say to that obvious statement. There would be a possible ass-reaming for sure, because logic meant nothing with a high-profile case. That fact that he was secretly pleased that the doctor's theory about the blood couldn't be put to the test caused him no small amount of guilt. It didn't change the fact, however, that at that moment, the patient's alien blood was disintegrating. The only live version was in the hands of an alien doctor back at Club Lux. He could only hope he'd truly hitched his wagon to the good guys.

* * * *

The gay gentlemen's club that fronted for a marooned group of aliens had a soothing quality to it that Trey couldn't deny. As he entered the quiet, plush place, the noise of the outside faded away. His fatigue, on the other hand, did not. He dragged his feet down the entryway to the main floor. It was early enough that no one was around. While the club was open to members twenty-four-seven, most men were either finishing up at work or heading home for maybe dinner or a change of clothing at that hour. Despite it being Sunday, rich guys worked all the time. That's what made them rich. He expected the place would be hopping in a few hours. He intended to be long gone and horizontal in his own apartment by then.

"Hey there, Sergeant Hottie."

Trey jerked back at the sudden appearance of the half-alien boy. "Christ, kid, don't startle me like that."

The boy, Demi, got closer, an impish smile on his face. "I'm sorry. Did I scare you? Do I make you nervous?"

The expression on the boy's face said that he thought he did and delighted in the knowledge. Trey wanted to deny it but didn't have the acting skills, certainly not when he was dead on his feet, so he didn't try.

"Beat it, kid. I'm here to see your uncle…or cousin. Whatever the hell he is." He tried to step around the boy.

Demi blocked him with quick movement that was almost too fast for a human to pull off. He frowned. "You're always working when you come here. Why not stay and play a while?" He pursed his lips in what he likely thought was a seductive pose.

Which it was, Goddamn it! "I'm busy. Your kind are making me so. I have no time to play, and besides," he added with a stern look, "if I did, it wouldn't be with you."

Demi ducked his head and clasped his hands behind him. "Oh, now you've gone and hurt my feelings. I'm only trying to be friendly."

Trey snorted. "Sure you are. You must give your fathers fits," he added with a shake of his head.

Demi batted his eyelashes. "Why not? It's boring being cooped up in here all the time."

"It's safer for you."

"I know," he whined, "but I'm not a kid anymore. I can take care of myself." He peeked up at Trey from under his lashes. "I bet I'd be safe if you took me out."

Trey barked out a laugh. "Yeah, right." The kid was about Trey's height, wiry-thin, yet probably stronger than Trey could ever be. "Run along now, Demi. The grown-ups have business to attend to."

The deliberate slight had the right effect. Demi's expression went from sultry to mulish. He tossed back his long, black hair. "I'm not as young as you think I am."

"Maybe." Trey looked him up and down. "You're too young, regardless, from where I'm standing."

With a huff and a glare, the boy twirled gracefully and strutted his cute ass away.

"God help me," he muttered.

"You know it's not Harry you have to worry about."

"Holy fuck!" Once more in the span of less than five minutes, Trey jumped out of his own skin.

Val gave him a self-satisfied look. "It's Lucien," he continued, as if he and Trey had been having a conversation. "He might appear mild-mannered, but he'd gut you like a fish if he could read your thoughts right now."

Trey grimaced and stood straighter. "What thoughts? The only one I have is how fucking screwed up this whole vamp thing is. The second user jumped to his death right in front of my fucking eyes."

Val's face went blank. "Indeed? That is both good and bad news, perhaps."

"Yeah, my thoughts exactly and I hate that. I'm a cop, for fuck's sake. It's my job to solve crimes, not cover them up."

"You must be very tired, Sergeant." Val was changing his mood and the conversation's direction rapidly.

"Why do you say that?"

"You're using the word 'fuck' a lot."

"Huh. As it happens, you're right. I've been up for almost two full days. I'd be home right now if not for the need to fill you all in on the latest and check on the progress with the blood analysis."

Taking Trey's elbow in a surprisingly supportive move, Val said, "Come. I'll bring you down to Harry's lab. We forget sometimes how vulnerable you humans are. You need a lot of sleep."

Trey was too surprised to do anything other than allow himself to be led. "You don't?"

"No, although we have no problem mimicking the human sleep pattern if required. Are you hungry?"

Now that he mentioned it... Trey's stomach growled. "I could eat."

Val released him and took his phone out of his back pocket. "I'll text Emil to bring you something in the lab."

"No need for him to go to any trouble." His stomach gave a loud protest.

Val flashed his teeth. "I assure you nothing would please him more than feeding you. A hungry person being in his orbit makes him very cranky, actually. You'll be doing us all a favor by allowing him to prepare you a meal."

"Well, when you put it that way..."

They passed through the main room and beyond the elevator. Val opened a door in the back hallway that Trey had never noticed before or used. A darkly lit, narrow staircase went straight down. After a moment's hesitation, he followed Val.

"It's perfectly safe," Val called over his shoulder. "You are one of us or you wouldn't be shown this part of the building at all."

A strong antiseptic smell greeted them before they reached the bottom. There was a door on either side of the small vestibule area. Each was closed and locked with a key pad. Val punched in numbers for the left one, opened the door and gestured for Trey to enter first. It was like walking onto a movie set for a mad scientist's laboratory. The room contained an array of tables strewn with strange equipment and bubbling glass vessels. Despite that 'double, double, toil and trouble' atmosphere, there were no noxious odors. The benefit of a great ventilation system, no doubt.

Harry, whom Trey accepted as being some kind of elder statesman despite his unlined skin and jet-black hair, was bent over a microscope. On the table around him sat beakers of weirdly colored liquid. Some of it also bubbled away while others sat eerily still. He hesitated, unsure of how safe any of it was for a human.

Val pressed his palm lightly against Trey's back. "It's all right. I wouldn't have brought you here if we weren't sure you aren't in any danger, either."

Difficult as it was, Trey hardened his resolve to trust these creatures. He approached the bench with more certainty. Before he reached it, the door opened again. Alex walked in with Quinn in tow. No surprise there. Trey had to wonder if the man let the boy out of his sight. *Then again, with a gorgeous boy like that for a lover, who would want to?* The redheaded brat, Mackie, brought up the rear.

Val folded his arms and glared at the boy. "What are you doing here?"

Mackie tossed his head dismissively at the man. "Alex invited Quinn and Quinn invited me." He mimicked the man's stance, his expression daring him to disagree with what the boss had allowed.

Oh man, is that brat leading the bouncer around by the dick. The thought gave Trey his first positive feeling for the day.

With a scoff, Val turned his attention to Harry. "So, what's the story?"

The older man's shoulders slumped with obvious fatigue. "I've isolated the compound, and it's some synthetization of our blood. When I mix it with human cells, courtesy of Kitty, it starts altering them on a molecular level. It appears to be trying to turn them into our species at a rapid pace that their cells can't handle. It simply, therefore, serves to destroy them."

"That squares with what the coroner said," Trey interjected.

Harry turned his tired gaze at him. "Yes. It's no wonder those poor men who've ingested it go on a rampage. They're being swamped with a surge of energy and strength they can't handle, while, at the same time, their brains are undergoing a metamorphosis that is literally turning them to mush. In short, they are going insane by human standards, while their other organs are being damaged beyond repair."

The man shook his head. "If they hadn't died the way they did, they would have succumbed to the process in short order. From what I've seen, this drug is lethal with one dose."

The room fell silent with that news. Trey was trying not to freak out at the idea of a deadly drug being peddled in his city. Maybe if word got out that no amount of the drug could be safely ingested, people would shun it. That kind of strategy would involve the higher-ups. He would have to take it to his lieutenant, who would kick it up the chain to the mayor's office and even the governor. How could he convey the information, though, without revealing its source? Damn, this secret society stuff was a pisser.

"Was that the intent?" Mackie posed the question in a quiet voice, his pretty face pinched with worry. He glanced around the room. "I mean, were they trying to change humans or kill them?"

Before anyone could reply, Val crossed the room and pulled the boy into an embrace. "Easy, boy. Deep breaths. This is why I don't want you here. You don't need this horrible information inside your head."

Trey could actually see the transformation. Mackie went from tense to relaxed in the span of a breath. He leaned against the bouncer's larger, harder frame in a pose of utter trust. "I can handle it."

The pushback was met by the very human response of Val raising his eyes to the heavens and shaking his head. But he held onto the boy and said nothing more.

"It's a fair question," Trey chimed in.

"The point with Dracul," Alex replied, "is chaos, however it can be caused. I doubt very much that he intended to create an army of converted humans. We can assume that he used many unwilling humans for experimentation before he released this drug. He knew what it would do."

"And this is all some kind of game he plays with you to amuse himself?" Trey's exhausted brain was working up a head of steam. He hated the idea that Boston was ground zero in this alien war simply because Alex and his crew were here.

"Not a game, Sergeant. Dracul takes all of this very seriously. His goal has always been to subjugate this world to make it his own. He went from being a drone in the hive to someone who had the ability to be not just a queen, but *the* queen. Always before, though, we were chasing him as he sowed discourse — as a whisper in someone's ear, planted evidence of disloyalty, a well-timed assassination. It was all too easy for him to get humans fighting each other. We did our best to clean up his messes and stop them from becoming worse."

"He's bringing the fight to us now more directly," Val added. "Although the course of his plan is as yet unclear, other than making our adopted city a combat zone."

Trey couldn't withhold his temper. "So leave! Give my city a break."

Once more, silence reigned. Trey immediately regretted his outburst, except not entirely. If all it took to make this horror show stop was the decampment of the Stelalux posse, then why not?

"Where would you have us go, Sergeant?" Alex asked the question while wrapping his arms around his lover's waist and pressing the boy's back to his front. "Isolation was our first effort, but that became harder to do as the human population grew. There is no place in the world now where we wouldn't put people at risk. Even if we tried, Dracul would go back to his old playbook and wreak enough havoc somewhere else where we'd have to come out again to stop him. I'm sorry. I failed your kind centuries ago. I should have seen Dracul's plans earlier and stopped him when I had him within reach."

Quinn turned within the embrace and lay his head on the man's chest. "You didn't fail us. You protect us." He glared over his shoulder at Trey.

Okay, now he felt like a douche. He rubbed the heel of his palms against his tired eyes. "Sorry. I'm running on too little sleep. I know you're the good guys."

"You need food." Emil had entered and he held in his hand a tray from which wonderful smells wafted. "Come on and sit here."

Trey followed the man to a small, empty table and sat on the chair Emil had dragged over to it. He lifted off the dome on the tray to reveal a plate with a six-ounce filet mignon, scalloped potatoes and buttered spinach. Trey's mouth watered at the sight and his stomach rumbled once more.

Emil grinned ear-to-ear as he took two bottles of water out of his pockets and put them on the table. "Sounds like I got to you just in time. There's lots of iron and protein there. Eat it all. And you need water. No more coffee tonight."

Picking up the fork and knife, Trey muttered, "Yes, Mom."

The jacked chef folded his arms and nodded. "Damned straight. Someone has to be, and where we come from, moms rule. Nothing better than your mother."

Trey was already in a coma of bliss from the first bite of his perfectly cooked medium-rare beef. He raised his hand in a gesture of peace and nodded. "No argument here," he said around his mouthful of food.

"Now that the pressing issue of Duncan's food deficit has been resolved," Val drawled, "what are we going to do about this new scheme of Dracul's?"

Still consumed by his much-needed meal, Trey gestured generally with his fork. "Yeah, what he said." Despite not liking spinach, he scooped up some because Emil was watching like — well, like a mom. He discovered he actually did like the stuff. It was only a matter of having it cooked correctly.

Sorry, Ma. He offered up the silent apology for dissing her cooking and wondered if he could discreetly get the recipe from the alien chef. Then he refocused on the discussion.

"We need a two-pronged approach," Alex was saying. "First, find and neutralize the distribution source. You take point on that, Val—with the good sergeant's help, of course." When Trey reluctantly nodded in agreement, the man continued. "Second, concoct some form of countering agent to neutralize the usefulness of the drug. We'll be counting on you, Harry, for that."

"Of course."

"Do you think you can?" Val asked.

The older man gave the bouncer a look that would have cut glass. "Indeed. I can only imagine who created this filthy thing to begin with. My biochemical skills are far superior to that insignificant drone's."

Trey was fascinated by the aliens' culture, despite his resentment over their existence on his planet. The way they referred to themselves mimicked bees, which was strange, considering they were so primate-like in their appearance. He couldn't really picture these huge men swarming around a hive while some queen popped out kids. The biology was confounding.

"What guy is that?" he asked, because why not do so? The more he learned, the better use he might be to protect his own people.

Harry made a sound like a violin being sawed in half. The screech caused Trey and the human boys to wince. "Jesus!"

"I beg your pardon," Harry said. "He calls himself Teo. He was a young botanist on our ship and easily swayed by Dracul's mutinous ideas. Just another one of us who got above his station, little shit." The invective was all the more amusing coming from the dignified man.

"He's no match for your talents, Harry," Alex agreed. "So, we have a plan. Let us hope that no more humans ingest that poison before we can find an antidote."

"About that." Trey wiped his mouth, surprised to see that he'd already inhaled most of his meal. "I'm going to have to go to my superiors about this. We already have a strategy meeting set for tomorrow morning involving my partner, Karl, and the two vice cops on the case. Hear me out," he added, when the aliens' mouths opened in automatic dissent. "Obviously, I'm not going to bring you guys up, mostly because I don't want to be put in McLean Hospital for observation. But, we have to try to get word out for people to stay away from this crap. We've got the name—vamp—from a human intelligence source of mine. No one believes it's actually made from vampire blood, either. So, I'm not giving up any secrets there. I've gotten pretty far using standard police work.

"We also have the coroner's report about what it does to a person's body, plus this too-smart-for-your-sake doctor who has already thought of taking blood samples in suspension for testing. I'm going to suggest that maybe the drug is fatal at any dose, like I'm some freaking chemistry savant all of a sudden. It's a logical inference and one others of my kind may have already made. I have no choice here, guys. Like it or not, my people are going to institute a third prong, using a public safety warning. Of that you can be sure."

Finished having his say, he started back on his food. Damn, he was already regretting that the chef hadn't brought dessert.

Emil leaned over. "I have a piece of Boston cream pie boxed in the refrigerator with your name on it."

Trey grinned. "Will you marry me?"

Emil laughed, the sound startling in the hushed environment of the lab. "As if I'm your type."

A brief image popped into Trey's head of a lithe boy with dark hair and cat-like eyes who might be older than he looked. It still freaked him out, so he shoved it away and winked at Emil. "For food this good, you could be."

"Gentlemen," Alex barked. "If the food flirtation is over...? We understand that you have to do your duty, Sergeant, and I don't have any objection to the idea. It will hopefully prove helpful. In the meantime, we all know the plan. Let's get to it."

Trey hurriedly shoveled the remains of his meal into his mouth. Val came up with Mackie attached to him like an appendage. The bouncer's expression implied he felt conflicted about the contact. There was no question, however, that the boy was right where he wanted to be.

"You're obviously dead on your feet, Duncan. I propose you contact me tomorrow whenever you can break free from your partner. I'm going to see how Logan has done, tugging at her sources. We can compare notes back here," Val said.

Finished, Trey stood and stretched the growing kinks in his body. "Fair enough. Let's hope this ends quickly."

The alien's face showed a surprising tiredness. "Quick is a relative term, Duncan. I can only say I hope it ends."

Chapter Eight

"I'm due on stage."

Val gave him a sideways glance. "I am aware. In fact, you are overdue. Just one of the reasons why I didn't want you downstairs."

Mackie couldn't suppress his irritation. "I'm part of this, you know. I have a right to be in on the plans, especially given how I'm practically a prisoner because of your stupid war."

Val stopped abruptly and turned to clasp Mackie by his upper arms. "If I could extricate you from it, I would. I'm no happier about your being stuck here than you are."

Mackie blinked up at him, trying to hide how much those words stung. "I'm sorry I'm such a burden to you."

"I didn't say that." Val let go and stepped back. "That was not my intended meaning."

"Seemed like it was to me," Mackie shot back.

"No, I... Get to work." He turned, then looked back over his shoulder. "I'll see you later. In your room."

Mackie couldn't hold back a grin of delight. "Are you going to choke me with your huge dick again?"

Val's face went into typical grim mode. It was a sight that sent a frisson of fear and pleasure up Mackie's spine. That expression usually led to delightful punishments. "That was a mistake," the man ground out.

Mackie batted his eyelashes. "Was it?" He knew he was acting like a snake charmer, trying to stay abreast of the deadly thing's movement instead of allowing it to strike, but that was kind of the point. He wanted to bait Val into action, to remind him of how good they were together.

"You think you're doing yourself a favor by goading me, don't you?" Val leaned in with a heated gaze. "You're not going to like your punishment tonight."

The warning shot right to Mackie's groin. His cock tried to harden and failed. His eyes went wide. "Oh, hey... I'm still wearing the cock cage." Val had removed the plug after Mackie's nap but hadn't liberated his dick. "You need to let me out so I can dance."

"Do I?" Val raised one eyebrow in a rare display of amusement. "I'll see you later, Mackie."

Mackie watched the retreating back, frowning. *Oh well.* He traipsed off to the dressing room, feeling happier than he had in months.

* * * *

"Someone's been naughty." Mr. Warren rapped his knuckles against the cock cage. "If you like chastity so much, I'd be happy to keep you in it if you would become mine."

Wiggling his ass against the pole, Mackie leaned over and smiled at the man. "I hate it, actually." That was partly true. He didn't like having his dick confined, but when Val finally allowed him release, the orgasms were always extra amazing.

He'd been receiving a lot of attention that night. Because of the cage, he'd been forced to put on fairly pedestrian boy-shorts, instead of a pretty thong. The outline of the hard plastic was clear for anyone to see, and the club members loved it when he was in chastity. They got extra pervy and generous with their money.

Really it was a win-win for Mackie. Plus, it served as a reminder that he belonged to someone. He was Val's boy, even if the guy himself was still too thick-skulled to acknowledge it. All in all, his plan of winning Val back was on the right track. He was thrilled and scared to death. What if it didn't work after all? A spanking and a flogging, an orgasm and one blow job didn't make them a couple again. It could all have been done out of duty on Val's part—or worse, pity. The only optimistic part of this was how clearly he'd gotten under the guy's skin. If Val was indifferent to him, would he be so emotional?

The song ended, starting Mackie's break. He hopped off the stage. Warren pressed a towel and a hundred-dollar bill at him. Mackie accept the one and gently rejected the other.

"You've been too generous with me tonight already, Mr. Warren."

Being able to turn away money was a testament to how financially secure he felt now. It made for a stunning change in his life. Thanks to Alex and Val, he'd managed to put away a tidy nest egg. Besides, at a certain point, a member's tips started to turn into bribes and expectations that Mackie couldn't, wouldn't, fulfill. He sensed that point had arrived with Warren.

The man leaned in to whisper in his ear. "There's so much more where that comes from. Let's go upstairs if you need to feel that you've earned it."

Mackie shied away, flashing what he hoped was a sympathetic smile. "I appreciate it, really I do. But," he added, cupping himself, "as you can see, I'm already someone else's boy."

Warren's face fell. "He doesn't deserve you."

"I can't argue with you there." Mackie shrugged. "What can I say? I, um...love him." Saying the words out-loud cemented them in his mind. Against all reason, he truly had fallen in love with an alien.

"You know where to find me if you come to your senses." With that parting shot, the man went back to the stage and ran his hand up the leg of the boy who'd taken Mackie's spot.

Rubbing the sweat from the back of his head, Mackie wandered over to the bar. He flashed a smile at Kitty and placed the towel on the stool before sitting down. Instead of bringing him his usual Coke, she placed a bottle of water in front of him.

"Val's orders," was all she said before moving away.

"Oh." Mackie unscrewed the cap and chugged half the cool liquid in one gulp. It was very refreshing, but he preferred the sugary caffeine of his favorite soft drink.

He finished the bottle on his way to the kitchen. He hadn't had any dinner, owing to the clandestine meeting. The chef greeted him with his usual good cheer. Before Mackie could ask for anything in particular, the guy ushered him over to the table and put down a bowl of brown mush and another bottle of water.

Mackie peered into the bowl. "What is this?"

"Porridge. The real kind, none of that processed crap. Took me a full hour to make it."

"Um."

"No sugar or cream. No add-ins of any kind. You get it plain. Val's orders," he added before Mackie could ask.

Mackie picked up the spoon, scooped a bit of the stuff up and let it plop down in the bowl again. "It looks disgusting. No offense."

"Nah, it's bland. That's all. Bon appétit, kid."

"Wait!" Mackie said when the man turned to leave. "Can't I have some raisins or something? That's healthy, right? Val doesn't have to know."

"Sure. I wouldn't tell him," Emil replied.

Mackie brightened for about two seconds before slumping in his chair. "I would." That was the problem with being a good sub. Mackie might act the brat, but he still respected Val's role as his Dom enough to be truthful with him.

"Like I said…enjoy."

He didn't. The porridge sucked and lay heavily on his stomach besides. He ate it, though, and drank the full bottle of water. After a quick clean-up and change of shorts in the dressing room, he returned to dance. His routine was perfunctory, though. He couldn't keep his mind on anything except what Val had in store for him later. The control over his food and drink was baby stuff, annoying for sure. It was only the warm-up, he knew. There would be more coming, things he wouldn't like. Eventually, Val would get around to something that made Mackie happy. All he had to do to get to that point was to endure.

Easy-peasy.

* * * *

Mackie was rethinking his bravado hours later as he stared at what Val had left for him in Mackie's private bathroom. Two bottles of disposable enemas stood lined up on the sink. There was no note. There didn't have to be. He knew what to do, and he hated it. Val's very thought, naturally. Depriving Mackie of what he liked and forcing him to do things he didn't was the perfect punishment for a brat like himself.

No one could make him do any of this. He could have grabbed a Coke and made himself a sandwich. Neither Kitty nor Emil would have stopped him. He could dump the enemas in the trash and greet Val with an unclean hole. The man wouldn't force the liquid up him. But his defiance would be a hollow victory because Val's ultimate punishment would be to leave Mackie alone, untouched, undisciplined.

And that would crush him.

So, he slipped off his shorts and tossed them into the hamper. He scratched along the edge of the cock cage where it chaffed him from hours of jiggling it. Eyeing the first enema bottle, he screwed up his courage and opened it. Then lying on the floor, he bent his left leg and positioned the lubed nozzle against his hole. With a grimace, he slid it in. After a year of taking Val's humongous cock, this thin piece of plastic barely registered. The solution he squirted up did. He loved warm cum coating his channel. This fluid, not so much.

He emptied the bottle nevertheless and started counting. The pressure inside his guts built slowly. Ignoring it, he made himself count out three minutes before getting up and relieving himself in the toilet. Then he took a shower before using the second enema. It was just as miserable as the first time, but he did feel clean as a whistle. Hopefully that would earn him a few brownie points.

As he had the time, he styled his hair. The shaved part was growing out nicely and as he studied himself in the bathroom mirror, he contemplated how he might wear it next. For the moment, it took a bit of gel to tame into something more sexy than wild. Eventually he was satisfied, so he returned to his room, settled on the bed and picked up a magazine to read. All he had to do now was wait.

* * * *

Val easily tracked Logan by her scent, at first. When he'd given Emil the orders about Mackie's food, he'd learned that the woman had left the kitchen within the previous hour. He'd followed her path on foot, as she'd been, but at a brisker pace than the human had used. It had taken little time to reach the T station she'd entered. Once in the crowded space, however, so many human smells made it harder to pick up the thread of hers.

He wandered around the platform, trying to be inconspicuous and knowing he failed. His size alone caught people's attention. As did his hairstyle choice, but damn he loved the clean lines and easy care that his Mohawk afforded him. His Hilfiger black bomber jacket and jeans were among the least expensive things he owned and still he didn't exactly blend into the crowd sartorially, either. He caught the eye of women and men alike. He saw both wariness and interest and ignored both.

Among the perfume, body spray, natural human odor and stale popcorn, he finally caught the smell that identified Logan. He followed it to the end of the platform and realized it went into the tunnel. He knew that some homeless made camp in the underground network that was intended for subway use only. It was dangerous and illegal to sneak back there, yet with the coming cold, it was done, nevertheless. It helped as well that there were unused portions of the system under the city that were accessible if one knew where to find them.

The homeless often did.

He waited until a train came and went before he streaked into the tunnel in its wake. From there, he followed both scents and sounds. He found Logan with a group of five other people of indeterminate gender and age huddling together in an alcove dangerously close to the tracks. Given the smallness of the space and the amount of stuff they had mounded around them, it was as warm a spot as any to hang out in. They all turned startled and hostile eyes in his direction.

Logan defused the situation immediately. "It's okay. I know him. What are you doing here?"

"I was hoping to catch up with what you've learned."

He squatted down to make himself less imposing. He wrinkled his nose at the fetid smells around him. Humans had evolved into a far more civilized species since his ship had crashed on the planet. Yet, they still had many of their society living without basic needs being met. He would never understand their ways.

"I hope that's all right. Matters have escalated, and the family is very concerned."

"What's he blabbing on about?" A male voice asked. The man sat in the corner, wearing a bulky camouflage jacket and a green watch cap pulled down low on his forehead.

"Like what I was saying," Logan answered testily, "the drug that's making guys crazy."

The man nodded. "Yeah, yeah, right. Heard of that, you know, when I was up top panhandling."

"Hard to miss it. That was some sick stuff," someone added.

Others nodded in agreement. "The mayor and everyone's freaking out." He chuckled. "They hate it when our kind make a mess in their pretty world."

Everyone else thought that was a funny statement, too. Val detected pot among the many smells. That didn't interest him, of course. He wanted to ask questions yet knew that would piss Logan off, and it was her standing in this part of Boston's community that would prove useful. He was only there to make sure she was still on the case and to report back to Alex. Although they considered Logan to be part of their hive, the woman didn't necessarily view them the same way.

"Yeah," Logan agreed, "no great loss having Newbury Street smashed up, but those two guys are dead now. And that kind of sucks. Anyone know them?"

"I did...sorta." This was from a young-looking female with her knees tucked under her chin. "I seen them around the Square. Harvard," she clarified, meaning in Cambridge, the city across the river. "I used to go there, you know. Those guys were panhandling in my spot.

I'm not sorry they're gone." She clammed up with that, resting her cheek on her knees.

"So, they hung out over there, huh?" Logan directed the question to the girl, but she got no response. She shifted back to the man. "Word is, it's called 'vamp'. Makes you feel powerful. A real rush."

"No, suh? Well, that explains all the bashing and carrying on and such." The man waved a dirty hand. "I ain't into that kind ah shit. I like being mellow. Give me weed every time. And thanks to the good citizens of the Commonwealth, it's legal now."

"Where would you go for something still illegal?" Val felt compelled to ask.

Crouching in a stinky niche of the subway system was wearing on him. Plus, he couldn't quite quell his desire to return to the club and see what Mackie was up to. Had the boy complied with his orders? Either way, Val intended to instill some stern discipline. The very thought had his cock stirring.

The man jerked his thumb in Val's direction. "Where'd you say you found this igit again? He's your brotha or something?"

Logan turned hard eyes on Val. "He's a pain in my ass, is what he is. Ignore him. Any line you can give me on whose dealing vamp, I'd appreciate it."

"You're not thinking of using that shit, are ya?" When Logan merely shrugged, the guy shook his head. "I got no idea. I like keeping a low profile."

No one else volunteered, so Logan stood and would have barreled right past Val if he hadn't moved out of her way. He followed her back to the station and out onto the street.

"I'm sorry if my presence proved distracting."

She didn't bother to look at him. "I said I'd let you know if I learned something. You don't trust me."

"It's not that." Not entirely, but it didn't seem wise to be totally honest on that point. Logan had come through for them when it had counted most. It didn't change the fact that she still acted more like a feral cat that let Emil feed her. Her mental health issues plagued her and so far, no amount of coaxing by the one guy she seemed to trust had convinced her to seek treatment. She was a wild card in the effort to fight Dracul.

She hunched into her jacket, one that Emil had given her and yet was already dirty and a bit smelly. "I got this. Even the street people who don't know me recognize me for what I am — one of them. You look like a cover model for *GQ*."

She did glance at him then, her eyes taking in his body with a dismissive sweep. "I bet that's your idea of dressing down."

Because it had been exactly that, Val felt defensive. "I was thinking that if I flash some green around, it might help loosen tongues."

Logan croaked out a laugh. "Sure, that would do it, except they'll give you false information for the sheer fun of watching you chase your tail. I've *got* this," she said again. "I'm going to Harvard Square to poke around. On my own," she emphasized.

Because Cambridge had come up more than once as a relevant location, it seemed like the logical step for her to take. It was possible that Logan could learn something the cops hadn't. Seeing the wisdom in her plan and sure now that she was doing what she could in their cause, Val didn't argue the point. "Fine, but shouldn't you have stayed in the T and ridden there?"

Logan shook her head. "Spoken like a guy who's used to getting around town in style. I'll get there my way. Don't worry about me. Haven't you got some pretty boy's ass to beat or something?"

Val stiffened at the taunt then let it go. Back on his home world, everyone knew everyone else's business. It was the nature of the hive. He'd become too used to the private ways of the humans. "As a matter of fact, I do. I'll see you back at the club."

With that, he peeled off and ducked into the first alley he found. He jumped up and grabbed hold of an old fire escape railing. He climbed quickly to the top of the building, crouched to listen if anyone might be about. Hearing nothing, he began his roof jumping.

There were few chances to navigate the city in this fashion. One had to be sure the humans were tucked away for the night as much as possible. Prying eyes were the biggest threat to his species' concealment. For him, the distance between the buildings took nothing to traverse. A human would be risking a nasty fall, not that they couldn't manage it successfully. Seeing him jump from one building to the next didn't automatically mean he had to be otherworldly, but it would be an instant YouTube favorite if his movements were ever filmed. He could only imagine Alex's reaction to that kind of spotlight.

Besides, at the moment, he needed to expend a lot of energy. So he leaped and ran at full speed. No human could move that fast, making what he did even riskier if detected. He couldn't help himself. He was too pumped over the idea of dominating Mackie. He'd missed their playing. It had become a way for him to let off steam, as the humans would say.

The constant need to rein in his natural strength and abilities took their toll. In the old days, he would have sprinted across desolate mountain tops. Or, hacked his way through battling warriors. Discovering the delights of the BDSM lifestyle had given him a better outlet in modern times. It was curious, but the amount of control he had to exert to play safely with his human partners left him drained and content, not frustrated.

That had been never more so than with Mackie.

Anticipation made him reckless. By the time he landed on the club's roof, he'd practically flown across the city. He crouched from a moment, catching his breath, a rare thing for him to have to do. Then he jumped down into the alley and entered the club by the side door. It was fairly quiet, it being a slow night and late at that. Those members who were left were making out with the boys in the lap dance balcony seats or one of the private rooms. He could hear each place where everyone was and avoided them.

He strode into the kitchen. Only Emil was left, stirring some massive pot of something. A sniff confirmed lentil stew. The man graced him with a glance. "Your boy is full of bland porridge and blander water."

"Great. Thanks."

"Don't mess with him."

Val stopped at the warning. "What?"

Dropping his ladle, Emil came over to get in his face. "That boy wears his heart on his sleeve. He loves you. So, I say again, don't mess with him. This time, you stick or don't do it at all."

Val held back his temper, understanding that his old friend was looking out for Mackie. "I'm only trying to help him get through this Dracul crap. The boy is scared and stressed. I can help him with that."

"Sure. A mission of mercy." Emil batted a meaty hand at Val. "You're full of shit. You love that boy as much as he does you. Why can't you admit that?"

"Because I don't." Val let his tone drop to sub-zero. This was not a conversation he was willing to have with anyone.

Emil's expression went from bearish to sorrowful. "I know it's hard, but Mackie isn't — "

"Don't say it!" Val warned, a sudden pressure on his chest making it hard to breath.

"Robbie." Emil's soft volume didn't hurt any less than an ice pick in Val's heart would have. "This is the twenty-first century, not the eighteenth. Everything's different now. Mackie grew up with vitamins and vaccines, antibiotics and healthy food. He's stronger than Robbie could have ever been, even with your blood in his veins. Don't let the past destroy what you have with Mackie."

Because he was very afraid he might destroy Emil and his beautiful kitchen if he stayed, Val bolted. He sprinted up the back stairs to escape his friend's well-meaning advice and his own haunted memories. Taking time only to grab a bag he'd packed earlier from his room, he went to Mackie's and threw the door open.

A naked Mackie jerked up from his pillow. The magazine he'd been reading slid to the floor. "Sir."

Val slammed the door shut. "In position on the bed. Now!"

Mackie scrambled to obey. Perfect form happened in seconds with his hands behind his back, knees spread and gaze downward. Val wanted to find fault with it but couldn't. So instead, he grabbed a hank of hair and pulled the boy's head back.

"Did you cleanse?"

"Yes, sir."

Because he heard a thread of fear in the boy's tone, Val eased back. He knew better. A good Dom stayed in control at all times. He let go and petted the boy's head. Then he placed the bag on the bed within Mackie's sight so that he could see what Val had brought.

First came the cuffs. He held them up. "This is a gift, a reward for doing what I ordered tonight. You won't have to worry about keeping your hands clasped together."

He slipped them onto Mackie's slender wrists, buckled them and attached them to each other. He tested the link to make sure it was secure. Next came a slender butt plug. It was there to tease, nothing more.

"Suck it," he ordered, holding it up to Mackie's face. The boy opened and wrapped his lips around the stiff plastic. Val fucked his mouth with it. "Make it good and wet because it's the only lube you're getting."

Mackie's eyes widened and he sucked and slurped it vigorously until Val pulled it out. "Bend over." When the boy complied, Val placed a hand on his back and slid the plug up his hole. "Tighten up. If you let it out, there will be hell to pay."

He watched Mackie clench his hole around the base of the plug. The sight of the winking flesh sent a shudder through him. His jeans got tighter as his cock responded to the stimulation. Ignoring his own need, he went back to the bag and pulled out a penis gag.

Val waggled it in front of Mackie's once-again-wide eyes. "Because you have such trouble keeping quiet. Open."

He shoved the gag into the boy's mouth, admiring how it made his cheeks bulge before he strapped it in place behind his head. "There. Now I don't have to listen to your bratty demands and complaints. However" — Val pulled out a red cloth — "you understand that in lieu of safewording, you're going to have to release this?"

Mackie rolled his eyes before nodding. That bit of silent disrespect earned him a nipple twist that caused the boy to bend over and grunt around the gag.

"You really try my patience, boy."

Val pressed the cloth into one of Mackie's hands, gratified when the boy clasped it. Not that Val expected him to use the signal. In all their play time together, the brat had never safeworded. Val feared that Mackie's childhood might have left him with a warped sense of pride. Val needed to keep a sharp lookout or risk hurting the sub.

"One last thing." He retrieved a black satin blindfold and positioned it over Mackie's eyes without further comment.

Stepping back, he regarded his handiwork. Yes, this is what he needed, Mackie entirely at his mercy. He could play with him any way he liked now. The boy wanted it, as well. His poor cock was mashed against the cage in an obvious effort of getting erect. The bondage and sensory deprivation aroused Mackie, and that's what counted. He did this for the boy, just as he'd insisted with Emil. Any enjoyment Val got out of it was secondary and of no consequence. He wouldn't lapse as he'd done the previous day. He'd been weak and had allowed Mackie to have his way. Val would not make that mistake again.

He would, however, make himself comfortable. He stripped off his jacket, shirt, boots and socks. His jeans stayed on, a reminder to his dick that it wasn't invited to the party. The bag contained an array of items. So many choices… Too many, really. Testament to how long it had been since he'd amused himself. He chose the Whartenburg wheel first. Val had been on the planet long enough to know this device had once been for legitimate, albeit ineffective, medical use. Now, it was a fun toy to tease a blindfolded play-partner with.

Val began his journey with the device in innocent places such as the front of Mackie's thigh. The wheel danced along the boy's skin, eliciting a quick jerk followed by a breathy sigh. The sensitive spots close to his groin made a bigger impression. Mackie bucked his hips forward. Val issued one stinging slap to his ass in admonishment. That kept the boy in place, for a while at least.

When Val ran the wheel across Mackie's abdomen, the almost concave surface undulated with delightful ripples. The boy was enjoying this far too much, so Val ran the sharp pins over a nipple. Mackie yelped around the gag and shied away. Another slap to his rump had him coming back into position.

"Stay still." Val issued the terse order in a thick voice. He was more affected by what he was doing than he'd intended or wanted. To punish them both, he ran the wheel over and over the same nipple.

Mackie whimpered and quivered yet didn't break his pose. A quick glance confirmed that he still clenched the red cloth. Val moved to the other nipple, his gaze feasting on the way the device caused the nubs to swell and redden. He opened his hearing to the rapid tattoo of Mackie's heartbeat. It pumped the boy's blood at racing speed through his veins. Val's memory of how delicious it tasted was a palpable thing. His fangs descended and his lips split wide with his laboring breath. His gaze fixed on the pulsing at the base of the boy's throat.

Mackie uttered a muffled shriek and jerked back once more. It shocked Val out of his reverie enough for him to see that he'd pressed the wheel too hard into the boy's skin. A few beads of blood welled up. Val dropped the instrument as his fingers became nerveless. His nostrils flared at the scent of fresh blood. Memories be damned. Here was what he craved, ripe for the taking.

He lunged forward and grabbing Mackie by the arms, pressed his lips to the boy's chest. Val lapped up the drops of blood, that salty treat coating his tongue. He closed his eyes in a moment of bliss and tried to regain control. He might have succeeded if Mackie hadn't moaned and rubbed his nipple against Val's lips in silent invitation. Val couldn't resist. He scored more flesh with one fang and feasted on the well of blood. Each time, though, his saliva closed up the scrape as he licked, so he had to open newer lines.

It wasn't enough. Like giving a man dying of thirst a dribble of water, this small taste of blood only served to incite his need. His control snapped. With a roar, he shoved Mackie onto his back. The boy's legs flew up, giving Val a chance to yank the plug out of the boy's ass. Tossing it aside, Val ripped his jeans open, freeing his cock. He splayed Mackie's legs apart wider, using his body, as he positioned himself between them. He shoved his dick balls-deep with one satisfyingly brutal thrust.

Mackie shrieked again, his head thrown back and his body arching against the assault. All that did to Val's fervor was expose that beautiful neck to his gaze and his fangs. He sank them into the jugular. The new source of pain had Mackie writhing. His hole clenched around Val's shaft.

Heedless and mindless, Val tugged at the vein. At the same time, he fucked Mackie's tight channel. He went slowly at first, taking the succulent blood down his parched throat and reveling at the way Mackie's swollen tissues caressed his cock. It had been so long since he'd done this, sucking and fucking at the same time. It was glorious, but he couldn't savor it.

Soon he picked up speed, drilling Mackie's ass with fast, deep strokes. He bottomed out every time and pulled back far enough so that only his cockhead remained before slamming it back in. He drew such large mouthfuls of blood that they had him choking in his effort to swallow.

Then he came, his orgasm erupting suddenly and painfully hard. His body reared up, bending Mackie almost in half. The boy's hole closed like a vise and a muffled scream met his ears. On the wane of his climax, he found the presence of mind to lap the puncture wounds closed. He gasped for breath and blinked to clear the fog from his mind.

With clarity came the sudden realization of what he'd done. He scanned Mackie's front to make sure he wasn't bleeding out. There wasn't a spot of blood marring his skin, Val having greedily drunk it all. *Fuck, I could have drained him dry.* He eased his dick out of the boy's ass and peered down. Relief at finding no obvious signs of damage made him dizzy.

But, that wasn't the whole of it. He was almost afraid to turn Mackie on his side and look at his hand. Once more, Val's head spun. The red cloth was still clenched inside the boy's fist. Whatever else Mackie might have felt about Val's loss of control, he hadn't safeworded without Val realizing it.

Small comfort. He didn't trust Mackie to know his own limits.

Val tugged the cloth free and released the cuffs. Having both their weights pressing on Mackie's arms must have been painful. He rubbed circulation in them briefly before removing the gag. Mackie sputtered and spit and licked his lips. Then he grinned.

"Are you all right?" Val demanded.

"Yes," came the breathless, sleepy reply.

"Did I hurt you?" Val slipped the blindfold off Mackie's head as he asked.

The boy smiled up at him with a dazed expression. "No. It was amazing." Emotion showed through the boy's lovely green eyes.

Val jerked back. He'd seen that look before — adoration to the point of worship. He'd been in this place where a human boy put his love and trust in him. The memory of it hurt so much that he rubbed his fist over his heart. No, he couldn't take it. Mackie didn't understand. That way led to death.

He stumbled off the bed. A scent caught his nostrils and made them flare. Mackie had climaxed. His dick had overcome its confinement and now Mackie's semen coated the inside of the plastic.

Mackie struggled to prop himself up. "Val?"

"Stay." He held his hand out.

He headed for the bathroom, his mind running through the things he needed — wet cloth, dry one, water — the things Mackie required after Val's hard use of him.

"You're staying, right?" The plaintive tone tugged at Val's guilt.

"Of course." He glanced over his shoulder. "I'm going to take care of you, Mackie. I promise."

Only that meant going back to keeping his distance. He couldn't be trusted with the boy. He should have known that about himself. That he didn't... That he'd had the hubris to think he could play the Dom and not get involved was unbearable. He hadn't felt such self-loathing since... No, that wasn't going to help. He would drive himself mad if he couldn't find a way to lock his emotions and needs down tight.

Worst of all, he would hurt Mackie. Again. It was already too late. The boy wouldn't understand, not now. Eventually, though, Mackie would come to realize that Val was poison to his happiness and his very life. The boy would accept that the best path forward for the both of them was to take divergent ones.

Chapter Nine

"Val's been avoiding me." Mackie made the complaint to Quinn as they leaned against the dance-floor railing, watching the boys on stage. Wednesday night was the beginning of the weekend for lots of people. The club was filled up with guys trying to get their freaks on.

"Really? He seems so attentive."

"Huh! Yeah, if you mean he makes sure I'm fed and watered, like I'm a horse or something. That's the extent of it, though. Oh, and, he took me out shopping yesterday and to my hair appointment. My own personal chauffeur, bodyguard and bag carrier. That service ends at my bedroom door, however."

It had been only a couple of nights since the jaw-dropping fuck and feed that Val had delivered. What had started out as an arousing, yet sedate, play session had ended in the ride of Mackie's life. The way Val had claimed his ass had left a deep ache that Mackie could still feel if he tightened his sphincter. The residual reminder of the night was helping him stay strong under the pressure of the battle, but its effects were waning.

He was still processing how he felt about being a feeding source for a real vampire, instead of the pretend one he'd always thought Val to be. He ran his fingertips along the jugular. There was barely any evidence of how the man had sunk his teeth in. "Does it make you come extra hard when Alex drinks your blood?"

Quinn's eyelids drooped. "Oh, yeah. I mean, I don't have anything to compare it to other than jerking off, but wow." He peered at Mackie. "Wait a minute. Are you saying Val drank from your vein?"

On a sigh, Mackie dished what had happened. He'd intended to keep the event private under the assumption Val wasn't ready to be open about their renewed relationship. Now that it seemed like Mackie had misinterpreted Val's intent, there was no reason to keep everything on the down-low.

"I didn't know if Val wanted that to be common knowledge," he finished. "And I was trying to be a good boy." He grimaced. "All bets are off now. He's retreated from any kind of play. Damn, I pushed him too fast."

Except he hadn't really been responsible for Val's epic meltdown that night. Mackie had been as surprised as he had been delighted with how the night had turned out. That was until he slowly realized that he was back to square one — or worse.

"What a jerk." Quinn scanned the room. "Why can't he accept how fabulous you two are together?"

"Beats me. Or, doesn't beat me. As in, I could really use a good spanking right now." Across the room, Warren smiled and raised his glass to Mackie.

"You've got at least one fan," Quinn observed. "I hear he is like a gazillionaire, never married. If you play your cards right, you could become Mr. and Mr. Frederick Warren." Quinn straightened. "Hey, you know what? You're like my best friend and I don't even know your full name."

"Mackenzie Fraser." Mackie made a face. "Not that I like using it. It reminds me of my family, and I'd just as soon forget them."

"Okay, so you marry the guy and become Mackenzie Warren. It has a nice ring to it."

Whirling around, Mackie leaned his back against the railing and pouted. "I'm not going to marry that man. I don't want to give him a lap dance, either. I want Val. Just Val. I love the stupid idiot, which makes me a complete fucking moron."

"Oh, sweetie, I'm sorry." Quinn wrapped his arms around his shoulders and rested his head against Mackie's.

But Mackie's attention was already taken by the sight of Val. He was walking briskly through the club in the tight-assed manner Mackie now knew meant the guy was trying not to bullet his way alien-style.

"Something's up." Straightening, he gently dislodged Quinn and headed after Val.

Quinn was right on his heels as they went to Alex's office. Kitty had beaten them there, as had Emil and Harry. And of course, Val stood to one side. Once again, everyone had their eyes peeled on the flat screen on the wall.

"Oh, no, not again," Quinn murmured.

Alex's head whipped around to face them. He gestured with his hand and Quinn fled to his side. The man embraced his lover tightly as they watched the drama unfold.

Mackie caught Val staring at him without expression. There was no invitation to join him. Hardly a surprise there. Although Mackie would have liked to have the comfort, he had his pride. He wouldn't ask when no offer had been made. Instead, he braced his legs and folded his arms to watch the misery playing out on the screen.

This time, there was no on-camera death, thank God. A naked African-American woman was screaming as four cops brought her down. She'd run riot through the Harvard Bookstore. It looked like a tornado had hit it. And while the station blurred out her private parts, it didn't keep one from seeing that blood was splattered over a fair amount of her. It was the glass, he realized. She'd broken windows and countertops. Whoever had filmed the scene must have been holding their phone right through the broken frame of the storefront.

As the woman was carried away, still screaming, the reporter came on with a split screen. He talked about how this was the fourth case of what police believed was the poisonous effects of a dangerous new drug. He reminded the viewers that both the governor and the police had only yesterday issued a joint statement warning against its use.

Kitty shook her head. "That poor, poor woman. What a horrible thing to do to anyone. Excuse me, boss. I'm going to go polish my bar." She strode out of the room, stone-faced.

Alex turned off the television. He'd seen enough. They all had. No one said anything for a few seconds until Alex turned to Harry. "Give me some good news."

"As it happens, I can. I've been experimenting with my own blood, Lucien's and Demi's. I think the key to neutralizing the effects of this drug is in the hybrid cells. So, I'm concentrating now on the boy. He doesn't mind, makes him feel useful and it lets me keep an eye on him. He has an interest in chemistry. That surprised me, actually." The man smiled with obvious pride.

"Great," Val chimed in. "So you think you can fix this problem and help that woman we just saw?"

Harry's face fell. "I'm not sure of that. I think I can *neutralize* it, not cure it."

Val shook his head slowly. "Meaning?"

"I can stop it from progressing, but I don't think I can repair the damage already done."

"It's something," Alex interjected. "We can perhaps find a way to get it to the humans. Duncan mentioned a doctor who seemed brighter than average. Maybe we can funnel it through him."

"Without his learning the source?" Val scoffed. "I don't see that happening, boss."

"It's a tangle, to be sure, and we'll figure it out once we get to that point. It might be enough to throw Dracul off this scheme once he learns we have something to counter it. There's no value in it for him unless it escalates. Please carry on, Harry. Let me know if you need anything."

The man left with a wave. He gave Mackie a sympathetic smile, as well, as he passed. That act of kindness irritated Mackie. This was all Val's fault. Now everyone pitied him because he loved someone too idiotic to acknowledge loving him back.

Mackie stepped forward. "Alex, is there anything I can do to help?"

"Yeah," Val replied. "Go back to work."

"I wasn't asking you," Mackie sneered.

Alex smiled at him. "No, thank you for the offer. Val is right, however inelegantly put. There's nothing for us to do except wait for Harry to brew his potion and for Duncan or Logan to find us the location of the drug source."

His kissed the top of Quinn's head with a tenderness that hurt Mackie to witness. "Waiting is hard, I know. But, there's nothing else we can do."

* * * *

Wales

"It took you long enough, Petru. You know how much I hate waiting." Dracul put venom in his tone because he did like to remind even the most loyal of men who was in charge.

"Your pardon, sir. I think you'll be pleased with my offering."

So saying, the man lifted the hood from the boy's head, exposing an exquisite beauty. His naked body had already met with Dracul's approval, all that milky-white skin pulled tight over a slender frame. The way he flailed in Petru's grasp, despite having his hands tied behind his back, meant he had a bit of spirit to him. Dracul would enjoy breaking him of it.

"He says his name is Brenin."

Dracul grinned. "As if I care. You are a slut for now, maybe a pet later, if you please me."

The boy blinked his doe-brown eyes back at Dracul. His short black hair stood up in sweaty spikes. That wasn't very appealing. Oh, well, it would grow. There was lots of time to shape the boy into something Dracul fully desired. In the meantime, the way the human's chest rose and fell on rapid breaths and the strum of his heart with fear were very fetching.

Dracul snapped his fingers and pointed to the ground. When the boy didn't move, Petru shoved him down. The boy winced as his knees hit the floor. Dracul's cock twitched at the sight.

"Where did you find him?"

"Coming out of a homeless shelter."

"Excellent." Parting his robe and his thighs, Dracul exposed his hardened dick. The boy's eyes went wide. Dracul smiled as he ran his palm up his length. "I trust you know what do to with this, hmm?"

The boy shook his head frantically and would have backed up but for Petru's grip on his shoulder.

Dracul tsked. "Oh, come now. Nothing too difficult. I only want your mouth." He'd leave what he hoped was a virgin hole for later. Taking time to savor delicacies was a strength of his. He prided himself on being disciplined.

When the boy still didn't move, Petru pushed him forward until it was either knee-walk over or fall flat on his face. The boy wisely chose the former. *Good.* Dracul liked boys with a bit of brains. Not too much, mind, but enough to train quickly and easily.

He spread his legs even wider in invitation. "I'm sure I don't have to warn you that if I feel teeth just once, you won't be allowed to keep them." The boy whimpered, a lovely sound that caused pre-cum to leak out. "Now, see? You've already paved the way for your lovely mouth to do its job. Come now. Don't be shy."

His arousal grew the closer the boy got. It was pure ecstasy watching the way the human reluctantly opened his mouth with teary eyes. He bent down to take only Dracul's cockhead past quivering lips. Of course, that lasted about two seconds before Dracul grabbed a handful of hair and impaled the boy's mouth on his shaft. The choking and gagging noises amused him for a few seconds before he let him up.

"Lick and suck, slut, or I'll choke you with it again."

The effort was tentative and artless, but he patted the boy's head in appreciation. He could afford to be magnanimous as a reward for good behavior. Carrot and stick had proven an effective training strategy with Dafydd. These humans were pathetically easy to control.

He turned his attention back to Petru. "What is the status of my boys?"

"They continue to feed the drug into the local population. There have been three deaths so far and the local government has started warning their people away from vamp."

"From what?"

Petru cleared his throat. "From vamp, sir. That is what your sons have been calling it."

"Ridiculous." Honestly, the human half of his sons made them stupider than need be. "Wait, what?" He straightened, sending his cock back down the new boy's throat. "Only three! What are my boys doing? There should have been wide-spread use of the drug before anyone realized what was happening. The streets of that backwater city should have been littered with bodies by now."

His pique caused his balls to tighten. Shoving the boy's head down again, he spilled his seed into the unwilling mouth. "Get me my phone."

Petru rushed off to comply. As the human struggled and gagged, Dracul fumed. *Must I do everything myself?* He poured all his anger into and through his cock, and when it was spent, he tossed the boy away. He lay sputtering and drooling onto the stone hearth.

"You're going to lick up every drop of that," Dracul snapped. "I'm surrounded by incompetence!"

"They only reflect your own failings."

Outraged, Dracul stood and growled toward the wan human lying on the bed. Dafydd stared back at him in defiance. Training notwithstanding, the boy had never learned to keep his mouth shut and his foolish opinions to himself. Dracul took a step forward, his palm itching to deliver a vicious rebuke. He pulled up short immediately, remembering why the boy still lived at all.

He changed direction. "You need a stern reminder of your place, *pet*. I won't risk the life you shelter, however, as he or they are far more important than you will ever be. But, then I don't have to. Let's bring back the ancient human custom of the whipping boy, shall we?"

He bent down and fisted the short strands of hair, hauling the human back to his knees. The boy started screaming before the first blow landed.

* * * *

"Do you have a moment, sir?"

Alex swiveled his desk chair away from the television. "Of course. I don't know why I keep watching that damn thing. There's nothing they can tell us of any use."

"It's hard to wait," Val agreed, taking a seat in one of the visitor chairs. "With four more deaths, there's more than a whiff of panic in the air. I don't understand why humans would continue to try this stuff with the warnings being issued."

Alex tossed his head back and stared at his ceiling. "You and I have been interacting with this species long enough to know there is often no logic to what they do. It's no surprise that so far the victims have been the young and the marginalized. Males in particular have always strangely tied their manhood into doing dangerous things."

Val did know that about humans. Two of the latest victims had been male college students, no doubt trying the drug on a dare. Duncan had told them that the police speculated the other two had been undergoing some kind of gang ritual of admittance. Sadly for all of them, no one had won any bets or prized positions, only a trip to the morgue.

"I hate to say it, but the one I'm worried about is the woman. Her survival is making it possible for that doctor Duncan mentioned to isolate the drug. Not that I wish any more ill than she's already suffered, but she might be the key to exposing our existence on this world. It would be ironic if Dracul causes our demise by doing the one thing that he and we have always agreed on — keeping our presence a secret." He choked out a laugh. "Sorry for being Captain Obvious. Waiting makes me squirrely. I think too much."

Alex flashed a smile. "I understand completely. I don't expect, however, that you came here simply to rehash what we know. What else is on your mind?"

Of course, Alex was always one to get to the point. Normally Val was as well. This conversation was going to be hard, because everything involving Mackie was. "When this latest battle is over, I want to send Mackie away."

"Ahh…" Alex sat forward and folded his arms on his desk. "This is a familiar topic of conversation, although surprisingly reversed. Haven't I been urging this very thing for the last couple of months? Mackie, himself, raised it only to have you shoot it down."

Val had expected this reaction and deserved it. "Yes, sir, you have, and I apologize for being so stupidly stubborn on this issue. You've been right all along. So was Mackie when he complained of being little more than a prisoner."

"Well, I would say I'm gratified to hear it, except now I wonder what has changed your mind. I have noticed, of course, since this latest aggression from Dracul began, that you've been running hot and cold with the boy. Mostly cold now. Glacial, one might say. What happened the other night?"

"I almost hurt him, badly." Val had trouble getting the words out because every time he relived his actions, he pictured all the different ways he could have ended up killing Mackie.

"I find that hard to believe."

"It's true. I-I lost control. Savaged him, in more than one way."

"Really? He seems fine to me. Not a mark on him other than the telltale signs of a feeding."

The observation reminded Val of how the warm, salty blood had coated his throat and satisfied the deep hunger that never left him. "I lost control," he repeated, choking a bit at the confession. "I could have bled him dry as well as ripped him apart with the brutal way I mounted him."

He lifted his gaze so that his captain could see his anguish. "At first, I thought I could keep him close and safe without getting involved with him again. When that proved unworkable, I convinced myself I could provide the discipline he craves and still manage to keep emotionally distant. I was wrong.

"Now I know that I have no discipline of my own when it comes to him. He'll be safer elsewhere. Yet I can't stomach the idea of handing him over to one of our cadre, either. That might not be fair of me, but knowing I might run into him and his new lover drives me to distraction. I'm not sure I could handle that and I wouldn't want to bring trouble to your command. There's already enough fighting between our two factions as it is."

"What makes you think if he went to live with one of my other men, they'd become lovers?"

Val merely blinked back at Alex in confusion. "Who could resist Mackie?"

Alex smiled. "Ahh... Of course. Forgive my obtuseness."

Val sighed. "In any event, I'm sure we can find a place for him to live where Dracul won't bother looking. As far as he knows, Mackie isn't mine anyway."

Alex shook his head and gave him the same look he had so many centuries ago. "Oh, my dear Valeriu, he *is* yours. Everyone can see that except you."

Now it was Val's turn to shake his head. "No. He can't be. Please, sir, I don't have the strength to have him near and not claim him. And, I don't have the courage to make him truly mine, either."

"Remember when we were picking our human names? We wanted to blend in with the locals, and though we thought it was strange that their names had meanings, we did each go for something we thought suited us."

"I remember."

Alex gave Val a wan look. "Because you have the uncanny ability to never forget, which makes you suffer perhaps more acutely than the rest of us" — he paused — "you chose a name that means 'strong'. It suited you then as it does now. One of my biggest fears when I realized that Dracul was plotting against me was that he would woo you to his side."

"Never!" Val issued the denial on a snarl.

Alex smiled. "Loyalty is the only thing about you greater than your strength. I was more relieved than I can say when you stuck with me."

"There was never any question of that, sir. And, I have only the one regret, as you know. That's why I'm begging you to help me deal with Mackie."

On a sigh, Alex sat back again. "I will, certainly. He won't like it."

"He'll do as he's told." He had to, or Val didn't think he could survive anything different.

"I can't imagine why you think that. That boy may be a natural submissive, but he's no pushover. Nevertheless, we'll figure something out."

Val was on the verge of expressing his thanks when Alex got a text. "It's Kitty. Duncan is here. She's bringing him back. Let's hope he has a line on the drug's source."

"And, let's hope it leads right to Dracul's whelps." He'd seen little of the hybrids, as Harry would call them. What he had made him keen on disposing of them for good.

"Hey, boss."

It wasn't Duncan who arrived a few seconds later. Emil came in as he issued the greeting with Logan in tow. Val hadn't seen her since that night in the T tunnel. She looked — and frankly, smelled — as if she'd spent the time since visiting homeless groups around the city.

Emil jerked his thumb in her direction. "Logan's got some news."

"So do I." Duncan trailed Kitty into the office, looking again as if he hadn't slept in a long time.

Behind him were Quinn and Mackie. *Of course. Why would I expect anything else?* He was on the verge of telling the boy to leave then decided it wasn't worth the confrontation. Val had no illusions, either, that he would win the argument. With Quinn heading straight for Alex's welcoming lap, there really was no logical reason for Mackie to be forced out. Val's discomfort didn't count.

Duncan dropped down on the couch. "Ladies first."

Logan made a rude noise in response but then got down to it. "I've found the source, the place the dealers are using as a home base. I can take you there."

"Where is 'there', if I may ask?" Alex's polite phrasing notwithstanding, he was demanding the information. "We — Val, Emil and I — can go on our own."

"You're not going without me," Duncan asserted.

"I have to show you," Logan insisted. "It's because you won't know how to access it without someone who already knows the layout."

Val faced her. "The layout of what?"

"The T. See... There's lots of hidden parts underground that aren't in use. It's in one of those, at Harvard Square."

"I've heard of that," Duncan replied.

"So have I," Val added. "I researched the area very thoroughly before we relocated here. Boston boasts the oldest subway system in the United States. There are forgotten places, as Logan says. You know the access route to where they're holed up?"

"Yup. We street people use them from time-to-time. No one hassles you down there. But I have to show you. It's too hard to explain."

"Fair enough," Alex replied. They all knew Logan could handle herself in a fight. Alex eyed Duncan. "What can you add to that?"

"Well, first off, I had the same info. Karl and I met with the Cambridge cops again this afternoon. They'd leaned on an informant and he'd told them the stuff was coming from somewhere in Harvard University's underground steam tunnels. He must have confused them with the T tunnels, though."

Val did the math in his head. "So, none of your police brethren will be looking in the right spot. We'll have a clear shot." The idea of taking down Dracul's sons and ending this latest round of war gave Val something to focus on other than Mackie. It also meant the boy would be leaving that much sooner. *Why doesn't that make me feel better?*

"Yeah." Duncan frowned and scratched the back of his neck. "I really hate all this sneaking around."

Alex inclined his head. "As always, we appreciate how difficult this is for you, Sergeant, and hope tonight will see the end of it, at least for now."

"I'd like to think so," the cop replied. "But there's no telling how much of that poison is out there. The other thing I found out is that it's being marketed differently, as a new and better version of Molly. You know, a form of Ecstasy or E. That explains the college kids." He shook his head. "Dumb bastards thought they'd be fine taking a less-lethal drug."

"Debbie would have thought that, too." Everyone turned to Logan. "That's her name, you know? The woman who trashed the bookstore."

"We did not know," Alex replied in a quiet voice. "I don't think anyone's come forward to say."

Logan grimaced. "I didn't know her well, but she was a vet, like me. Can you fix her?"

Alex shook his head. "I'm sorry. I don't know. I can promise you, though, that once Harry finds an antidote, we will do our best to get it to her."

"She's heavily sedated on the psych ward," Duncan offered. "No one's guarding her because it's a lock-down unit and she's restrained besides. I bet I can get something past Dr. Paz, though."

"All right," Alex said, standing and setting Quinn down on the floor. "Let's gear up."

Mackie, who had been uncharacteristically quiet, said, "Wait. What about us?" He gestured toward Quinn, then himself. "What can we do?"

"Stay here." Val issued the order before Alex could open his mouth.

"Yes," the boss confirmed with a narrowed gaze at Val. "That would be best. Your presence out there would distract us," he added when Quinn started to object.

"Oh." The boy hugged Alex briefly. "We understand. Be careful."

Alex brushed a kiss against the boy's lips as if they were the only ones in the room. "Always, dearest boy. Always."

"Hey, Duncan," Emil called out. "You had dinner yet?"

The cop rubbed his stomach. "Now that you mention it, no."

"Come on. You too, Logan. Can't fight on an empty stomach. We'll meet you at the back door in thirty, boss."

As the others left, Mackie stood staring at Val for a few seconds before moving to bring up the rear of the column exiting the room.

"Wait." The word popped out of Val's mouth. With the boy and Alex already in the room and the end of the current crisis in sight, it made sense to talk about his future. Val didn't need a half hour to get ready, anyway.

Mackie eyed him suspiciously. "What?"

Val took a deep breath for courage, itself a cowardly act. "I've been talking to Alex about where you should go once this thing is over."

Mackie's eyes widened. "When what thing is over, the war with Dracul?"

"Just this round of it. You won't be in his sights, if you ever were, while he licks his wounds. It will be the perfect time to relocate you."

"Relocate me!" The boy whirled to face Alex. "What do you intend to do with me?"

"Val has made a valid point that as you and he are no longer…involved, it makes sense to get you settled somewhere else, somewhere Dracul has no interest in."

"Oh, I get it. You and *Val* have the rest of my life all planned out, huh? You're going to shunt me off to 'no one's ever heard of this God forsaken place' Idaho or something. And I'm supposed to be grateful, is that it?"

"I don't understand. Only a few days ago you raised the issue of leaving. You said you felt imprisoned."

"That was different. I meant moving to an apartment instead of living at the club. And besides, things have changed since then, h-haven't they?"

Val saw the hope and confusion in the boy's eyes. Val had hurt him, again. He'd allowed Mackie to think they were in a relationship once more. "No." He made his tone final and implacable, making a quick cutting wound instead of drawing it out.

Mackie's jaw tightened and his eyes hardened. "My mistake."

"We're doing this for your own good." The words sounded weak to Val's own ears.

"Really? Is that what you tell yourself? Like when my parents were going to send me to a special school to cure me of my sexual *confusion*. Beatings and praying hadn't worked, so they tried to rid themselves of their problem the same way you are."

"No, it's not like that." Val knew something of Mackie's history. The way his family had treated him had always made Val want to hunt them down and mete out some of their own vicious justice. "We'll make sure you're situated to your liking and take care of you financially. It won't be like when you had to run away." Val could see tears forming in the boy's eyes. Damn, he should have thought of how this might remind the boy of his family's betrayal. "You'll get to pick where you want to go."

Mackie eyes spit fire. "Gee, thanks. I appreciate having a say in my life. And, fuck you for thinking my concern is the money. Did it occur to you that I might have found a home here? I have friends and admirers and a skill for making money. If I get a say, then I choose to stay in Boston."

"You can't!" Val's temper snapped in an instant. Couldn't Mackie see how hard this was on him, too?

But, the boy was focused on Alex. "You're onboard with all of this? It's your club. Are you kicking me out?"

Alex looked pained as he replied. "Mackie, please understand. This is for your own good."

"Bullshit. It's because he can't handle having me around, and he can't fucking commit." Mackie punctuated by jabbing his finger in Val's direction. "Well, fuck you, Val. And fuck you, Alex. Fuck the whole damn place. You just tell me when the coast is clear and I'll be out of your hair faster than a seven-foot-tall alien vampire. Good thing I never unpacked. But, you don't control me and you don't own the whole damn city, either. I can live wherever I want."

Val closed his eyes a second to gain control. "Mackie, please. We know you're upset, but don't do anything rash. We can help you financially and physically."

"I don't need your help. I can earn a living. If nothing else, I can always go back to sucking cock in alleys." He shot past Val — or tried to.

Val reached out to grab his arm. "Wait!"

Mackie turned hard, dried eyes on him. "*Let. Go.* You're not my Dom anymore. You're not my *anything*."

The venom in the boy's voice drowned out the hurt. It was still there, layered under the bravado that the human's past had forced him to adopt. It would have taken nothing for Val to lift him up and tie him to his bed, but that wasn't the way for a Dom to treat his sub — or former sub. There would be no consent given for such an action. Much as he hated to do so, he forced his fingers open and watched the boy flee the room.

Alex said nothing for a few seconds in the boy's wake. "He's upset. We'll talk to him again later. Quinn will help, I'm sure."

Val couldn't imagine anyone would be able to say anything to change Mackie's mind. The boy was a brat after all, stubborn and unruly.

Not my problem.

He turned cold eyes on Alex. "Let's go show Dracul's boys whose city this is."

Chapter Ten

Mackie took one last look at his kohl-rimmed eyes, blushed cheeks and red lips and decided that he had achieved the perfect look. He turned this way and that to check out the effect of the HommeMystere Britney high-neck bra and thong. His body was just the way he wanted it — slender and sexy. He walked a knife-edge between boy and girl.

Val would hate it.

Let him. Mackie was no longer concerned with what turned on his ex-vampire lover. Many of the club members would appreciate his non-binary appearance and pay dearly for the privilege of watching him dance — and touching him. There would be lots of touching from now on. Val and Alex had made it quite clear that Mackie had to set his own course or run the risk of losing his hard-won autonomy. Being independent meant having the money to do so. Starting that night, he was going to maximize his earnings, regardless of what it took.

"Hmm, looking fierce there, girl," Shawn said as he came out of the bathroom.

Mackie didn't correct the boy's female reference. Mackie flashed him a smile. "Thanks, sweetie. Let's go break some hearts."

Mackie put a swing to his hips and entered the main room. He took a second to make a song request from Kitty. "*Numb*, please. The *Encore* version."

Kitty gave him the once-over and shook her head. "Fine."

Mackie could feel the eyes of all the club members milling around as he sashayed his way over to the far-front stage. He hopped onto it during the last bars of the current song and grabbing the pole, struck a pose inspired by Marilyn Monroe with lips pursed and legs spread. Having no dress to hold down, he grabbed his junk. Every man in sight fixed their gaze down there. When the song started, he slowly navigated the stage, giving everyone a good look at his whole pretty body. Then, as the tempo picked up, so did he.

He let his thoughts drift, moving to the rhythm of the song and emptying his head of worry. He could lose himself in the music and the flow of the dance. He forced his muscles to move and contort his body in time to the beat. The pole, as always, became an extension of himself. The lyrics told his story more eloquently than he could have ever expressed. And, as he played to his audience, treating each man as if he were the only one in the room, accepting their pawing and money, he cleansed his mind and his heart of Val.

There was one man in particular who captured his attention. He edged out his competition, staking a spot by the stage and making sure that he touched whatever part of Mackie he could reach as Mackie went through his routine. The man's eyes showed adoration and his hand fisted not twenties, but hundreds.

Sliding one leg high on the pole in a vertical split, Mackie leaned down and gave the man an 'O' face. "Hi, Mr. Warren." He grinned provocatively before twirling away.

By the time the song ended, his thong was stuffed with the man's appreciation. Warren waved one more bill in Mackie's face. He bent over and snatched it up with his painted lips. Then he took it out again and stuffed it down into the pocket of his thong.

Warren's eyes lit up. He snagged Mackie by the top of his bra and pulled him closer. "I've got ten more where that came from if you meet me upstairs after your set."

Mackie fluttered his lashes. "How can I resist?"

With that promise made, he went into his next routine, not really caring what Kitty played now that his feelings had been purged with the first one. Plenty of men stuck by him, and he gave each one as much attention as he could. By the time he was due for a break, he'd worked up a sweat. Someone offered his hand to help him down, while another flourished a handkerchief. Mackie used the square of cloth to dab his skin dry before handing it back with a quick peck on the cheek.

Another man brought him a cold bottle of water. Hands roamed shamelessly over his lace-covered chest and patted his ass. The men were treating him with such courtly attention, albeit with a whole lot of naughty thrown in, that he knew his new look had struck the right chord. It had led to even more money being stuffed down his thong and invitations for private assignations. He made vague promises to everyone, mindful of his date with Warren. He would find a way to satisfy all of them. The way things were going, he would only need to keep this job for a few weeks to pad his nest egg and find a new place to work and live.

The reminder that he was being kicked out of the club and Val's life sent a stab of pain through him. Pushing it aside, he flirted with his admirers for a few minutes before heading up to the second floor. He found Warren lounging in a lap-dance chair, sipping a drink and sporting a hard-on in his silk slacks.

A moment of hesitation pulled him up short before he shoved the concern aside and plastered a smile on his face. "Hello there. Sorry to keep you waiting."

Getting up, Warren snaked out an arm and snagging Mackie by the waist, pulled him against his body. He rubbed his erection against Mackie's stomach. "I saw you down there, letting those other guys fondle you."

Mackie swallowed past a frisson of worry and licked his lips. "Boy's got to make a living."

"Not if you were *my* boy." Warren traced his tongue around the shell of Mackie's ear. "If you were mine, I'd set you up in a condo and all you'd have to do all day would be shop and keep your hole ready for my dick."

Mackie shivered a bit in revulsion.

"You like that idea, don't you," Warren said, misreading Mackie's reaction.

Not that Mackie could explain why he'd had it... It wasn't that Warren was unattractive. It was something nameless about him that made Mackie want to push and run away. *No, not nameless. He's not Val.* That was a stupid thought, though. He didn't have Val any more. He needed to get that straight in his own mind and be sensible.

He forced himself to look up at the man with desire. "Sounds like the perfect life."

Warren's expression softened. "Not exactly though, huh? I mean you like it rough, don't you? That BDSM stuff?"

"Well…"

"It's okay. I've been reading up on it. I can give you that, if you want. I can be your Dom."

"Really?" It was kind of sweet that the guy had gone to the trouble and was willing to try it for Mackie's sake."

"You don't have to." Mackie wasn't sure he was into it without 'he who could not be named'.

"I want to try. You're worth the effort." Warren pressed a chaste kiss on Mackie's lips. "I've reserved one of the playrooms. Let's go."

"I'm not sure."

"A thousand just to give me a chance to please you." He held up a wad of cash in his hand.

At that moment, Mackie felt more like a whore than he'd ever done sucking cocks in alleys. He wanted to refuse because he'd moved past that life—or, he thought he had. Then he remembered how he was really on his own again. Either he accepted money from Alex and Val or from Warren. What difference did it make, except that at least this way, he was earning his money? In a weird way, there seemed to be more dignity in offering his ass up to Warren then allowing someone who didn't want him any more to pay his way out of pity or a sense of duty.

Fuck that.

Pasting a smile on his face, he said, "I'd love to."

Warren beamed with happiness and gratitude, just the kind of response that made Mackie feel wanted and appreciated. He linked his arm through the man's and led him out of the room and down the corridor that contained the playroom. His steps hitched only a moment when he saw that they were going into *the* room, the one where he and Val had always played. The supersized equipment would make it harder for Warren, a mere human, to access whatever part of Mackie he wanted. But, oh well. Not his problem.

Inside the room, the music was muffled unless one turned on the speakers. Warren didn't. Instead, he let Mackie go and started stripping off his jacket. "Okay, boy. Take all of those bills out of your panties. I don't want to see other men's money."

"Yes, Sir." As Doms went, the guy wasn't half bad. His voice was steady and his tone authoritative over all. Mackie pulled the money out and stacked it in a neat pile on a table. He gave Warren the courtesy of a standing submissive pose and waited for his next order.

"Okay." The man rubbed his hands together and pursed his lips. "We need, um, a safeword, right?"

"Yes, Sir. It's red, Sir."

Warren nodded. "Good. So, ah" — he darted his eyes around the room—"up on the spanking bench. I'm going to paddle your ass." He grinned broadly.

Mackie batted his eyelashes again, trying to appreciate how hard the man was trying. He padded over to the bench, shoved aside sudden memories threatening to swamp him and climbed up. But when Warren started to cuff Mackie's first wrist, something within him snapped.

"Red!" He reared up, his chest heaving. "Sorry," he added with a hard swallow.

"It's okay," Warren rushed to reassure him. "We have all night. Take your time."

Mackie reached up to clasp the invisible lump in his throat. "I just need a moment." He flashed the guy a grin. "I'm nervous."

"Me too," Warren admitted. "Say… I have something to help, maybe."

"What?"

By way of answer, Warren went back to his suit jacket and took out a flask. He brought it back and opened the cap. "Here's a little high-octane bourbon. It might do the trick."

Mackie wasn't sure what the man meant, but as he was determined to go through with the play session, he reached for the flask. He took a tentative sip, grimaced at the harsh taste, then took another larger one. The burn eventually morphed into a slightly floaty feeling. Normally, he didn't drink when playing. It wasn't recommended, but he needed the Dutch courage for this one night.

He took a few more sips then handed it back. By the time he got into position once more, the liquor's effect had started to change. He didn't feel relaxed or sleepy. He felt powerful.

* * * *

"This way." Logan propped open the old door with the warning sign and stood aside for the men to pass.

Val wanted to go first. As Alex's enforcer, he considered it his duty to always put himself at the pointy end of the spear, as the humans would say. It didn't sit well with him for his captain to be the first thing their quarry might see and attack. But, he'd also long ago given up trying to protect Alex. The man had his own way of doing things and that meant running into danger, not away from it or hiding. So, Val had to be content with this secondary position. Immediately behind him was Duncan, with Logan bringing up the rear. She carried the duffle filled with the necessary items to destroy the stash of drugs. Val would have preferred for Emil to be with them, but Alex had decided at the last minute to leave him at the club — just in case. If Dracul launched some kind of direct attack, Harry and Kitty wouldn't be enough to keep everyone safe.

The old subway tunnel was dank and musty. It reminded him of a dead thing, ravaged by time and infested with vermin. A rat scurried across Alex's path, its beady eyes shining off the beam of Alex's flashlight that was for the benefit of the humans. It cast weird shadows on the walls.

Val would bet that students who knew about this underground world must dare each other to explore it at night, when they were drunk and feeling braver than usual. The dirt offended Val's senses, but otherwise, he felt invigorated at the idea of meeting up with Dracul's boys. The scene with Mackie had left Val with a murderous need to tear someone to shreds.

Not that he could afford to think of the boy at the moment. On the drive over, he'd replayed the scene in Alex's office dozens of times over, despite his efforts to put it aside. He kept seeing Mackie's hurt expression underneath his obvious anger, kept hearing the boy's vicious words, as well, hurled at him because Val had been clumsy in broaching the topic. It had happened because of Val's own lack of courage and desperation to shove the boy as far from his orbit as possible.

I'm weak.

He lambasted himself because it needed doing. His lack of discipline had led to one boy's death. He would not allow it to cause another to lose his life.

The sound of voices reached his ears. Alex heard it too, and they both snapped off their lights and flattened against the wall. Duncan and Logan followed suit, although Val doubted they could detect the sounds. With Alex still in the lead, they inched forward. From what Val remembered from his investigation into the area, this old part of the subway contained a large room that was sometimes used by the transit authority for storage. He could only assume they were reaching that point.

"I'm telling you that I don't like to be fucked with." The human voice, heavy with a Boston accent, was pissed. "You told me this was a cheap, better form of Molly, but my customers are ending up dead. It's that vamp shit, ain't it?"

"What do you care?" The silky voice with the Welsh accent sent Val back more than a hundred years when he'd first encountered proof of Dracul's fatherhood. "You get paid either way."

"I don't if my customers are all dead."

"We pay you well enough, regardless." This second voice was a little different, the twin for the one Val had tangled with before.

"Not enough."

"You're trying to renegotiate the terms of our deal? You're not the first to do so." The menace in the response should have made the human man shut the fuck up.

It didn't. "I don't give a rat's ass what you've done in the past. I'm saying if you want me to keep pushing your shit through my pipeline of street dealers, you need to up my cut."

A loud growl reverberated through the tunnel. It was the right cue for them to rush forward. Around a bend, a muted light gave a clear view of two of their kind and a smaller man squaring off. Dracul's rabid pup had grown since Val had last seen him, his brother equally big. There was little of their human father to be seen.

The dealer was frozen in place, having finally realized that he'd gone into business with monsters. The twins' fangs were down and they loomed over the man, ready to tear him apart. Alex's, then Val's, arrival captured their attention. They turned their heads as one and hissed.

"So like your father," Alex drawled. "No finesse. Always looking for the easy way out of any problem."

That was all the talking that was going to be done. Val had already come abreast of his leader, fangs down, blood up. As the first twin sprang for Alex, Val did the same to the other brother before he could follow suit. The human found his feet, and taking out a gun, backed away from the fight.

Val paid no attention to him, keeping his focus on the prey. He had height and weight on the murderous boy. Plus, Val was no hybrid. If being half-human caused the guy any weakness, Val wouldn't hesitate to exploit it. Fighting to the death was the goal. There was no room for mercy, as he knew his opponent had none. Unless Val killed him, Dracul's son would be a constant threat to the lives of those Val cared about.

"Drop it!"

Duncan's order hit Val's ears just as he and Dracul's son clashed. A shot rang out, then another. A human cry barely registered with him. All of Val's attention was on the living locomotive trying to bring him down. The boy was a worthy opponent, grabbing Val by the arms to swing him against the wall. There was strength in that effort, although not enough. Putting his weight on the balls of his feet, Val stopped the momentum.

He bent low and crashed his shoulder into the boy's sternum. Grasping him by the neck, he flipped him up and over. A bellow whipped dust in his eyes. He roared back and lunged to grab the guy by the lapels of his leather coat. Nearby, Alex was waging a similar war. It took effort, but Val had to block concern for his captain from his mind as he'd done many times before. War had been a common event in their lives on this planet. He had to trust that they would both be victorious. If not, he would kill both of Dracul's sons — and gladly.

A hundred years had made the hybrid boy bigger but not a better fighter. Val threw him against the nearest wall. The structure shook, raining cement dust on them. A fissure cracked open where the bricks had taken the brunt of the crash. Val used his bigger body to pin the boy into the dent he'd made before he could move away. Fangs flashed and raked Val's cheek. Blood welled up and dripped down, but that only increased Val's determination. He grabbed the long tail of the boy's hair, wrapped it around his fist and pulled.

This was why Val had long ago adopted a shaved Mohawk. Long strands were a liability in a fight. The boy howled as Val yanked his head to one side, exposing his neck. Val lunged to bite into the jugular. The boy proved slipperier than expected. He went lax in Val's grasp at the last minute. Val's fangs pierced the side of the boy's face.

There was still the sweet taste of blood, of victory. He sank his fangs through the flesh and pulled a chunk free. It turned to ash in his mouth almost immediately. A vicious kick to his crotch had him grimacing. Then a sudden hard yank left him with a fistful of hair. Dracul's son scrambled away, head and face bleeding.

With a snarl, Val started to pounce and finish him off. Someone called out his name. *Logan.* But when he turned, he saw the woman helping a wounded Duncan. Her warning was for Alex. The other twin had the guy pinned under a large wooden crate that had fallen or been pushed down. Alex was already freeing himself, except that the boy had a knife poised over him.

Of course, Dracul had never fought honorably, either.

Val roared and raced over to knock the guy and his weapon away. The boy flew in one direction and the knife in the other. Its blade missed Alex's chest, yet grazed him. Val forgot about chasing down either of his enemies and instead dropped to his captain's side. He ripped off the man's shirt and lapped at the long laceration. He ignored the sound of pounding feet behind him.

"Fuck!" Alex yelled. "They're getting away."

Val didn't even bother to look over his shoulder. He needed to make sure that Alex's wound was tended. His species might be far superior to humans physically, but they were hardly invincible. It wasn't until he was sure the wound was closed sufficiently that he jumped up and pursued the twins.

They had taken off through the tunnel on the other side of the room. He couldn't see them, yet there was only one way for them to go. Sensing it was useless, he still chased them. He came up onto the street at the other end in time to see an SUV speed away. He bit back a roar of disappointment and ducked back into the tunnel before any humans noticed him.

In the room, Alex crouched in front of Duncan. The cop had a cloth tied around his upper arm. Logan was quietly placing the incendiary devices Harry had provided to destroy the drug cache. The human dealer lay obviously dead on the ground.

"I'm telling you it's fine," the cop was saying. "Logan did a fair job at a field dressing and I'm going to have enough to explain as it is. I can't have this miraculously healed flesh wound added to the mix."

Alex turned angry eyes on Val. "Damn, vicious little pup! He should never have gotten the drop on me with that crate or that knife. I'm getting too old for this shit. I assume they got away."

"Yeah, and don't ask me to apologize for coming to your aid."

Alex lowered his blazing eyes. "I won't. For Quinn's sake, if nothing else, I thank you." He sighed and looked around. "I hope this is all of it."

To Val's eyes, it seemed to be too large a quantity to not be all the drugs Dracul's boys had brought to the city. "I suppose they could have a lab here."

Alex stood and helped Duncan to his feet. "We're going to have to hope Harry has concocted something to counteract it so they won't bother making more, regardless. Are you about ready, Logan?"

"Yes, sir." She toed the nearby body. "Do we bother bringing him with us?"

"Nah," Duncan answered. "If my story is going to be that the dealers set this stash on fire before I could stop them, then I can't have had time to drag a dead perp with me, not with my arm this way."

"Well, then…" She flicked a switch, and the packages she'd scattered ignited. Smoke quickly started filling the small space.

They rushed out, the journey taking mere minutes, due to the urgency and lack of secrecy. Duncan was already calling the fire in by the time they reached the outside. Staggering to a nearby curb, he dropped. "Yeah, I'm clear of it, and yeah an EMT wouldn't hurt. Thanks. I'll keep the line open so long as you get someone to call my partner, Detective Karl Anderson." He glanced at them over his shoulder and mouthed 'go' before slumping and putting his head in his hand.

Val hated leaving the guy. There was nothing they could do and would only raise more questions than they or Duncan wanted to answer. So, he, Alex and Logan made a beeline for the non-descript SUV they'd come in. Val slipped behind the wheel and tried not to fume too much over their partial success. He'd failed, and that was something he never took well. Saving Alex's life had been paramount, naturally. It didn't change the fact that this latest battle wasn't entirely over.

"We'll get another chance at them," Alex said, obviously sensing Val's anger. He pulled his phone out of his pocket and frowned as it vibrated in his hand. "What is it, Kitty?"

Val had no trouble hearing the woman's words. Or, really two words — *Mackie* and *trouble*. He floored the gas pedal and flew.

* * * *

"This is what it's like to be a god." Mackie twirled around the ledge, marveling at how magnificent the cool breeze felt on his overheated skin. "No. Not a god, an alien." He giggled. "A vampire alien."

"Please, Mackie, come over to me." Quinn's bright blue eyes were so clear, even though it was dark out. Everything about Mackie's body was better — sight, hearing, smells — and the way his blood sang through his veins, making him stronger and faster... He was invincible. Everyone should undergo this transformation.

"Oh, Quinn, sweetie, you should come here. Take a look at how wonderful the view is."

Swinging around again, he peered down. There was a small crowd gathered, looking up at him. He felt so pretty...and admired. People adored him. Men desired him, all except one. Then again, he didn't count because he wasn't really a man.

He threw his arms up. "Fuck Val! I am fantabulous, aren't I?"

"Sure you are." That was Emil talking.

He smiled over his shoulder. "I love you, Emil. You're always so good to me. You cook for me."

"That's right, Mackie. Come down and I'll make you anything you want."

Sticking a finger in his mouth, Mackie thought hard. "I want... I want...to fly." He spread his arms wide again and closed his eyes. He could do it. If he walked off the ledge, he would take off and go anywhere he wanted. He would finally be free. No one could stop him or make him do anything he didn't want to.

"I'll be free." He gave voice to his thoughts and felt the surge of power. Opening his eyes again, he shouted down to the crowd. "No one can tell me what to do. I am Mackenzie Andrew Fraser and I don't have to take shit from anyone."

"I didn't know your middle name was Andrew."

The voice was a like a slap. Whirling back to stare at the roof, he saw the man. The alien. The vampire. The one who'd ripped his heart out and stomped it to dust. "What are *you* doing here?"

"I want you to come inside now, Mackie."

He shook his head hard, making himself dizzy. He staggered for a moment. Someone screamed and a loud grunt expelled past Val's lips. Mackie grabbed the sides of his head with his moist hands. God he was sweating. *Gross.* And, it felt as if his bones were moving around under his skin.

"Go away. You make me sad and I want to be happy. I don't need you anymore. I'm amazing all on my own."

"I know that. You are the strongest person I've ever met, Mackie. You've survived and thrived when others would have folded in despair."

Mackie dropped his hands. "That's right. And now I'm powerful. More than you, I bet."

Val's nostrils flared as he took a deep breath and let it out. It was amazing how easy it was to see and hear everything. "Mackie, please listen to me. You're on that drug. You know, the bad one that makes people do dangerous things."

"You're lying." Mackie put his hands on his hips. "I'm not stupid. I only had a little bourbon."

"Warren crushed what he thought was Ecstasy in it to make you more pliable."

Mackie frowned. "He wouldn't do that. Unlike some people, he *likes* me. He's going to give me a castle in the sky." He ran his hand down his front, liking the way his body tingled with the touch. "He thinks I'm pretty."

"Because you are pretty. Beautiful, in fact." Val's voice was thick with emotion — or was that arousal?

"You want me." He blew a kiss.

"Always." Val took a step closer.

"Don't come near me," Mackie warned with a jab of his finger in the man's direction. "You don't want me. You're trying to get rid of me."

Val took another step before stopping. "Because I'm bad for you. I can't give you what you want, what you deserve."

"Coward!" Mackie screamed the insult out into the whole of the city.

Val struggled to keep himself under control. Every fiber of his being screamed at him just as loudly as Mackie had done to run to the boy. *Grab him before he goes over.*

He kept himself in check with difficulty. He'd never been terrified in his life. Afraid, yes, worried out of his mind. He'd known helplessness during Robbie's long labor. This feeling, though, that he couldn't take a deep-enough breath to keep from passing out, was new. The synapses of his brain kept misfiring, making it hard for him to reason. All he could think over and over was, *He's going to fall. He's going to die.*

Val forced air into his lungs. "You're right. When it comes to you, I am a fool and a coward."

Mackie cocked his hips in a provocative pose. The ridiculous black lace bra and panties should have been a turn-off. They weren't. He could see easily why so many men coveted the boy when he blurred the already fuzzy human gender line. "What do you care if my middle name is Andrew?"

The question startled Val. He could have ignored it, considered doing so. Then he decided that Mackie deserved the truth. If Val had given it to the boy from the beginning, they might not be in this terrifying position.

"Because it is my son's name."

Mackie raised his eyebrows. "You have a son?"

Even after centuries, the wound was still painful, although not quite so raw anymore. Or, maybe his fear for Mackie overshadowed it. Regardless, it was time for the truth. "I did, although he never had a chance to draw breath." Val took a noisy one of his own, trying not to be swamped by the memories of the day he'd burned his lover and their son.

"Oh." Mackie's face fell and his bravado drained away. "That's so sad. Who gave birth?"

"Robbie." He hadn't said that name out loud for centuries. That, too, was painful to do but not as much as he'd feared.

Mackie's eyes went wide. "He was like Lucien?"

Val knew there was a crowd below, watching and waiting. The blare of sirens had heralded the arrival of the fire department and the cops. He didn't care, though, who might be listening or what his words might mean to them. Nothing mattered except Mackie getting off that damn ledge and over to Val's side where it was safe.

"Yes." His breath hitched. "I am responsible for their deaths, you see. I won't let that happen again."

Mackie blew out a breath and put his hands on his hips. "Well, that's just stupid." The way he swayed so casually on the ledge caused Val's stomach to drop. "I mean, if you think the same thing would happen to me… Well, it won't. Because, first of all, I never agreed to have your baby. And second…I'm invincible." He whirled around to once more peer down.

Val's stomach turned. He took a few tentative steps closer to the boy, mindful that he could be the one to send him over the edge if he acted rashly. "Please, Mackie. You're not. That's the drug talking. Please, I'm begging you to step back. Come to me." He stuttered to a halt when Mackie stared over his shoulder at him.

"Why should I? You don't love me."

Val would have said anything to save the boy. What came out of his mouth, however, was the hard truth. "Yes, I do."

Mackie shook his head. "Not the way I need you to."

"Perhaps not, but I'm willing to try. I'm not sure I understand the emotion the way you do. I can learn. A sub can teach his Dom, after all."

Mackie slowly nodded his head. "Okay... I like that idea." The human's words gave Val a moment of relief. "I'll start by showing you how strong I am."

With that cryptic remark, Mackie spread his arms and stepped off the ledge. Screams bellowed up from the street, but they were muffled sounds to Val's ears. His inner howl was making far too much noise. Indifferent to his centuries-old habits of holding back his true nature, he flashed forward and followed Mackie off the roof. He caught the boy halfway down, wrapped his body around the flailing frame and twisted.

By the time they landed, Val's back had taken the brunt and he'd cocooned Mackie within his embrace. Val had expected to smash against concrete. Instead, he was enveloped in a jump cushion. The sounds of clapping reminded him that he was among humans. It didn't really matter. Mackie was safe, at least from being killed in the fall.

Hands reached in, pulling them out. Val held tight to Mackie, who writhed, although weakly. The firefighters struggled to separate them. He heard the well-meaning humans try to get through the fog of his terror for the boy. On some level, he knew they wanted to help but his more primitive self didn't want to let the boy go — ever.

"Val! Release him. Let the EMTs do their job." It was Kitty shouting to him. Her voice cut through the chaos in his brain. He forced his eyes to open. She loomed over him, shoving the emergency personnel aside. She grabbed Val's arm. "They need to get him to the hospital, okay?"

"No." Val tightened his hold and stood on shaky legs.

She zoomed in close to his face. "Harry will meet you there. He can help now. Do you understand?"

The meaning of her words cut through. He nodded and forced his fingers to release Mackie's twitching body that sagged at the same time. He let the EMTs take Mackie and lay him on a stretcher. It was the hardest thing he'd ever done.

Chapter Eleven

"Thanks." Duncan winced as Karl helped him put on his jacket. "I appreciate your coming with me to the hospital, but I'm good getting myself home."

"Fuck you."

Pausing briefly as he slid his injured arm through the sleeve, he eyed his partner. "Was it something I said?"

Karl narrowed his eyes. "It's something you didn't say." He paced away as much as the small emergency department pod would allow. "What the hell, Trey? You've been acting weird since this killer drug tied into the Murphy murder, and tonight you sneak off on your own to chase a lead. You could have been killed. Why did you freeze me out of it?"

Trey shrugged the jacket fully on, relishing the bite of pain because he deserved it and the dressing down Karl was giving him. He so wanted to spill it all about the vampires who are really aliens and their endless war. The only thing holding his tongue back was the fear he might end up on the psych ward, or worse, off the force.

If he couldn't lend a hand with his position, it put his species and his planet at greater risk.

He blew out a breath and ran his hand over his head. His mind registered the realization that he was still overdue for a trim. "Look... I'm sorry. I was chasing what I thought was a stupid lead from an unreliable source." He gave his partner a sheepish look. "I knew you had a date and didn't want to disturb your plans over nothing."

Now he felt like a complete shit for making it sound like it was Karl's fault for having a social life. "It won't happen again." And, that was a lie. "I really need to get home and horizontal. Can I retract my earlier bullshit statement about getting there on my own and ask for a ride?"

Karl grimaced. "Yeah, sure. Asshole," he added, but with a grin.

As they made their way to the exit, the typical moans and groans and beeps and whirrs of the place became drowned out by a wailing that struck a familiar chord. Trey stuttered to a halt just as the doors swung open and EMTs rushed in with an incoherent redheaded boy strapped to their gurney. A frantic giant with a Mohawk tore in after them, while hospital personnel tried to hold him back.

"Jesus, fuck," Karl muttered.

Trey pushed forward, grabbing his badge out as he did so. He held it up for the nurse and the orderly to see. "I'm a cop. Let this man through. He's the patient's fiancé, plus I need to talk to him."

The orderly threw up his hands, and the nurse said, "Fine. But he needs to keep himself under control. The EMTs damn near tossed him out on the ride over."

"Yes, ma'am." Trey put himself in Val's path. It was like standing in front of a moving train. He didn't so much as stop the man as ended up being pushed along himself. "Val, what happened?"

He turned crazed eyes on him. "A club member slipped Mackie that drug to make him more pliable for playing."

"Fucking hell." Trey turned to Karl. "Do me a favor and go to the club and see if that fucker is still there. I want his ass in a cell."

Karl nodded. "On it. What's his name?"

"Warren," Val spit out, still moving.

Trey was no longer trying to slow him down. He picked up speed to stay apace. "I'll make sure Paz gets called in on this."

"He can't help, but I think Harry finally can." He slowed enough to grab Trey by the arm and haul him up on his toes. "We need him to help Mackie. Understand?"

"Absolutely. I promise I'll make it happen." How he would honor that vow, however, Trey had no idea.

* * * *

There were a lot of sounds in a hospital, the middle of the night notwithstanding. Humans were a noisy species. A hive by comparison had a quiet hum to it and little else. His species only became loudly vocal when in stress or conflict. Val had long ago learned to tune out the things he didn't need to hear. He wondered, though, while he watched helplessly as Mackie thrashed within his restraints, if the boy wasn't being tormented by noise he didn't know how to block.

The transformation wrought by the drug had already begun, of course. Warren had told Kitty about how Mackie had broken through his cuffs. She had briefed Val as they'd raced up to the roof about the way Mackie had shimmied up poles and overturned tables, all done while he'd laughed insanely and avoided their efforts to catch him. There was no question that the body Val knew so well was transforming into something different—and ultimately fatal.

He reached over to smooth the boy's hair from his sweaty face. It did nothing to soothe either of them, and Val felt that failure like a knife twisting in his gut. He couldn't help his sub find peace in his confines or pain. Val was impotent and a failure. He'd confessed his feelings when it was too late. Because of his cowardice and selfishness, another boy was going to die.

A soft knock caught his attention. The human doctor who had been too smart about the drug entered. He gave Val a nod before checking Mackie's medical information and the machines that surrounded him.

"There is no change in his condition, if that's your purpose." Val delivered the information in a low tone, not sure what Mackie could hear. He also wanted the well-meaning man gone. The only person Val pitted his hopes on was Harry.

The doctor, Paz, grimaced. "I know. It's just a thing we do. I promise you that our lab is working on the blood we took. We hope to learn how to counter the effects of the drug. It's a surprising synthesis of unknown compounds." The man gripped the metal guard rails on Mackie's bed. "I'm off my shift and promise to stay here with you and help keep him comfortable."

Val supposed he should say something to try to shake the man off track and get him out of the room. He couldn't muster the energy. What did it matter? Let this world know of his people's existence. Let Dracul's schemes come to light. Val only knew that he would fight until his dying breath to avenge what had happened to this lovely boy. Mackie had only wanted to be appreciated for who and what he was, to be loved.

The door opened, taking his attention once more. Duncan came in first, followed by Emil and, thank God, Harry. The doctor carried what Val recognized as the old-fashioned doctor bag the man had acquired over a hundred years ago.

Dr. Paz started to object. "Sergeant Duncan, who are these men? I haven't authorized any other visitors."

No one responded. Instead, Duncan took up a position against the closed door, Emil headed for the doctor. In a quick, but still human move, he had his hand over Paz's mouth and had him pressed up against the far wall and out of the way.

"My most sincere apologies, sir, for this rude aggression," Emil said into the man's frightened and angry face. "I assure you it is necessary and won't last long. I hope." He gave the man a shallow bow.

That was all the attention Val gave them. He trusted Emil to keep the doctor in check, although what they would do with the man afterward was something he couldn't think about. Harry had put his bag down and was checking Mackie's vital signs.

"He's in extremity, but I may be able to stop the progression. He took out a vial of murky liquid and filled a syringe. "Val, I have to warn you that this is untested."

"I understand."

"Do you, my friend? I could end up killing him."

A shudder ran through him. He stared down at Mackie's beautiful face, twisted in pain and anguish. "He's already dying." He lifted his gaze to Harry. "I heard someone tell the doctor out in the hall that the woman from Cambridge had died. Mackie has very little time left, and better he die now and quickly than slowly in agony."

The words practically choked him. Harry didn't question him or make him repeat himself. He simply shot the antidote into Mackie's IV. Behind Emil's hand, Paz made some sound of outrage. Val ignored him. He kept his focus on Mackie's face. It didn't take long, only a few minutes, before the boy's features smoothed out. The thrashing slowed, then stopped. The squiggly lines of the machine he was hooked up to slowed, as well.

"This is good," Harry said, a smile crossing his face. "I think it might be working."

More time passed, and most of the signs of Mackie's condition improved. Val dared to look at Harry. "I think you've saved him." Val's hope was short-lived when he saw the look on the man's face. "What?"

"It seems that I've neutralized the drug, yes. Remember what I told Logan? I don't think I can reverse the effects." He shook his head. "I can't tell the damage done to his body without doing a scan." He glanced over his shoulder. "I would need someone in the hospital to authorize it."

Val placed his hand against Mackie's cheek. It still felt hot. "It's bad. It must be, given how long it was in his body. There's no point in putting him through anything when we basically know the answer already."

He sat there feeling helpless, not wanting to see the looks of pity on everyone's face. It was the same as it had been with Robbie, although this time Val would witness the death himself. *I'm so sorry, my love. I brought you to this end.* He had, too, as if he'd fed his blood to him and changed Mackie's body himself.

Change.

Val raised his gaze to Harry. "He's half changed, isn't he?"

"I suppose...in a way."

"What if I do it all the way — not reverse the damage but override it. Complete it?"

Harry rubbed his chin. "I-I don't know. I can't say that it would work. I don't know enough about what we've been dealing with." He shrugged. "You can't make matters worse, though, I suppose."

That was enough for Val. He wasted no more time. He dropped his fangs and scored his wrist with one. Again, Paz made a muffled noise, although this one was more like a squeak then a yell. Beads of blood welled up. Val placed his hand over Mackie's face. A drop fell onto his chapped lips. Mackie's face screwed up and he turned instinctively away.

"No, baby. You need this." Val clasped the boy's head to hold it in place and pressed his wrist against his mouth. "Drink, Mackie. Come on."

The blood dripped down the human's chin. Val realized he was going to have to bring his Dom out if he stood any chance of getting this mad scheme to work.

"Open up, *boy*. Fasten your lips around my wrist and suck. Treat it like you would my cock," he added in a low, seductive voice close to the boy's ear.

That did the trick. Mackie opened his mouth and latched on like a baby — or a good sub. Soon he tugged at Val's vein in earnest, drawing the blood down his throat.

"That's it, baby. Good boy."

Val's cock hardened. His pulse beat in time to the rhythm of Mackie's sucking. Val's breathing became shallow and quick. The sensation of an orgasm built as his balls tightened and his dick twitched. Mackie moaned around his mouthful of Val's wrist, the sound sending a wave of pleasure straight to Val's groin.

He'd forgotten this. Feeding a lover was almost as powerful as taking from him. "Yes, that's it, greedy boy. Suck me dry."

He curled his fingers around the strands of Mackie's hair and leaned forward. His climax was almost upon him when Harry lashed out and grabbed his wrist. He pulled it away from Mackie's mouth. The sight of Val's blood coating the boy's lips was almost enough to send Val over the edge.

"Val!" Harry's voice was like a vice on Val's dick. "Enough. Human stomachs are delicate things. Too much blood will make him sick and he'll vomit it up." He stared back at Val with a mild-mannered expression.

Val pulled himself under control. Licking his flesh closed, he nodded in appreciation. "Thank you, Harry. I'm not myself right now."

"I would say that you are yourself for the first time in a long while, actually. No matter. Let's get this boy home where I can keep an eye on him."

"Do you think it worked?" he asked, standing.

"Time will tell. You can feed him again later."

Val nodded in assent, already embarrassed at how he'd lost control, yet looking forward to another chance to have Mackie tugging on his vein again. He put down the safety bars and gathered Mackie's limp form with the bedding wrapped around him. Already it seemed as if the boy was calmer and sleeping naturally. Maybe that was wishful thinking.

He turned and caught sight of the human doctor still pressed against the wall and muted by Emil's hand. "Shit. Duncan, can you please figure this out?" he asked, jutting his chin in their direction.

"Sure. I'll have a little chat with Dr. Paz if you'll lend me Emil?"

"I can drive us home," Harry offered.

"I'll see you later," Emil chimed in. "Sorry, sir," he said to a wide-eyed Paz. "This indignity won't last much longer. And you are in no danger. You have my word on that."

Val doubted the doctor was relieved by Emil's words, but that was not Val's concern at the moment. He needed to get Mackie home to the club — Val's bedroom, to be exact. He waited until Duncan had confirmed the hallway was empty before striding out of the room. His path was clear — that night and forever. He would make Mackie well, then he would make him *his*.

Trey played doorman, ushering a determined Val and a hopeful Harry out with Mackie cocooned in Val's arms, as safe as he was ever going to be. Now all Trey had to do was get Paz to believe that. The doctor stood like a statue, Emil's captive. The cook shot Trey an encouraging smile, clearly not interested in taking on the task of educating and coopting the man to the aliens' cause.

Trey really wished he'd taken up his own doctor's offer for pain meds a couple of hours before. With a sigh, he joined the other two men across the room. He met Paz's hostile glare with a firm nod. "Okay, doc, let me tell you a tale that you're going find hard to believe."

First, he switched his attention to Emil. "Would you mind providing a little show to my tell?" He made a circle with his finger around his mouth.

Emil frowned, then his eyes lit up. "Oh, sure." He opened his lips and flashed his fangs at the doctor.

Paz freaked and tried to break through the wall against his back. His fingers scrambled against the plaster and he yelled through Emil's finger gag.

"It's okay," Trey jumped to reassure him. "He's not going to hurt you. These are the good guys in all of this. Give me a chance to explain. Emil," he added without taking his gaze off the doctor's face, "please take your hand away."

"You sure, Duncan?"

"Yes. Dr. Paz is going to hear me out before he starts screaming for help. Right, doc?"

Paz glared at him for a few seconds before nodding. Emil slowly removed his hand, although he still boxed the man in. The doctor licked his lips and took a few deep breaths.

"Okay," he said in a surprisingly strong voice. "I'm listening. It better be good, though, otherwise I'll have you all in jail. And that boy needs to be in a hospital."

"Believe it or not, he's getting the best possible care, but I appreciate your skepticism. I was where you are now not long ago. I made the decision to keep what I'm about to tell you secret because it's the right thing to do."

"I'll be the judge of that."

"Yeah," Trey conceded, "you will. So…this all starts a thousand years ago."

* * * *

Val only paid attention to who came into his bedroom because he was surprised it was Demi. Harry and Quinn were frequently in and out. Alex had also come in to check on Mackie and to reassure Val that Duncan had somehow put the lid on Dr. Paz, not that Val cared. He knew he should, but nothing mattered to him except Mackie opening his eyes and proving a steady diet of Val's blood had counteracted the ravages of Dracul's drug.

"Why don't you go take a shower. I've got this."

Val shook his head. "I'm fine."

Demi tsked. "That's an obvious lie. You're a mess. When was the last time you changed your clothes?"

"What does it matter?" Val had lost all track of time."

"You won't do Mackie any good if you run yourself into the ground. You've given him so much blood in the last few days that you're starting to look haggard. You need more food and water — and rest."

Val gave the boy only a second of his attention. "Everyone brings me what I need. And, I sleep fine on the floor." He hadn't dared share his massive bed with Mackie for fear of accidentally doing some harm to him. "If you're worried about me, bring me something up from the kitchen," he added.

"If that's what you want." Demi raised the covers by Mackie's waist.

"What are you doing?"

"Checking his catheter and making sure his bag doesn't need changing." He glanced at Val. "Don't worry. My father taught me what to do. I've been helping him with his medical stuff for a year or so now."

"I didn't know."

Demi chuckled. "You think all I do is make my parents crazy and dance around the stages when no one's looking?"

"Yes." It was an easy, automatic answer.

Demi laughed out loud before clapping his hand over his mouth. "Sorry. I don't mean to be a nuisance now. I really want to help."

Val, as usual, was concentrating on Mackie, watching his every move for signs that he was improving. So, he saw the twitch of the boy's lips and how his head turned in Demi's direction. "No, it's fine. I think Mackie might like that you're here."

"I don't know why. I've always been a pain in his ass."

"You're too similar. Both brats." He managed to work up a smile for the boy.

Demi sighed as he smoothed Mackie's bed covers back down. "I suppose that's true. I only hope I can find as good a Dom as he did."

Val looked up sharply. "He didn't. Find a good one, I mean. I failed him. His lying here is proof of that."

"You know, no one tells me squat around here, and I'm just this dumb hybrid kid and all. But if you had actually gone through with sending Mackie from your life, I would have joined a monastery and made fruit cake for the rest of mine. It was never going to happen, Val, and you're not responsible for what that moron Warren did."

The man's very name caused fury to surge through Val. If he'd been able to leave Mackie's side, he would have skipped a shower and food to find time to force a fistful of vamp down the man's throat and drop his crazed remains in the harbor.

"He made a terrible Dom."

Val froze, momentarily unable to accept where that observation had come from. Afraid that his mind might be cracking under the strain of worry, he slowly shifted his gaze from Demi to the head of the bed. Mackie was awake. He lay there, blinking owlishly up at Val. Then his trademark sly, bratty grin broke out. "I don't know what I was thinking going with him to our playroom."

Val was struck dumb, unable to muster up any rational response. Relief made him weak like nothing else had ever done.

"I'll get my father." Demi left the room in a blur of movement.

The boy's alert response pushed Val to act, as well. He leaned over and cupped Mackie's chin. "Baby, how do you feel?"

Mackie frowned. "I'm thirsty."

"There's water right here." Val fumbled for the bottle on the nightstand.

"No." Mackie licked his lips. "Blood. I want your blood."

Once more, Val froze. Mackie's request was the last thing he would have expected. "Are you sure? Do you understand what you're asking for?"

"Yes," the human replied in a hushed and needy voice. "I don't know why, but I do know it's what I crave right now. Please, Val, feed me."

The pleading left no room for doubt. Val's fangs dropped down without coaxing and his cock punched up against his fly. He crawled onto the bed as he opened the vein on his wrist. This time, when he pressed it against Mackie's lips, the boy needed no coaching. He fastened his lips around the weeping slit and began pulling with sure tugs. As always, Val's cock reacted as if it were being sucked. This time, however, with Mackie awake and looking at him with heavy-lidded eyes, Val gave free rein to his arousal.

He flexed his hips to hump his erection against Mackie's thigh. "Do you understand what this does to me? How it's a sexual act? Do you consent?"

Mackie slanted his gaze sideways and moaned his answer. He pushed down the covers, exposing his naked body. He also had gone hard, despite the catheter invading his dick. The flexible rubber did nothing to inhibit the blood engorging the shaft. But when Mackie moved to pull the tubing out, Val stopped him by bending his knee and using it to block Mackie's hand.

"Easy, baby. You might hurt yourself. Once you've finished feeding, Harry can safely remove it." Mackie grunted in frustration and narrowed his eyes. Val chuckled at the reaction. "We've never tried sounding play. Perhaps you'll enjoy the sensation of being aroused and coming with something inside your dick."

"Hmm." Mackie responded by undulating his body against the side of Val's knee. He reached up, grasped Val's forearm with both hands to hold it tightly against his mouth.

"That's it. Slowly now. Taking my vein will intensify the orgasm, but I won't let you hurt yourself."

Mackie proved to be an adept student, as always, allowing Val to hold him in place. They found a rhythm, each humping the other in careful sync. So many times in the last few days, Val had suppressed his need to come, not willing to use Mackie without his full awareness. It had left Val's balls aching and his nerves frayed with pent-up longing. With the sucking at his vein to spur his orgasm, Val lasted no more than a minute. The climax tore through him, causing his head to snap back on a roar.

Mackie followed a second later, his body arching up. Cum spurted out, the flexible tubing proving no match to the force of his orgasm. It coated the catheter and sent flecks of sticky fluid onto the boy's flat stomach. Even Val's jeans took a hit. He reveled at the sight, proof that his boy was on the mend.

And still, Mackie sucked down Val's blood. Reluctantly, Val freed his hand and licked the wounds closed. Mackie made a mewling sound and pouted. Val pressed a kiss to those delectable lips, tasting his own blood.

"Don't fret, baby. There will be more later. You need to be careful about how much you consume. It can be hard on your human stomach." He rolled off the bed. "Stay there. I'll clean you up before Harry gets here."

Mackie watched Val cross over the large space to the bathroom. Val's room. Mackie felt at peace for the first time in months. This was where he belonged. As he lay waiting as commanded, he called up his memories of what had happened. He remembered everything from the time he'd drunk what he'd thought was only bourbon until he'd taken flight off the roof of the club. He shuddered at how he'd nearly killed himself. There were even some bits and pieces of his experience at the hospital. He needed help, though, to understand how he'd come to this bed and why he craved Val's blood.

When Val returned with a wet wash cloth and towel, Mackie lay patiently as the guy wiped up the semen. "Will you tell me what happened, please?"

"Of course."

A knock, followed by Harry's entrance, put an end to the discussion. The kindly alien doctor smiled down at Mackie. "So, you are awake and feeling the need for blood, heh?"

"Yes, sir."

"Well, that's good news, the best we've had in days." He gently proceeded to remove the catheter. "There. You should urinate now to help flush out any possible bacteria."

"Here. I've got you." Val didn't help Mackie rise so much as pick him up and carry him into the bathroom. Then he stood Mackie in front of the toilet and tried to hold his penis in place.

"I can do that part, thanks." Mackie slapped Val's hand away, embarrassed by the intimate attention. There was nothing sexy about peeing, at least not in Mackie's estimation.

He winced at the burning sensation. "I don't think I want to try sounding. It's weird and uncomfortable, although it might have made the orgasm stronger. Or, was that only the blood?"

"A bit of both, I'd say." Val made like a rock wall for Mackie to lean against. "Makes me want to introduce medical play into our repertoire, actually. If I use a sound, it will be more solid and can be used to keep you from coming."

Flushing the toilet, Val turned Mackie around. He placed his hands on Mackie's shoulders as he peered down at him. "That's assuming you want me to stay your Dom. My feeding you is entirely free of conditions."

Mackie's stomach dropped. "I thought you wanted me back."

"I do!" Val gathered him up in his arms and claimed Mackie's lips in a bruising kiss. "Forever and always," he added when they finally came up for air. "Let's get you lying down again so we can talk."

Harry was already gone. Mackie's legs were unsteady and despite having a belly-full of Val's blood, he still felt hungry. Val helped him lie down and tucked the covers around him as if he were a little kid. Mackie didn't mind the attention. He felt wanted and cherished again. He worried, however, that perhaps all of this was due to misplaced guilt on Val's part. Mackie was desperate to get the man back, but only for the right reasons. Pity wasn't acceptable.

Val pulled out his phone and texted a brief message. "I've asked Emil to bring you a plate of food."

Mackie didn't try to hide his appreciation. "How did you know I was hungry?"

"You haven't eaten anything solid in days. Harry gave you IVs of fluids and I fed you my blood. Nothing solid has passed your lips, though, so I assume you're ready for something substantial."

"I am, thanks. You always have taken good care of me, Val."

"It has been my pleasure to do so—and my shame that I failed lately, especially that night you sought Warren for what I should have been giving you." When Mackie started to object, Val hushed him with a finger. He sat on the edge of the bed, his body pressed comfortingly against Mackie's hip. "I see more clearly now, and I would like to continue to be the Dom you want and need for the rest of our lives, if you will permit me."

The man looked strange to Mackie. He saw uncertainty in Val's expression and that wasn't something he had ever seen before. Reaching out, he took Val's hand in his. "Of course, I want that. As long as you are doing it because you want to, not because you think you should."

"You think I'm here out of duty?"

Mackie looked away and gnawed at his lip. He could still taste a lingering bit of Val's blood there. He should have been disgusted. Instead, he found he loved it. "It's what I'm worried about," he confessed.

Val rubbed his thumb along the back of Mackie's hand. "I would have done — and will continue to do — anything to keep you safe, except lie to you. What do you remember about being on the roof?"

"Everything."

"What we said to each other?" Val's voice conveyed his skepticism.

"Yes. That drug made me stupid-crazy, but it didn't affect my memory. I remember feeling as if I were invincible. The power surging through me was amazing." He paused to take stock of how his body had felt at that moment. "Kind of like I do now, although I know I'm not like Superman or anything. I just have this sense of tremendous well-being."

"That's my blood. It's already changing you. It simply does it slowly and safely compared to what that drug was doing." Val paused and focused his gaze on where their hands joined. "I'm sorry I didn't give you a say in what's happening to you."

"I'm not complaining. I like how I feel, believe me. But, I guess I am confused about how it came about. Did Harry concoct something to counteract the drug?"

"Yes, and as he predicted, it stopped the damage from progressing yet didn't have the power to reverse that which was already done." Val took a deep breath. "It was out of desperation that I tried feeding you my blood. It seems to have worked," he added with a smile. The guy had so rarely used that expression that Mackie was struck for the first time by how beautiful Val was.

Mackie let out a breathless giggle. "I think so. And," he added with all seriousness, "I'm glad you did. I'm not afraid of changing like Lucien did. I can tell it's going to be awesome."

Val closed his eyes briefly with a painful expression. "I hope so. I must confess I'm scared to death for you."

"Because of Robbie."

"Yes."

"Tell me about him, please? And about Andrew. I don't want you to worry that I'll end up like them."

"It's impossible for me not to. I killed them both, you see."

Because he could see that he meant it, Mackie tugged him down for a hug. "Lie here next to me while you explain why you think that."

"All right." To Mackie's delight, the big man snuggled up against Mackie and let him be the one to give comfort for a change.

"Robbie was a beautiful boy with red hair and a quick smile. A bit of a brat, too, although that wasn't something one spoke about back then."

Mackie stroked Val's head. "Back when?"

"Eighteenth-century Scotland. Men lay with other men secretly then. I could see Robbie wanted me as much as I him, but it took some wooing for him to get past the norms of his society. It was actually easier for him to accept that I was a creature of the night than it was natural for two men to find pleasure in each other. The idea of my coming from another planet was beyond him. He thought the sky was heaven and believed he loved a blood-sucking demon, not an angel."

"He must have loved you a great deal, regardless," Mackie observed, trying not to be jealous of a long-dead boy.

"He did. And in my way, I loved him, too. He allowed me to drink from him and quickly agreed to drink my blood, as well. I was always amazed at how much he trusted me. That trust led to his death. His human body didn't handle the unnatural state for him of carrying a young. The birth killed him outright, despite Harry's best effort. The baby, born too early, in any event, was stillborn."

Mackie hugged him tightly and showered his face with kisses. "I'm so sorry, Val. But you can't blame yourself."

"And who am I to blame?"

"No one. Sometimes life sucks." He sniffed back sudden tears. "I spent a lot of years hating first my own nature then my family's reaction to it. I hated that I had to run away to save my sanity, and I hated the men I used to stay alive when I was on the streets. Eventually, I realized that all that negative emotion wasn't making my life easier. Blaming myself and others wasn't going to make things better."

Val traced his fingers along Mackie's collarbone before cupping one of his pecs. "When did you come to that realization?"

"Around the first time that you beat my ass with a paddle until I was flying in a blissful cloud of subspace."

Val chuckled and rolled over to brace himself over Mackie. "Really? I did that for you?"

"And more."

"Here I thought I was only giving you discipline and a roof over your head."

"That too." Mackie reared up to kiss Val. "I love you, and I'm not afraid to change into whatever it is I'm going to become. Someday, I'll give you a son. I'm strong, Val. Healthy. I won't die. I promise."

"I won't let you. I promise."

They spent the next few minutes reacquainting themselves with one another. Val had always been a generous and virile lover. Now he showed a tenderness that Mackie had never expected. Their arousal built slowly with long, passionate kisses. Val invaded Mackie's eager mouth, conquering it. Mackie gladly surrendered under the assault, wrestling Val's tongue with his own and using his teeth to grate and nip.

With a growl, Val tore off his shirt, keeping his lips on Mackie's face and neck. He feasted his way down Mackie's body to take a nipple in his mouth, even as he ripped his jeans down his legs. Mackie cried out and arched his back when Val bit the nub hard.

Then the covers were gone, and their bodies collided flesh-to-flesh. Val reached between them as he once more claimed Mackie's mouth. He clasped both of their dicks in his big hand and pumped them in unison. Mackie heaved and groaned down Val's throat. The orgasm rose fast, the way it had before. He would have come in Val's fist, except the man tightened his grip enough to hold it back.

Mackie yelled in frustration and pounded his fists on the bed. Val half growled, half chuckled before wrenching away. Mackie made a grab for him to stay, but all Val did was reach for the nightstand. He pulled out a bottle of lube and reared back to slick up his dick. He hissed at Mackie, his fangs gleaming a sharp white, as he jammed two fingers up Mackie's hole to grease the way.

Mackie raised his legs up high, parted them and bent his knees in silent invitation. Val lunged forward, shoving his cock in balls-deep. Mackie cried out and threw his head back to expose his neck. Then he clutched at Val's massive shoulders as the man's fangs sunk in almost as deep as his dick.

The pain was exquisite. Mackie came in a blinding second in which all he could feel was his balls emptying and his heartbeat syncing with Val's. The pulsing shots of cum coating his insides from Val's sudden release added background sensation to that rhythm. He felt covered by heat, drenched with warmth. The tugging at his jugular became a pounding in his head — a litany of *mine, mine, mine* except it was Val's voice he heard, not his own.

He belonged to this man. This alien. This vampire. His Dom. He was claimed and taken, and nothing would ever be the same again. Nothing would ever keep them apart again.

This was love, even if those words had not been spoken.

Chapter Twelve

Val's firm grip kept Mackie's nervousness at bay. It was silly, really, but something about meeting the doctor who had cared for him with the whole alien-vampire issue laid out in plain sight made Mackie anxious. He hadn't been living with this secret for long, yet now that he and Val were in a committed relationship, the urgent need to keep it weighed on him.

Val squeezed Mackie's hand. "It will be fine. Duncan vouches for the man and he just wants to see for himself that you are cured."

Mackie didn't feel as reassured as he would have liked. "Does he understand why I'm okay?"

He gnawed at his lower lip, uncertain if he should push Val on the meeting, given that the man had already set it up. Although they had discussed how they both wanted to cement a twenty-four-hour Dom and submissive lifestyle, they hadn't hammered out the details. It wasn't clear to him how much he should challenge Val's authority. On the one hand, having Val take on responsibility for Mackie's life let Mackie relax and let go of worry for the first time ever. On the other hand, Mackie was no mindless doormat. As much as he trusted Val and Val's judgment, Mackie couldn't turn off the instincts that had served him well so far.

"That's a fair question and one I can't answer. We'll have to see what Duncan has told him, not that the cop is privy to all our secrets. As far as I know, the cop doesn't understand the implication of your drinking my blood."

"Oh." Mackie felt eased by that knowledge.

He was still trying to come to grips with the idea that his body was already changing. Despite his initial bravado about it, he had moments of real fear about becoming something different, alien in its own way. He couldn't detect any difference, yet Harry had kindly given him the low-down on what this alien blood slushing around Mackie's insides was doing to him. He instinctively palmed his abdomen, as if he could discern ovaries and a uterus growing somehow within the confines of what had always been a flat and fit area. He took heart in the knowledge that Lucien looked trim, even after having given birth.

Val raised Mackie's hand and kissed the back of it. "Please don't worry. I can always use condoms to ensure you won't breed unless you're ready to."

"Oh." Mackie smiled up at him. He was finding Val to be solicitous and sensitive in unexpected ways. "Does that work?"

"Why wouldn't it? The barrier method has always kept sperm from meeting egg." He grinned. "Although I'm delighted if you think my semen has the power to break through latex."

Mackie hip-checked him. "Stop fishing for compliments. I'm already aching from the last few days."

It was a sweet, dull discomfort that reminded him to whom he belonged. He loved being fucked by Val, as much as he did giving and taking blood. The only thing that had marred their time together was how Val had refused to do anything more. Mackie was itching for a full-on scene, involving pain and bondage. Val, with Harry backing his position, had forbidden anything strenuous until Mackie had regained full health after his multi-day confinement. Mackie had spent a week mostly lying in bed. He was itching to restart his normal life. Val had promised that after this interview with the doctor, they'd play. Mackie was already locked in chastity, and the confinement only served to pique his desire.

Val pulled him up short outside of Alex's office. "I don't want you to worry about anything. You have the power to stop this interview any time simply by saying so."

"Thanks. I'm fine, and if this doctor can help us in the war, then I'll do whatever it takes to keep him as an ally."

"My brave boy." Leaning down, Val pressed a kiss against Mackie's lips. This was something new in their relationship — casual affection. He liked it. Val seemed relaxed around him in a way that he had never been before.

With a perfunctory knock, Val opened the office door and ushered Mackie through. The boss was seated behind his desk as usual. Quinn graced his lap, again per usual. Harry occupied one of the visitor's chairs, while Duncan lounged on the couch. The cop was looking more and more at home at the club. A slender, impeccably groomed and handsome Latino sat next to the cop. His tension was obvious in the set of his shoulders and the way his gaze darted suspiciously at them.

The moment his eyes fixed on Mackie, however, his expression softened. He rose gracefully and focused his attention only on Mackie. "Amazing. It is as they say. You're cured."

Before Mackie could reply, Val dropped his hand in order to pull him into a tight sideways embrace. "Before I permit you to question my boy, I want assurances as to your commitment to keeping our secret."

The doctor's pretty brown eyes narrowed. "Your permission? Your boy?" He looked at Duncan. "What the fuck, Sergeant? You said nothing about these *beings* taking control over humans."

Duncan rolled his eyes and sighed. "It's not like that. It's some kind of kinky thing they're into. For Christ's sake, Val, explain it to him before this meeting gives me any more heartburn than it already is."

Mackie decided that now would be a good time to step in. If Val didn't like it, well…he could take it out on Mackie's hide later. Which, when he thought about it, made the whole thing that much more appealing.

"Val's my Dom…Dr. Paz, is it?" Mackie smiled brightly at the man, putting a little coquettishness into it. He knew how to work a man, and damn if the doctor's expression didn't get that kind of glassy-eyed look Mackie had seen on plenty of men's faces before.

"We're into the BDSM lifestyle. I'm sure you've heard of it," he clarified.

Paz nodded. "Yes, of course." He coughed. "I suppose I have."

"It has nothing to do with Val being an alien. That's just a weird perk." He shrugged helplessly and leaned against Val to show how comfortable he was with his big, bad, Mohawked alien-vampire lover.

The doctor's eyes took in the entire scene. After a few seconds, he nodded. "I understand, although I still want to make sure that you are all right. I can't do that if I think you're under this man's control. I need honest answers from you."

"I get it. Come on, Val. Try to drop the grim factor down a few notches and let's go sit."

Val merely grunted, but he also did as Mackie asked. He dragged him over to a visitor's chair and plopped them both into it. Or, rather, Val's ass hit the chair while Mackie's hit Val's lap. He didn't mind in the least. Cozying up to the big guy's chest, Mackie smiled brightly at the doctor.

"Please ask me any questions you'd like."

"Thank you." The doctor returned to his seat. "But, to reassure your...um, everyone, I am committed to helping your cause. Sergeant Duncan has told me a fantastic tale, and I can't deny the evidence of my own eyes. I am first and foremost a scientist, so I'm willing to keep my knowledge to myself if I have access to the kind of information you have that would help my people. Humans," he clarified, as if anyone had any doubt as to his meaning.

"You would also have a hard time getting anyone to believe you," Val pointed out. "Duncan came to that conclusion a few months ago."

The doctor stiffened. "Yes, there is that. I have a couple of samples of strange synthetic substances and that's all. My one living patient from the drug poisoning is uncooperative and has taken himself out of my care."

"Sorry," Mackie said with a shrug.

"He's also unwilling to press charges against the guy who spiked him with it," Duncan chimed in.

"I've had a talk with Mr. Warren," Alex said. "I can assure you he is most contrite. There is nothing you could do to him that would be worse than his own self-recriminations." He flashed his teeth. "Of course, it might have been me who put the fear of God into him, as you humans would say."

Mackie heard and felt a faint rumble from Val's chest that might have been a chuckle. He'd told Mackie that Warren had been banned from the club. When pressed, he'd also assured him that Val hadn't hurt a hair on the man's head. Nothing had been said about Alex, however.

Mackie turned suspicious eyes on Alex. "He's still alive, isn't he?"

"Of course, dear boy. I merely conveyed a heartfelt message from Val, who didn't want to leave your side, naturally. I believe Warren has decided to seek life and pleasure elsewhere. He won't be found in the Boston area ever again."

"Huh." Mackie decided that, all things considered, he could live with that answer, although in truth the man's stupid actions had inadvertently given Mackie his heart's desire. He turned his attention back to Paz. "So, what would you like to know, sir?"

"How are you feeling?"

"Fine, thanks. Great, actually."

"Because of the alien blood you've been drinking?"

"Yes, sir. That's what Harry and Val tell me, anyway."

"No more hallucinations or feelings of grandeur?"

"I don't think I can fly, if that's what you mean."

The doctor smiled. "Yes, I mean things like that."

He was gorgeous. Mackie thought he caught a gay vibe and wondered who at the club might be a good match for him. Now that Mackie had found his happily ever after, he wanted it for everyone.

The doctor shifted his focus to Harry. "Can you explain to me what drinking your species' blood did to counteract the drug?"

Harry didn't answer right away. He looked at Alex instead, an unspoken reassurance to proceed. Alex inclined his head. "The idea of feeding Mackie was Val's. He did it on instinct, to be frank. It was my newly-manufactured drug that stopped the damage being done by the one Mackie had ingested. I hadn't worked out how, if at all, I could reverse the effects. What Val did was continue the process in a natural way that we have found to be relatively safe for humans."

"I'm afraid you've lost me already," the doctor confessed.

"He's changing me." Mackie blurted out the information, then shrank against Val as he worried he'd gone too far. Val gave him a reassuring pat on the arm.

Paz. "Into what?"

"It's difficult to put a label on it," Harry said.

"Please try."

"His body is changing into something that will be ostensibly human, yet with influences from our species."

"Meaning it does...what?"

"It will lengthen his life span, for example."

"And?" Unlike Duncan, the doctor was not going to accept easy or incomplete answers.

"It will allow Mackie to gestate Val's male offspring."

The room went totally silent as Paz and Duncan absorbed that information. Mackie caught Quinn's eye and they shared a grin. On a purely juvenile level, this consorting with aliens was wicked awesome.

"Jesus, Mary and Joseph," the cop finally said. "Demi."

Harry nodded. "Just so."

Duncan scrubbed his face. "Fuck me, as if this whole thing couldn't get any weirder."

Paz frowned. "Who is Demi?"

"My son," Harry answered simply, then stood. "Dr. Paz, why don't you come and see my lab? I'll be happy to show you how I came up with the countering agent. If there are any more poisonings, we want you to be able to claim you made the breakthrough on your own."

The doctor stood as well. "I actually have nothing against that plan. I want to protect my people from this scourge." He looked around the room. "Gentlemen, your secret is safe with me for now. But my cooperation is predicated on your being the good guys in all of this."

"And, so we are," Alex reassured him. "Proof of that starts by giving you access to Harry's work. We are mindful of how hard it is for you—both of you," he added with a nod toward Duncan, "to keep this secret from your people. Others of your kind have allied with us before you, and we sincerely hope you will be the last."

With an uneasy detente created, Harry led the doctor out.

Duncan got up. "I guess I'll be going. I still have a pissed-off lieutenant and partner to deal with. We're trying to make sure all the drug's gone, too. We haven't found another stash and there have been no new cases of drug use. Fingers crossed that those two goons have left for good."

Mackie cocked his head to look at Val. "They must have run off, right? Would they stick around to make more trouble?"

Val ran his hand up Mackie's arm in reassurance. "They've likely gone home to their father to lick their wounds and make excuses for their failure. They won't stay away forever, though."

"What will they do now?" Mackie asked before Duncan could.

"That, dearest boy, is an excellent question," Alex replied. "I wish I could give you an answer. Dracul's next play is anyone's guess."

"We'll be ready for him, no matter what, though," Val said. "Please don't worry."

"I won't." Mackie relaxed against Val's broad chest. That was the good thing about having a Dom. Worrying was Val's job.

* * * *

They walked to the playroom without speaking. Val cupped the back of Mackie's neck, controlling him with a light pressure, reassuring him in the same way. If Mackie's dick hadn't been locked in a plastic cage, it would have hardened from that contact and the anticipation of what was to come. As it was, he'd already started his descent into subspace. He knew Val would take care of him.

Val guided him into the room, placing the lights on low and shutting the door quietly behind them. It felt as if they were alone in more than simply in the playspace. It was as if no one else existed at all, only the two of them. Mackie emptied his mind of all thoughts of war and enemies. At that moment, the world consisted of his Dom and how to please him.

"Take off your clothing and go stand facing the wheel." Val's order was softly spoken, yet the power behind it raised goosebumps on Mackie's skin.

He carefully did his Dom's bidding, slowly removing each article and placing them neatly on a nearby table. His natural impulse to be a brat was suppressed for this scene. It was a solemn occasion, a reaffirmation of their relationship. Mackie was determined to be the best sub he could be. There would be time later to bait his Dom. They had a whole lifetime together. Many, actually, given the way Val's blood was changing his body.

He walked over to the wheel attached to the wall. The many straps and handles allowed for different types of play. What did Val have in mind? An unexpected swat to his butt made him squeak.

"You're thinking. Stop that. Here and now, that is my job. Yours is to obey."

"Yes, Master." Mackie hid a smile behind a proper response. He couldn't help it — and got another, harder smack for his efforts.

"You're not taking this seriously enough, boy. I will remedy that. No more talking."

Val took control over Mackie's body. He raised each of Mackie's arms and buckled his wrists to the wheel. The height of the confinement forced Mackie onto the very tips of his toes. The strain didn't last long because Val then placed Mackie's feet on the padded footplates that elevated him to compensate for their height difference. Val tightened the strap to stretch Mackie's arms more, though, before securing his ankles. He didn't attach the chest harness, however, so there would be no being hung upside down. Mackie was a little disappointed. The head rush was awesome, although right side up usually meant being fucked from behind, so there was that to look forward to.

Val pinched a bit of Mackie's ass hard enough to make Mackie whimper. "What did I say about thinking?"

Mackie took a shuddering breath and closed his eyes. He cleared his head the way Val wanted him to and focused on listening to his Dom's commands.

No more came. Instead, Val went about manipulating Mackie's body however he wanted. He left for a few moments and came back with a lubed butt plug that he shoved up Mackie's ass without warning or prep. Mackie swayed against the sudden burn and took deep, shuddering breaths as he adjusted to the painful invasion.

"That's to get you ready for my cock later."

Those words made Mackie's hole clench. He shuddered deliciously, too. That's all he allowed himself to do, mindful of his Dom's admonition to stay in the moment.

"I'm not going to strap it in place because I know you'll keep it inside. If you don't, that will be the only thing you'll feel in your ass for a week. Understand?"

Mackie nodded and clenched again to make sure the plug stayed lodged. Val rewarded him with a soothing pat on the ass and murmured, "Good boy."

Next came a ball gag, the hard, round of rubber stretching his lips wide. The second Val had that strapped around Mackie's head, he slipped a piece of red cloth in one of Mackie's hands. There was no need to explain why. Mackie gripped the fabric, but he was also determined not to let it go.

"We're going to start this new chapter in our lives with a new lesson on trust. I'm going to take everything from you — voice, sight and hearing. You will be mine to do with as I please. There is only one way you can stop me, as you well know."

There was no question in any of that, so Mackie made no response. He merely stood pliantly as Val slipped a blindfold over his eyes and headphones over his ears. Mackie stood in the silent dark world that his Dom had created for him, waiting for...he didn't know what.

Until the first blow struck.

It was more of a whisper than anything with real heat. Val wanted to warm up. He'd left Mackie utterly helpless and the sight of it sent Val's own arousal flying high. Such a beautiful sight — his boy bound, gagged and rendered senseless. Val could stand there all day simply looking — or touching. His fingers itched with the need to caress all that soft, warm human skin. His dick would gladly drill it for hours.

But being a Dom meant caring for his sub. Mackie needed and deserved his own pleasure. Val knew what would work best to achieve that state for the boy. He had his best floggers in hand, using the suede tails of one to tease Mackie's ass. The soft swishing back and forth against the skin would be driving Mackie both crazy and into the first level of subspace — or the second level, given that the boy's cock clearly strained within its confines. It was heady stuff knowing that even the promise of play was enough to do that.

He flicked the flogger a few times across each side of the ass before settling into a figure eight. He warmed the globes of Mackie's ass to a pretty pink hue before adding the second flogger into the mix. Val loved the rhythm of the difficult Florentine technique, finding it hypnotic and helping him achieve his top space quickly. Having played with Mackie many times, he knew as well when to increase the speed and hit with more force. His boy could take a lot. With his senses temporarily robbed, the only thing Mackie would have to focus on were the strikes against his ass.

Val didn't want his sub getting too settled, however. He started delivering a stinging blow every so often. The force of it sent the boy rocking forward within his bonds and crying out through his gag. Val checked Mackie's hand, and while the boy's fingers clenched and loosened a few times, he didn't drop the piece of cloth.

"That's my boy." He said the words to himself as Mackie couldn't hear. Val's balls ached and his dick begged for release. He ignored them both.

Patience would be a sweet reward. Fucking Mackie too soon was indulgent. Val had more discipline than that. Mackie counted on him to. He would keep building the pleasure so that when release finally came, it would be that much more amazing.

He continued with the flogging, careful to keep his arms moving in sync. Mackie's ass had turned bright red and bruises would form from the beating. Val would enjoy seeing them for days to come, and he knew from past experience how Mackie would delight in preening before a mirror to watch how the color of the marks would change as they healed. Every man in the club would know that Mackie belonged to Val.

The thought of other men staring at his boy caused a sudden fury to rise within him. Mackie was *his*. No man should ever touch him again. The mere thought of someone like Warren pawing at Mackie's beautiful ass made Val's fangs descend. He landed a viciously hard blow on one cheek. Mackie screamed and arched against his bindings. Still, he clutched at the cloth.

Val tossed the floggers down, playtime being over for him. He ripped his jeans open and freed his cock. It pulsed against his hand, even as Val grabbed the plug in Mackie's hole and yanked it out. He replaced it with his dick in one, long thrust. Mackie again cried out and stiffened before a shudder racked his body from head to toe.

After wrapping his arm around his boy's waist, Val pulled the headphones off. "You are mine," he growled. "No one will ever have this ass again. I will kill anyone who dares touch it."

He punctuated his claim and his threat with short, hard jabs of his dick. He scraped his fingers along Mackie's silky abdomen, brushing against the hard plastic of the cock cage. He growled again before tearing the thing off. A hot, hard cock sprang forward.

"This is also mine." He squeezed until Mackie screamed and pounded his forehead against the padded wheel. "Don't you dare come until I tell you."

With that warning issued, Val concentrated on his own pleasure. He closed his eyes and reveled in the way Mackie's tight channel gripped his shaft. He pulled out slowly, letting the tissues try to keep him in. He stopped at the point in which the head of his dick stretched Mackie's puckered hole. He held it there, knowing that he strained the limits of the human's flesh. Then he plunged it back in up to his balls.

He fucked his boy in earnest, working up to a pace that skirted the edge of what a human body could absorb. His pelvis smacked against the heated globes. The tactile reminder of the beating increased Val's arousal. He couldn't hold back any longer. Glancing once more at Mackie's hand, Val bent his head. The throbbing beat of Mackie's heart called to him. The pulsing at the base of the boy's throat taunted him.

He struck, fast and hard, his fangs sinking into the flesh as if it were no more than air. Mackie's scream egged him on, as did the flow of warm, salty blood. Val drank it down as if for the first time, slaking that thirst that was never truly satisfied. He tugged at the vein as he drilled Mackie's hole. The bucking of his hips sent the boy's dick sliding through his grip. The shaft twitched against his fingers in an unspoken plea.

Now was the time. Val let himself go, his cum spurting up into his boy, coating the grasping channel and slicking the way. His thrusts stuttered as he lost control. He choked on the flood of blood he sucked down. With a flick of his thumbnail through Mackie's slit, he forced the boy to join him in the mindless pleasure of the climax. Sticky cum covered Val's fingers. He let the dick go and slid his hand up Mackie's torso, leaving a trail of fluid.

Spasms rocked Mackie's body. He twisted and jerked in Val's embrace before going limp. Val came to his senses and retracted his fangs. He licked the puncture wounds closed so as not to waste a drop of his boy's precious blood. The red cloth fluttered past his head, alarming him. He made short work of freeing Mackie from the wheel. He held the boy in the crook of his arm as he removed first the gag, then the blindfold.

Mackie blinked up at him before raising his lips in a ghost of a smile. Val returned the look and gave him a quick kiss.

"That's my good boy."

Lifting him in both arms, he carried Mackie over to the couch. He wrapped him in a blanket and lay him down. Val's dick hung out, ready for round two. He stuffed it back into his pants, wincing as he forced the zipper up. Time for more fun later. Now, his boy needed him. He brought a clean cloth and a bottle of water back to Mackie. The boy's eyes were fully open.

"Don't try to speak," he said, kneeling by the couch. "Not yet. Drink first."

He held the bottle to Mackie's lips and made sure he took in a few sips. When he was satisfied that enough water had made it in for the moment, he put the bottle aside and wiped Mackie's sweaty face. The blanket had undoubtedly absorbed the cum, so he didn't bother to do more than that. Later, they'd shower together. And yes, he assured his dick that it would get another chance at one of Mackie's holes.

He joined his boy on the couch, resting Mackie's head on his lap. He indulged himself by petting Mackie's head. "How are you feeling?"

"Drained," the human answered in a sleepy voice. "When can we do it again?"

Val laughed. It was a strange sensation for him. It had been a long time since he'd felt free to enjoy himself. He ruffled Mackie's hair. "Greedy boy. Your poor ass will need some time to heal up, although if you are a very good boy, I'll let you suck my cock later."

"Hmm," Mackie purred and rubbed his head against Val's crotch. "Promises, promises."

"Stop that!" Val gritted his teeth against the renewed hard-on. "Here... Drink some more."

Between them, they finished the bottle. Val went for another and cuddled a refreshed Mackie. The weight of the boy's body on Val's dick was sweetly painful.

"Was I a good boy?"

Frowning at the wistful question, Val said, "You know you were."

He lifted Mackie's chin with one finger and brought their lips together. Kissing was a hard thing for Val. He worried that he was too forceful, so he pressed gently. When Mackie sighed, he slipped his tongue inside and made a languid sweep before letting go.

"You make me proud. You make me happy." The confession was also hard, yet if he and Mackie were going to have any kind of future, Val needed to make himself vulnerable again.

"I love you, Val." The simple declaration, said with a clear gaze, humbled Val.

"As I do you. It's important that you believe me, Mackie. I may not be good at saying it or even showing it. I'm not sure you and I have the same view of what that means. But I promise you that I will do my best every day for the rest of our lives to prove it to you."

"Oh, Val." Mackie rested his head against Val's chest. "I know you do. You don't have to do anything special to convince me of it."

"That may be, yet here is one thing I can think of. One moment."

Val put Mackie into a sitting position on the couch before walking to a drawer where he kept toys. He reached deep inside and pulled out the small box he'd placed there earlier in the day. He returned to Mackie's side and knelt on the floor.

"This is for you, if you'll have it." He held the box up and opened the lid.

Mackie blinked rapidly a few times, convinced he was hallucinating. Inside the box Val held was a platinum band with a row of rectangular pavé diamonds running through the middle. He reached out to touch it, then snatched his hand back.

Val chuckled. "It's yours, baby. Take it out. Please."

With his heart threatening to burst out of his chest, he did as Val asked. His hand shook as he gazed at the ring he held. "What is this?" His voice shook, too.

"The woman at the store called it a man-gagement ring, but I'm thinking of it as a wedding band." He shrugged. "You can call it whatever you want, so long as you let me put it on your finger."

Mackie swallowed hard and passed the ring back. "Please do."

Val took Mackie's unsteady hand in his strong one and slipped the band onto Mackie's left-handed ring finger. It fit perfectly. "Oh, Val." The next thing he knew, he was flying into Val's embrace. Tears flowed freely and he didn't care.

Val hugged him hard. "I assume this means you are accepting my proposal, clumsy as it was."

"Fuck yes!" Mackie pulled back and beamed back at him. "Is this really a thing with you guys? Marriage, I mean?"

"It's different on my home world, but it's how it's done here. And I want this for you, for us." A cloud passed over Val's eyes. "I wasn't able to do this for Robbie. I couldn't give him the respect and protection of my name and wealth. It gratifies me that your species have evolved enough for me to bind us legally."

Mackie worked to wrap his mind around what Val was offering. "I hadn't expected marriage. It was enough that you wanted me."

"Oh, Mackie, it shouldn't have been." Val cupped Mackie's face. "You deserve every happiness. Your family was foolish to think you anything other than perfect."

The tears really started to flow. Mackie swiped at them, sniffed and laughed. His emotions were overwhelming him, especially as he came down from subspace.

"This is too much for you now." Val frowned and swept him up again. "Drink."

Mackie obeyed because he trusted Val to know what was best, not that he wasn't going to give the guy a hard time on a routine basis. But playing the brat was too much fun for the both of them to give it up entirely. For the moment, he acted the good boy. He drank and rested and planned.

"Could we have the wedding here, do you think?"

"Of course. Alex will be delighted to play father of the groom for you. And Emil will treat us to the best reception meal and wedding cake imaginable. Everyone will be happy for us. I promise you that."

"And I'll finally have a family who loves me." He sighed and melted into Val's arms. "I can take your name."

"Of course, unless you want me to change mine to Fraser."

Mackie gave that notion a second of thought. In that brief time, he let go of his past and the family that had made him feel broken and unwanted. "No. You, Alex and everyone else are my family now. I want to be a Stelalux officially." Throwing his head back, he gazed up at Val, pouring as much of his love as he could in his expression. "I'm your boy, Val. Forever and always. In sickness and in health."

"Until death do us part" — Val brushed his lips against Mackie's — "which won't be for a very long time."

Epilogue

Wales, Dracul's castle

"Idiots! I'm surrounded by incompetence. You had a simple job and you fucked it up. How is it possible for you to have come from my loins? There is clearly too much of the weak slut in you."

Dracul flung his hand in Dafydd's direction, his face mottled with rage, his eyes burning red. Spittle flew from his mouth. The objects of his fury stood mute, not offering an excuse for their failure.

Well, at least they learned something from me. Dafydd watched his hated 'husband' spew his venomous wrath at their sons without fear for himself or them. Not even seeing the ruined side of Cadoc's face moved him to pity. He had long ago resigned himself that the boys he'd labored to bring into the world were wholly their alien father's. No doubt the boy had deserved the scarring and was lucky to have survived. Next time, and there would be one, both of his sons would probably die. Dracul saw them as disposable, like everyone else around him.

Dafydd didn't worry about that. He had nothing left in him to feel anything. Dracul had beaten and raped all emotion out of him, except for one—hatred. That burned bright in his heart, as did the hope of revenge. He placed his palm over his abdomen where one or more babes grew anew. As much as he'd tried to avoid this from happening, he found the alien life inside gave him a strange sense of strength.

A whimper from the new boy lying next to him caught his attention. Dracul's latest victim still shook and wept from the brutal fucking Dracul had subjected him to. He understood well how the boy felt. Disbelief was turning into despair.

Dafydd reached over and brushed sweaty hair from the boy's face. "Hush," he whispered. "He likes hearing your pain and misery. Don't give him the satisfaction." When the boy merely blinked back at him, he added, "Don't lose hope."

Dafydd smiled yet said nothing more. He couldn't trust anyone with his thoughts—with his plans.

Dracul threw a bottle of wine against the hearth, the pieces of glass flying into his silent sons. "I was mistaken to give you a chance. You, Bran, in particular, are a bitter disappointment. I put you in charge."

He cracked his fist against the boy's face. Bran took the blow and said nothing.

"Get out of my sight before I tear you to pieces and throw them to the dogs."

The boys wasted no time in leaving the room. The one saving grace was that Dafydd would probably not see them for a while, if ever again. It was a sad thing to hate your own children. Then again, he really felt nothing at all for them.

Dracul paced away before turning to glare at Petru. The steadfast lieutenant didn't so much as flinch. He never did, and Dafydd studied the man's stolid demeanor for inspiration.

"I suppose you're feeling vindicated. You advised against sending them."

"I feel only your keen disappointment, sir."

"Huh! You've always had a silky tongue, ready with the right words. I wonder what you really think." When Petru remained silent, Dracul chuckled. "Too smart to let me know. It matters not. You have always been loyal, regardless, and you were right. So, go ahead and take your bow. Then send for Marius. I'm done playing games with Stelalux."

And there it was… The next level of war was coming, an escalation that would bring those across the ocean to their knees if they weren't ready for it. Marius was a weapon Dracul used sparingly. Dafydd stroked the boy next to him to keep him quiet in the wake of such menacing words. There was no sense in calling attention to themselves. Dracul would be back to bed soon enough to work off his fury in the few ways that gave him pleasure. It would be a hard night all around.

Want to see more from this author? Here's a taster for you to enjoy!

Alien Slave Masters

The Captain's Pet

Samantha Cayto

Excerpt

Joel Porter owed his father a debt of gratitude. The son of a bitch had done one thing right for his only child. He'd taught him how to hide his fear. As Joel walked through the Travian space station, he kept up his mask of indifference, even though his heart raced and sweat trickled down his back. The place was huge, cavernous with a mile-high ceiling, ringed all the way up with corridors. Every meter of the docking bay and beyond teemed with people. No, not people. Aliens. And not only Travians, although most were, but other creatures that defied his imagination. How had his own race of humans ever managed to miss discovering the variety of life existing beyond their backwater galaxy?

Even though he wore clothing for the first time in what seemed like forever, he felt far more exposed than he had while naked aboard ship. Back there, nobody paid any attention to him. He'd been one of a dozen human slaves milling about, something the crew had become used to seeing. He'd belonged to Firth, too, a senior officer respected and even feared. No one had dared bother Joel. Here, as he walked next to the floating stretcher carrying Firth to the infirmary, just about everyone they encountered studied Joel as if he were a bug in a jar. They stopped and stared and even leered at him, his species having never stepped foot in this part of space before.

Joel wouldn't give them the satisfaction of showing how afraid their attention made him. He wanted to drop his gaze and shrink away. Pride alone stopped him. Weakness, once shown, was a liability that couldn't be easily erased. So he stood with his spine straight, looking ahead and pretending he didn't notice any of them. He felt a tug on the leash attached to the hated collar around his neck. Back on the ship, he'd been allowed to wander around without it. Not here.

He looked down at the male nominally holding him close to the stretcher by the tether. Firth looked back at him with a tight smile. His eyes conveyed that he knew how uncomfortable Joel was and wanted to reassure him. Joel hated being on the receiving end of any kind of sympathy. That the alien understood him well enough to realize how Joel felt irked him. Unlike his friend, Wid, Joel hadn't fallen for his master. At best, he and Firth had settled into a kind of uneasy détente — not even friends, yet not exactly enemies, either. And while he didn't want the alien to feel sorry for him, Joel cared enough about the male to worry about *him*.

Some serious illness that Joel didn't understand had taken hold of the guy to a degree that the phenomenal healing waters onboard the ship weren't enough. He needed treatment that could only be provided by the kind of medical personnel found on a station. Instead of gifting Joel over to another officer, Firth had asked Captain Kell for permission to take Joel along. So, here they were, slowly making their way to the medical facility in the company of what Joel assumed was the Travian equivalent of EMTs. Joel had been excited at the prospect of getting off the ship. Now that he'd arrived on the station, he wasn't so sure that he wouldn't have been better off staying behind. At least on the ship, he knew his place. Here, he had no idea what to expect.

The trip took forever—endless halls, right turns, left turns, down open-sided lifts that caused Joel's stomach to drop, and up moving inclines that threatened to topple him over. Always, aliens swarmed around them. Most were Travian males in their red uniforms. They dwarfed Joel, the average one topping seven feet. At five-ten, Joel felt like a child next to them. But the weirdest thing wasn't the Travian soldiers. He'd lived with them, after all. It wasn't even the other aliens, strange as many of them were with nonhumanoid features and skin colors he couldn't even name. No, the thing that freaked him out was seeing Travian females. They also fascinated him.

Given their rigidly segregated society roles, no females served in the occupying forces on New World Colony Seven or onboard ship. Wid had seen Kell's wife a few times by hologram and had described her generally, but nothing compared to the reality of it. Very nearly as tall as the males, the Travian females seemed to float around. They moved with such eerie grace. Their flawless movements were even more impressive given the elaborate gowns they wore. The material alone had to weigh a ton. Their hair and makeup matched the complexity of their clothing. Unlike the males' hair, a few braids here or there weren't enough. There were dozens of whip-thin ones intricately twisted and twirled in patterns. Beads and baubles were woven in as well. Their 'face paint' looked exactly like that—paintings. Not merely simple color enhancements, but stylistic patterns and shapes. How long did it take these creatures to get dressed in the morning?

Because his own mother had died within the first year of colonization, Joel had little experience living with women. He'd rarely seen the women on New World Colony Seven dress up and never in anything fancy. Life had been hard, work endless on the colony, with little time for frivolity. No one had the luxury of having many things that were purely decorative. He was used to practical women, not these colorful creatures that caught and held a man's eye. Wid had said the Travian females ruled, but Joel found that hard to believe. These females looked like they did nothing other than spend time on their appearance, providing their males with provocative sights. He couldn't help but turn his head and gape as one female floated by him with her breasts essentially uncovered.

A sharp jerk on his leash forced him to turn back.

"Don't stare," Firth admonished in a raspy voice that signaled his failing health.

Seriously? How could Joel *not* with so much female flesh on display? While he'd been fed a steady diet of Firth's cock until Kell had rewarded him and the other boys with a choice, Joel had never acquired the taste. He liked girls, always had. It had been forever since he'd seen even a glimpse of female breasts, and as nice as his girlfriend's had been, they hadn't looked like *that*. Still, he didn't want to upset Firth. The guy looked terrible, shrunken and even paler than the creature normally was. He also didn't want to disrespect him in front of the other Travians.

"Yes, Master," he said in a rushed, low tone. God, how he hated calling the alien that.

Firth rewarded his effort at meekness and obedience with another tight smile, not fooled in the least. The travel had been hard on the guy. Joel breathed an inner sigh of relief when they finally entered a room with obvious medical equipment and set Firth up on a stationary platform. Firth's fingers relaxed their grip on the leash, but of course Joel didn't try to move away. He stood by the alien's head, his back to the wall and waited for… He didn't know what. A male dressed entirely in a dark, skintight uniform fussed over Firth for a while, taking readings, giving him an injection. It seemed to ease Firth a bit as his muscles relaxed and his expression looked less pained.

Joel wondered idly if his days were about to be filled with standing around while the medicos did whatever they needed to do to make Firth well. He also wondered where he'd sleep. On the floor probably. He eyed it critically and figured he'd slept in worse places as a boy. Any time his father had been on a bender, his anger—fueled by alcohol and looking for its favorite punching bag—Joel had taken off and spent the night anywhere he could find. A sterile floor, hard yet free of vermin, ranked pretty high in comparison. His thoughts short-circuited, however, when the door slid open and he caught sight of another male joining them.

Words inside his brain fled, replaced by compelling images that registered in flashes of awareness. Large. Very large, tall and broad. Authority striding in on two long and massive legs. A face with strong, masculine lines framed with inky-black hair tied back in braids at each temple. Dark eyes that pierced Joel with a 'don't fuck with me' expression before dismissing the human pet with a flick of his lashes. In that second when their gazes met, though, fear skittered up Joel's spine. He instinctively pressed against the wall until he reminded himself that he didn't show fear, and he forced his body to relax.

The male walked up to Firth's platform and gave a brief nod. "Engineer Firth, welcome to the station. I'm sorry for the reason behind it, but I have assured High Command that you will receive the best of care here."

Firth raised his head a fraction to return the salute as best he could.

"Thank you, Commander Arath. Captain Kell asked me to convey his personal regards."

With his arms clasped behind his back and his legs braced wide, the male, Arath, seemed to loosen up his fierce aura a fraction. "I served as a cadet under Kell. I was very glad to hear that he'd weathered some unpleasantness recently on his ship."

Joel couldn't hold back his snort of disgust at the categorization of the mutiny by Kell's first officer as a mere *unpleasantness*. All of the humans had suffered under that mutiny and if not for the efforts of their pets, Kell and his loyal crew wouldn't have survived. And yet Joel still wore a freaking collar around his neck.

The only reason he wasn't standing there stark naked was because of the females on the station. Firth had said it would be improper for Joel to walk around with his dick swinging in mixed company. The sort of clingy lounge wear he'd been given hardly constituted clothing in his mind. He wanted to be home, on Seven, back with his girlfriend, Dawn, if she hadn't hooked up with someone else in his absence. Instead he stood here like part of the furniture.

Except his rude noise had been heard and although he couldn't see Firth's reaction, Arath nailed him with another look that threatened to turn Joel's guts to water. Before the alien could issue any kind of admonishment—if he'd even intended to—the door slid open once more.

A female glided in, wearing a dress so elaborate that it practically had its own identity. If she'd stopped walking and the dress had kept on going without her, Joel wouldn't have been surprised. Made of fabric in various hues of blue, the gown had a stiff, low-cut bodice constructed of what appeared to be gems, not fabric. The poofy skirt billowed out around her, dropping all the way past her feet. A long train trailed across the floor in her wake as she passed Arath and came to stand on the other side of Firth's platform.

Her multi-plaited hair had ribbons and more jewels woven throughout, and it pulled her beautiful face back in sharp relief. Her eyes, forehead and cheeks were all heavily made up, painted with designs of blue accented with silver. The makeup was laid on so thickly, he expected it to crack when she smiled down at Firth. Strangest of all was her jewelry—earrings and a necklace that looked to be made of some kind of metal, sharp and seemingly dangerous to be lying against soft skin. It made him think of the porcupines he'd seen once in a zoo back on Earth. How the hell did Travian males cop a hug without impaling themselves?

"Engineer Firth, welcome to Outer Ring Station Twelve. We are humbled to be of service to such a fine warrior." The female issued her welcome in a melodious voice, soft and sweet, even to Joel's cynical ears.

Arath took a step closer to the platform on the side Joel stood. He got the feeling the alien intended to box him in. "May I present Governor Lalith," he said, with his gaze fixed on Firth. Joel wasn't fooled. He'd been prey often enough at home to know when he was being tracked.

Once again, Firth lifted his head as much as he could and nodded at the governor. "Ma'am, I thank you for your kind hospitality."

God, all this drawing-room formality made Joel want to roll his eyes. He didn't dare, for his own sake and for Firth's.

"We are more than happy to provide the care you need. I would wish you a speedy recovery, but alas, we both know your treatment will be long and arduous. I will say instead that I hope it will ultimately prove successful."

Wait. What? It sounded like Firth might die. That couldn't be true. He'd have said something about that, wouldn't he? Jesus, he might not have fond memories of Firth raping him, but he didn't want the guy to die. Besides, what would happen to Joel if he did? As if he'd asked the question out loud and called attention to himself, the female turned her gaze toward him. Her expression morphed into something far more familiar to him—distrust with a hint of disgust.

"What is this creature doing here?"

Firth wheezed out a brief cough. "He's my pet, ma'am. Captain Kell was kind enough to allow me to bring him."

The female's eyes raked Joel from head to foot before dismissing him. She bestowed a benevolent smile on Firth, however. "That was very kind of him, I'm sure. Unfortunately, this station is not equipped for the containment of lower life forms kept as pets. It's a security matter. I'm sure you'll agree, Commander." She turned that harsh stare to Arath.

The big guy inclined his head with obvious respect and interestingly, he seemed to dial down the natural menace he exuded. That is, until he swiveled to glare at Joel. Then the "I can snap you like a twig" attitude came roaring back. Once more Joel had to fight to keep himself appearing unfazed. The guy looked as if he were picturing shoving Joel out of an airlock. *Holy fuck.* Not even when Joel had been a small kid had his father elicited the kind of heart-pounding fear this creature did. He certainly made Firth look like a big, soft teddy bear in comparison.

"Indeed, ma'am. From everything I've heard about these humans, they aren't to be trusted to act rationally. Their continued occupation of our outer world proves that."

Joel clamped down on his molars to keep from saying anything. *Asshole.* Seven had been totally uninhabited when his colony had landed. The Travians wanted to kick out the colonists for no purpose, expecting them to go back to Earth. Yeah, like that was even possible.

"I can have security put it in detention until Firth has recovered."

Joel seethed at being referred as an *it,* yet realized speaking up wouldn't do him any good. Fortunately, Firth did it for him.

"If I may, ma'am, my pet is well-trained and has done nothing wrong. I wouldn't have brought him if I'd realized he'd be locked up."

Joel shot Firth a look of gratitude, although the commander didn't appear so convinced. Luckily the male didn't get to make the decision.

"Hmm," the governor said. "You are correct. It would be uncivilized to confine the creature without provocation." She turned to Arath. "Commander, you will take the pet for your own."

The big guy couldn't hide his surprise. Even Joel could tell he hadn't expected her to say such a thing and he didn't like it.

"Your pardon, ma'am. You wish me to take ownership of the human?"

"Yes. It's the best solution. Engineer Firth is not in any condition to control his pet or even make use of it." She turned her gaze to Firth and softened her expression. "I'm sorry. You know your pet is of no use to you during your treatment. It will only get in the way here. Commander Arath is the best choice for taking it."

The translator inside Joel's head had no trouble keeping up with the conversation. He understood perfectly well what was being said. It just took a few more seconds for the import of the governor's words to sink in. He'd been traded off to another Travian, one that didn't have to adhere to Kell's edict about gaining consent from his pet.

"No, wait," he blurted out.

Only Firth paid him any mind. "It's for the best, boy," he said in a tired voice. "I was being selfish trying to keep you with me."

Joel looked down at him with mounting terror. He couldn't become that monstrous male's pet. "Please," he pleaded in a low voice that made his pride cringe. "I won't cause any trouble. I'll just hang out here, in the corner. No one will have to worry about tripping over me. I promise."

Firth sighed. "Not my decision, pet."

Joel saw resignation in the male's eyes. And he became aware that the governor and commander had been conducting their own sidebar over the ruling. The female, of course, had prevailed. *Women speak and men obey*, according to Wid. The evidence lay before Joel in Arath's expression. He looked furious, but he nodded at the governor in acquiescence.

"As you say, ma'am. I will ensure it behaves."

"Excellent." The smile she shot him appeared genuine, as if she couldn't tell the effect she'd had on everyone else in the room. Or, she simply didn't care. "Good day, gentlemen." With a brief nod, she floated out of the room.

Silence filled her wake for a few seconds before Arath strode the few steps necessary to extract the leash from Firth's lax hand.

"We will leave you to your rest, Firth."

The older male released his slight hold on the leash. He didn't look at Joel when he said, "So long, pet. Be good for your new master."

That was it? After the time they'd spent together in such intimate ways, all Joel got was that brief send-off? He didn't have time to work up too much outrage or even analyze why in the hell he'd care. A yank on his collar propelled him forward to keep up with the commander. As he picked up his pace to prevent himself from being choked, Joel felt the familiar fear well up inside him. Where was this alien taking him and what would happen when they reached their destination?

About the Author

Samantha Cayto is a Boston-area native who practices as a business lawyer by day while writing erotic romance at night—the steamier the better. She likes to push the envelope when it comes to writing about passion and is delighted other women agree that guy-on-guy sex is the hottest ever.

She lives a typical suburban life with her husband, three kids and four dogs. Her children don't understand why they can't read what she writes, but her husband is always willing to lend her a hand—and anything else—when she needs to choreograph a scene.

Samantha loves to hear from readers. You can find her contact information, website details and author profile page at http://www.pride-publishing.com.